POPULAR PUBLICATIONS — FACSIMILE EDITIONS

Terror Tales #7
(March 1935)

Starting in 1934, editor (and publisher) Harry Steeger unveiled *Terror Tales*: perhaps the flagship magazine in Popular Publications' so-called "Weird Menace" lineup of titles. Running for almost 50 issues, *Terror Tales* showcased some of the best suspense, mystery and terror stories to see print in the pulps. This facsimile of the March 1935 issue contains stories by Arthur Leo Zagat, E. Hoffmann Price, Nat Schachner, Raymond Whetstone, Arthur J. Burks, Mindret Lord, and George Edson.

Authors:

Arthur Leo Zagat, E. Hoffmann Price, Nat Schachner, Raymond Whetstone, Arthur J. Burks, Mindret Lord, George Edson

Illustrators:

John Newton Howitt, Amos Sewell

1

TERROR TALES

Volume Two   March, 1935   Number Three

Cover Painting by John Howitt
Story Illustrations by Amos Sewell

Published every month by Popular Publications, Inc., 2256 Grove Street, Chicago, Illinois. Editorial and executive offices, 205 East Forty-second Street, New York City. Harry Steeger, President and Secretary, Harold S. Goldsmith, Vice President and Treasurer. Entry as second-class matter pending at the post office at Chicago, Ill., under the Act of March 3, 1879. Title registration pending at U. S. Patent Office. Copyright, 1935, by Popular Publications, Inc. Single copy price 15c. Yearly subscriptions in U. S. A. $1.50. For advertising rates address Sam J. Perry, 205 E. 42nd St., New York, N. Y. When submitting manuscripts kindly enclose stamped self-addressed envelope for their return if found unavailable. The publishers cannot accept responsibility for return of unsolicited manuscripts, although care will be exercised in handling them.

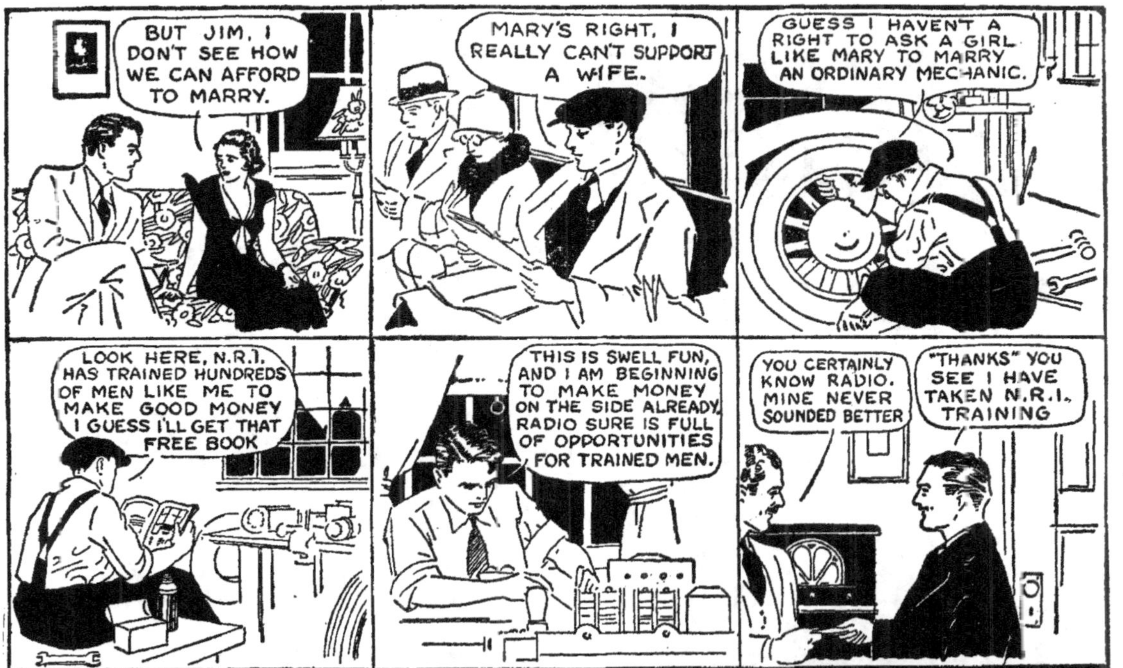

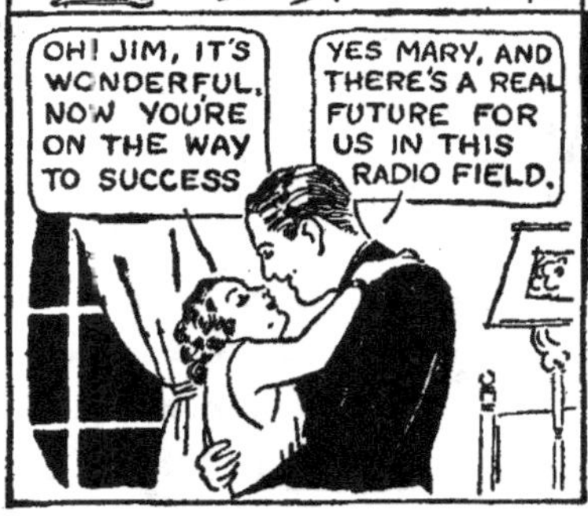

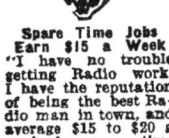
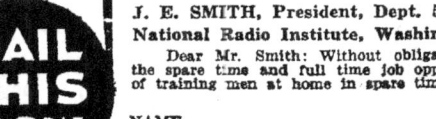

3

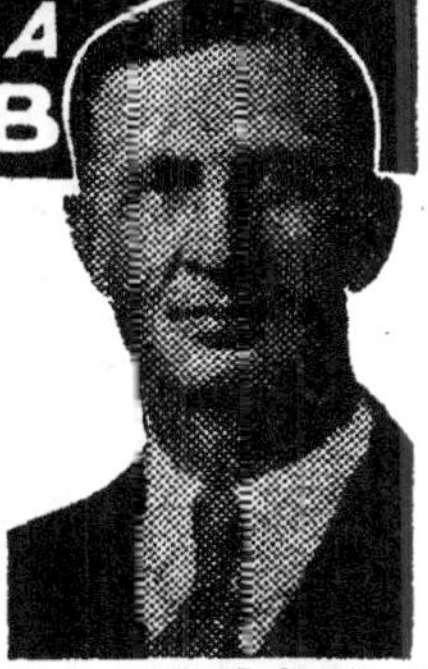

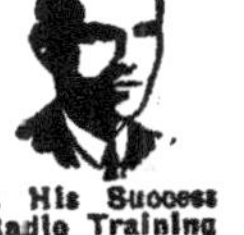

Adventure

Starting in the February 15th Issue

A NEW SERIAL OF INDIAN DAYS
THE WOODS RUNNER
by Hugh Pendexter

•

Also—these good stories: HOT PAPA, U.S.N. A Complete Novelette about the Navy's Most Dangerous Job, by GEORGE BRUCE. MAN FROM HORSE HEAVEN by WILLIAM S. WELLS. THE SORRY JEST by ARTHUR D. HOWDEN SMITH. LIFE ON A HELL SHIP by CAPTAIN WILLIAM ALFORD. THE HARBOR KLEPTOMANIAC, by RAYMOND S. SPEARS—and many others. The February 15th Issue is on Sale February 1st.

Easy as A-B-C

Here's a Queer Way to *Learn* Music!

NO teacher—no monotonous exercises or confusing details. Just a simple, easy, home-study method. Takes only a few minutes—averages only a few cents a day. No "grind" or hard work. Every step is clear as crystal—simple as A-B-C throughout. You'll be surprised at your own rapid progress. From the start you are playing real *tunes* perfectly by note. *Quickly* learn to play any "jazz" or classical selection—right at home in your spare time.

Free Book and Demonstration Lesson

Don't be a wallflower. Send for Free Booklet and Free Demonstration Lesson. These explain our wonderful home study method fully and show you how easily and quickly you can learn to play at little expense. Mention your favorite instrument. Write NOW.

U. S. SCHOOL OF MUSIC
3673 Brunswick Bldg., New York City

Pick Your Instrument

Piano	Violin
Organ	Clarinet
Ukulele	Flute
Cornet	Harp
Trombone	'Cello
Saxophone	Piccolo
Mandolin	Guitar
Banjo	Accordion

Sight Singing
Harmony and Composition
Voice and Speech Culture
Drums and Traps
Automatic Finger Control
Juniors' Piano Course

Most Amazing TYPEWRITER BARGAIN

10 DAY FREE TRIAL OFFER

FREE HOME TYPING COURSE

NEW REMINGTON PORTABLE only

10¢ A DAY

FIRST TIME! Remington's new purchase plan now lets you buy a genuine latest model Remington Portable No. 5 direct from the factory for only 10c a day. Not used or rebuilt. Not incomplete. A beautiful brand new regulation Remington Portable. Standard 4-row keyboard, standard width carriage, margin release on keyboard, back spacer, automatic ribbon reverse; every essential feature found in standard typewriters.

With your machine we send you *free* a 19-page course in typewriting. Teaches touch system quickly, easily. Soon you dash off letters quicker than with pen and ink. You also get a handsome, sturdy carrying case free.

FREE TypingCourse Carrying Case

10-DAY FREE TRIAL OFFER

The amazing low price and easy terms now make it possible for you to buy this genuine complete Remington Portable for only 10c a day. But we cannot guarantee present prices long. Higher wage scales, rising cost of materials, everything points to higher prices. So we say, "Act now . . . while our liberal offer still holds good!"

You Don't Risk One Cent

Try this typewriter in your home or office on our 10-day FREE TRIAL OFFER. Then, if you do not agree that it is the finest portable *at any price*, return it at our expense. *You don't even risk shipping charges.* Don't wait. Mail coupon now. It's the best chance you've ever had to own so complete a machine for so little money. So act NOW!

CLIP COUPON NOW

Remington Rand Inc., Dept.   193-8
Buffalo, N. Y.

Please tell me how I can buy a new Remington Portable typewriter for only 10c a day. Also enclose your new catalog.

Name _____

Address_____

City_____ State_____

5

CRAWLING

By Arthur Leo Zagat
(Author of "Riverfront Horror," etc.)

The men who were to have helped Ann Travers and her injured, helpless husband had driven madly away, fear's clutching fingers at their throats. Now Ann was alone on the desert—alone with him of the gaunt, Satanic features, and with the crawling horrors that slithered up from the grey moonlight to feed on human flesh! . . .

ANN TRAVERS awoke with a start. She lifted her head from the rough tweed of Bob's overcoat shoulder and looked dazedly around. The roadster's motor still thrummed the mo-

notonous song that seldom had been out of her ears in the long week since they had left New York. Her husband's blunt-fingered, capable hands still gripped the steering wheel. The desert still spread—

MADNESS

A Complete Mystery-Terror Novel

bare, utterly lifeless—from horizon to horizon; and running interminably under the hood there were still the two faint ruts in the sand which the thin-lipped filling-station attendant in Axton had pointed out as the road to Deadhope. Yet Ann was uneasy, oppressed, aware of a creeping chill in her bones that matched the anomalous chill of the desert night.

"Awake, hon?" Bob broke the silence.

"We're almost there. Not much over a mile more."

Ann's lips smiled, but her weary eyes were humorless. "I don't believe it. This trip is never going to end. We're going on and on . . ."

"Wrong again. A mere five thousand feet from here, the gang I sent ahead to get things ready is waiting to greet their boss—Mrs. Travers."

How Bob loved to mouth that title. She hadn't gotten used to it yet—one doesn't identify a new name with oneself in a week. . . .

All at once now, Ann realized what change had occurred to weigh her down with vague fear since she had drifted off to sleep. The stars that had been close and friendly, their myriads a vast, coruscating splendor in the velvety black bowl of the heavens, now were pale, infinitely distant in a sky suffused with heatless, silvery radiance, forerunner of a not-yet-risen moon. The spectral luminance silted down to paint the undulating, gaunt plain with weird mystery, and long flat shadows of mesquite bush and cactus barred the vibrant glow with a network strangely ominous.

Bob leaned forward, flicked a switch on the dashboard. The headlights boring the night dimmed. "Save battery," he muttered, in explanation. Then, grinning, "Show my employer how economical her mine-superintendent can be."

Ann twisted to him. "Bob! I don't want to hear that sort of talk any longer. The silver mine Uncle Horvay left is as much yours as mine. More, because it's just so much dirt except for your wonderful process. There hasn't been anything taken out of it for years."

The man threw an arm up in mock defense against her vehemence. "All right. All right. I'll be good. Give me a kiss."

Even while Bob's lips clung warmly to hers, Ann's eyes strayed past him. Ahead, the horizon was close, much too close, as if the road ended abruptly in a vast uncanny nothingness. It was just the crest of a rise, she told herself fiercely; but she could not rid herself of the eerie sensation that they were plunging on to a jumping-off place, a Land's End over which the car would hurtle to fall eternally into some abysmal chasm.

Under the steady thrum of the roadster and the sough of its tires there was a hissing sound, like the breathing of

some unseen monster. It was the whispering of countless grains of sand sifted along the desert by the wind, but it added to the spine-prickling certainty of impending disaster in Ann's mind. This strange, grim land resented their intrusion, their intention to reopen the old wounds in its bosom that long ago had healed. Once before it had lured men with false promise into its deadly gullet, had spewed them out broken in pocket and health, grey with the patina of defeat. Now it was warning them to turn back—before it was too late.

Ann started at a new sound that filled her ears. It was a roaring from ahead, from the secret region beyond the ridge-crest. It was the thunder of an approaching engine, a ponderous engine plunging through moon-hazed night at breakneck speed.

The tremendous apparition on that too-close skyline was startling despite the trumpeted warning of its approach. The huge truck lurched over the ridge, careened down the road, hurtled straight at them. Bob's horn blared raucous warning. Ann glimpsed his pallid, lined face, his blanched hands fighting the wheel. The truck blasted down upon them like a juggernaut, an avalanche of destruction. Ann screamed. . . .

THE gigantic front of the bellowing projectile loomed right above her. In that age-long, frozen instant of imminent demolition Ann saw the utterly white countenance of its high-perched driver: his eyes that bulged with a terror blinding him to the presence of the other car, of anything but some stark inner vision from which he fled; his twitching, bitten lips. She screamed again, more in horror at that which she read in the contorted visage than from her own peril.

Her shrill keening penetrated the brain of the truck driver. His big-thewed arms jerked, the careening vehicle swerved, scraped past the edge of the roadster's fender. The swaying body of the dirt-truck, altitudinous above her, was crowded with husky, brute-jawed men. They were rigid in the grip of the same terror that invested their chauffeur. Their livid faces were color-drained masks straining through the dust-cloud that swirled after them. Their eyes were deep-pitted coals ablaze with black flame. The truck skidded . . . .

The picture of soul-shattering, fearful flight flashing on Ann's vision exploded in a grinding crash, a thunderous detonation of metal on metal, of bursting tires and smashing glass. She hurtled, asprawl, through a whirling world, thudded down on stinging, breath-expelling grit.

She looked up through dazed eyes. The truck was already yards away, its breathless haste not slackened at all, the red eye of its tail-light penduluming in short arcs as panic speed magnified the slight inequalities of the desert road. The sideward, yellow spray of the tiny lamp spattered, not on a license plate, but on an incredible figure hanging by clenched, bony fingers from a bracing truss under the truck's tailboard and hidden by it from the terror-stiffened men above.

Ann saw the man clearly. The grisly fingers by which the rag-garmented, dust-greyed apparition was suspended from the catapulting vehicle seemed to probe her brain with horror. Skeleton-thin, he streamed out behind the hurtling lorry like a bedraggled pennant; whatever of clothing had covered his pipe-stem, bounding legs was torn away and they were greyed to the hue of putrescent bone. His feet, flesh-stripped as they dragged through the dirt of the turnpike, trailed two lines of scarlet blood.

Then the truck was gone. Only a low-lying band of drifting dust-cloud and two scars on the desert's silvered surface showed that it had even been. Two scars between which thirsty sand drank red moisture, till no trace remained to testify that the grisly figure she had seen, or thought she had seen, was real.

The truck was gone! The meaning of that impacted on Ann's bewildered mind. As on the trackless sea, so in the desert waste the unwritten law of Man's obligation to his fellow in distress is stringent, inflexible. To have ignored it as the occupants of the lorry had, in rushing heedless from the wreck they had caused, stamped them as utterly vile—or inflamed by such devastating panic as had stripped humanity from them. . . .

The sound of a groan cut into Ann's consciousness. She rolled toward it.

THE roadster was on its side, smashed to a jumble of twisted metal, burst rubber. Ann realized that only by the miracle of a lowered top had she been thrown free. Threshing arms, a body twisting up from chaos, falling back into it, showed her that Bob had not been so fortunate.

A sob tightened her throat. She pawed sand, pushed herself to her knees, heaved erect. The ground rolled like a tidal swell, staggered her, reeled her to a grip on the crumpled car-side. Bob groaned again, and she saw his twisted torso, the pale, tortured oval of his face.

"Ann!" His voice was a husked, hoarse whisper, pain-edged. "Ann! You're—you're all right?"

"Yes," the monosyllable squeezed from between her icy lips. "But you—you're hurt, darling. You're terribly hurt."

"A—little." Bob gasped and collapsed to the sickening sound of grating bone. "I—can't—get free."

His eyes sought Ann's face. Agony flared in them, was obscured by drooping, bloodless lids. Suddenly he was so motionless, so filmed over by the spectral moonlight with the very hue of death, that Ann's heart stood still and her skin was an icy sheath constricting her trembling body. But his cheek was warm to her darting palm; his nostrils quivered with pain, and a muscle twitched across the taut cords of his stretched-back neck.

Ann's teeth gritted. Her lips tightened to a grim, thin line. Her husband's right leg was strangely askew. Its ankle, making a nauseatingly awkward angle with its calf, already was swollen to twice normal size and the foot was caught between gear-lever and emergency brake. No wonder he had groaned in anguish, no wonder he had fainted!

The next few minutes greyed to a blur of feverish activity, of muscle-tearing effort. How Ann accomplished it she never knew, but somehow she extricated Bob, somehow she lifted his hundred-eighty pounds free of the wreck. At last he was stretched out on the sand. Ann loosened his shoe, got it off. Then, staggering back to the car to pull seat-cushions out, she improvised a bed for him. She tugged and pushed at his inert frame till he was as comfortable as she could make him. She paused then, stared down at his big-boned face, appallingly white against the black leather.

Bob's eyelids flickered open, revealing hot torment. "My boy," Ann sobbed. "My poor boy."

There was something besides pain in those queerly glittering eyes—an appeal, an urgent demand. "What is it, dear?" the girl gasped. "What do you want?"

The croak that came from him was unintelligible. But his arm lifted, motioned waveringly to the breast pocket of his coat.

Ann realized what worried him. She slipped a hand between the warm roughness of the fabric and his pounding heart. Paper crackled at the tips of her searching fingers. She pulled it out, the en-

velope containing the essential formulae for the process that would make profitable the working of low-grade ore from the abandoned mine at Deadhope. She pulled it out and held it up for Bob to see.

His mouth twisted, and his eyes signaled imperatively. Ann slid the envelope into her bosom, felt it crackle against her breast. After he had proved the worth of his process, Bob had told her, he could sell it for vast sums. Until then he must keep it secret. There were interests. . . .

But her husband was once more unconscious. Her own limbs were water weak. She sank down beside him, squatted there, holding his hand in hers. Exhaustion welled up in her like a dark sea.

CHAPTER TWO

The Crawlers

THE moon was risen now over the ridge whence had catapulted the juggernaut of terror and destruction. It hung low in the sky, a great orange globe. It was so close, yet so infinitely far. It watched Ann's distress with an impersonal stolidity and she was small, terribly small, in the unpeopled immensity of the desert, in the hush weirdly emphasized by the whispering of the restless sands. What else did the moon watch, there over the hill, there where the ghost town of Deadhope had spawned horror which had sent hard-faced, stolid men careening through the night in a paroxysm of terror?

Ann tried to wrench her mind away from fear, tried to tell herself that she ought to see what she could do for Bob's broken ankle; that she ought to bathe his face, pimply with the cold sweat of pain even in his coma. In a minute she would —in a minute, but just now she must rest. She was so tired, so tired, and her body was one gigantic ache. And she was terribly afraid. Not only because of the breath of death's wings that had brushed so close. Not only because of Bob's hurt, his helplessness. But because of that which she had read in the faces of the men on that truck—because of that which had trailed behind the vehicle as it rushed away!

Recalling these, a pall of dread closed down, somehow visible in the sheeted moonlight lying spectrally on the limitless, lifeless waste around her. Lifeless? Was it some trick of the half-light, of her tired eyes, or was that shadow, that one way off there on the horizon, moving? . . .

It *was* moving. It was something gruesomely alive, undiscernible, flat against the sand, something that slithered slowly, that slithered over that ridge to the east, that vanished over the earthfold beyond which was—what?

Ann's scalp was a tight cap on her throbbing skull. That which had crawled along the desert surface, how long had it lain there? How long had its shadow lain immobile like the other shadows, shorter now, of the water-starved, grotesque foliage of the barrens? How long had it watched there, buzzard-like? Had it now gone to call its fellows, certain that there would soon be carrion here for them to feed upon?

"Ten thousand men laboring an hour apiece! That slide rule's warped . . ." Gibberish in a hoarse, parched voice pulled her head around to Bob's sweat-wet face, to his open, staring eyes. *"DX over DY multiplied by cosin thirty degrees and you get two kilograms of Ag O Cl."* His hand was a burning coal in hers, his lips were black, cracked. He jerked up to a sitting posture, his other arm flung up over his head, and he screamed: *"Ann! I've got it! I've got it, Ann! We're rich. We're rich!"*

"Bob. Bob, dear. Lie down. Be quiet." The young wife had both hands on the delirious man, was trying to wrestle him down. But fever-madness contorted his face, and with the strength of madness he tossed her about, fighting her.

"You can't have it!" he screeched, in that awful voice that was not Bob's voice. *"You can't have my secret. It's for Ann. For Ann, I tell you. I won't give it to you!"*

The desert silence took his shrill cries and quenched them, but they rang on in Ann's ears, and in her veins the blood ran cold with fear for her husband, her lover. Even as she fought to save him from his fever-demented self, tears streamed down her face, and sobs racked her. Oh, God! What was she to do? What could she do for him? If he got away from her . . .

As suddenly as it had come, the paroxysm of delirium passed. Bob slumped down. One word, one word more rasped from him. "Water . . ."

Water! He was burning with fever. Water would relieve him, water for his dry throat, water to bathe his torrid brow. Ann clawed to her feet, fought weakness, fought exhaustion to get to the car.

Water! The cans had torn loose from their straps on the crumpled running-board, the cans all travelers in the desert must carry. Here they were. Here in the sand was the red-painted one for gas, there the blue one for oil. The white one! Good Lord! Where was the white can, the water can? Breath sobbed from between Ann's lips as she spied it, flung farther than the others, blending with the silver of the sands.

She tottered to it, bent to it, got hands on it and lifted it. It was light! *Too light!* Oh, God! Oh, merciless God! The depression it left in the sand was wet, though rapidly drying, and a gash in the white side of the round can showed where the water, more precious than a thousand times its weight of silver or platinum, had run out. *There was no water!*

THERE was no water, and on the pallet she had improvised for him Bob, her Bob, tossed and rasped out his agonized demand for—water. "Ann," he husked. "Ann. I'm burning. Water. Ann, give me water."

The distracted girl licked her own dry lips, let the mocking canteen slip from her powerless fingers, stood statuesque, rigid, numbed by a disaster more overwhelming than all the intangible fears crowing around her had foreshadowed. To be waterless in the desert ! Even now the fever-wracked, thirst-tormented man was threshing on his bed of pain, was crying for cooling liquid to assuage the fire within him. What would it be when the sun came blazing up over the horizon to pour down its torrid beams on the shadeless, waterless waste? What would it be when the air, so chill now, quivered with insupportable heat and the sands became a fiery furnace, a searing hell?

Water! Old tales crawled out of the past to trail their awful warning through her anguish. Tales leathery-visaged Uncle Horvay had told, come from the Purgatory of his depleted mine to find a year or two of brooding sanctuary in her home. They had haunted her dreams, those stories of men creeping, creeping through the thirsty, interminable miles of the desert, black tongues hanging from blackened mouths—stark, staring mad after hopeless struggle and ripping their own veins to drink relieving death at last. One gibbering, skull-like visage seemed to form in the ambient sheen of the vacant night as it had gibbered at her in nightmares then. It changed to Bob's square-jawed, bronzed countenance, changed back again to a mask of horror. Her larynx constricted to a soundless scream.

"Ann !" Bob's cry came like the cry of a frightened child, through the shell of despair encompassing her. "Ann ! Where are you? *Ann !*" He was sitting up, was staring about him with glittering, frightened eyes. He stared right at her and did not see her.

She got to him, knelt to him. Her arms were around him. "Bob !" she sobbed. "Bob, dear. Here I am. Right here."

"Ann," he whimpered, clinging to her. "Ann. Why don't you give me some water? I'm so thirsty. So terribly thirsty. And my foot hurts so."

Fever and pain had made of her strong, brawny husband a little, frightened child. Agony tore at her heart, clawed her brain.

"Help me, Ann. Help me."

"Of course I'll help you." The girl got steadiness into her voice. "But you will have to be brave." She loved him. Only now did she know how love strained in her every nerve, in her every sinew, how it yearned to him. She got his head down to her palpitant breast, held it there. He was quieter, his upturned eyes more reasonable. She would have to chance telling him. "Listen, dear. Our water is spilt. I'll have to go and get some more. I'll have to go and get help. I'll have to leave you, but it will be only for a little while."

"Leave me ! Alone?" Fear flared in the pain-filled orbs that were fastened on her face. Then it died away. The lines of Bob's face hardened, the lines of his mouth firmed. "Of course. Deadhope is only over the hill." He lay more heavily against her breast. The fever was sapping what little strength he had left. "Kane . . . foreman. Tell him . . . hurry. I'll be—all right—till he—comes." Bob's voice trailed into silence. His eyes were closed. He was asleep.

Ann slid him gently off her lap, on to the seat cushions, pulled his overcoat together, buttoned it with shaking fingers.

She stood up and slipped out of her own warm garment to roll it and push it under his head for a pillow. Her lips brushed his and he smiled in his sleep. Muttered, "Ann. Darling."

Then she was erect, was walking away from him, the desert sands clogging her footsteps. Walking toward the crest of the road-rise that now was silver-edged, shimmering as though it were the crest of a long sea-swell. Deadhope was over the hill. Deadhope from which two-fisted, hard-faced brawlers had fled in an extremity of blood-curdling terror. Deadhope where some awful menace lurked, more fearful because she could not know, could not guess its nature.

Deadhope where water must be, water and some conveyance, perhaps, that would enable her to carry Bob to shelter.

Behind lay mile upon mile of unpopulated, barren country. Only in the mystery ahead was there any reachable possibility of help for Bob. And so, although apprehension lay a leaden weight within her, and fear clawed her with gelid talons, and her veins were a network lacing her shuddering form with icy dread, Ann Travers stalked like a lonely specter through the ghost-grey moonlight. And far out on the desert another shadow that had lain motionless and watching, moved imperceptibly and slithered over the edge of the ground-swell to carry ahead word of her coming. . . .

ANN climbed the ground-swell as though she were moving through some transparent, thick liquid. Though quite invisible, it resisted her slow advance so that she had to force through it, fighting for every inch of progress. It was barely a hundred yards to the summit of the rise, yet it was an endless journey as within her fear shrieked, "Look out! Danger ahead! If those men

could not fight it, how can you hope to? Turn back. Turn back before it is too late!" Thus fear. And love answered, "Go on! Go on! At whatever peril to yourself, you must go on. Bob will die if you do not. Bob will die." Love, conquering fear. *"Go on before it is too late."*

She reached the last tiny rise at last, hesitated a moment, shuddering with cold dread, took the final step that brought her up and over the summit. Stopped again.

The desert pitched more steeply than it had climbed, so that it descended into a vast hollow filled with moonglow, ghostly, evanescent. It seemed brighter here, and momentarily Ann could see nothing but that all-pervading, silver-grey radiance investing sky and earth alike with brooding mystery. Then she made out the grey bowl of sand merging with the grey bowl of the heavens so that their joining was indiscernible. Far at the other side of the hollow, a maze of darker lines resolved themselves into gaunt, shattered timbers hazily outlining what once had been houses, dwellings.

Like silhouetted skeletons they rose, those ghastly beams, like stripped skeletons of a dead town. Here a tall chimney leaned askew, still faithful to a hearth that never again would gather about itself laughter and merriment. There the collapsed roof-poles of a more ambitious structure stabbed through a space that must have been a dance-hall, perhaps the very dance-hall Dan Horvay had cleaned out one mad and brawling night. . . .

Ann's gaze pulled away from the ghostly town, pulled nearer. Midway across the lower plain an angular-edged black blot lay athwart the shifting, luminous sands, somehow incongruous to the color-drained, incorporeal, dreamlike scene. This was the long barracks, Ann guessed, erected by the men Bob had sent to prepare the mine for its reopening, the men who had been driven away from here by some supernal terror. And her heart leaped as she saw, in the ebony side of it facing her, a yellow oblong flash out, an oblong of light, and across it shadow move.

Someone had been left behind! Someone alive! Someone who could help her! The girl forgot her dread in exultation, sprang into motion. She was running down the side of the hill, her lips formed to a call. . . .

The call was never uttered. Ann's heels dug into the sand, braked her to a halt. Her hand came up to her frozen lips, stifling that cry. A nightmare paralysis held her rigid on the hillside, and the affrighted blood fled the surfaces of her body, sought the warmth of her pounding heart. Only her eyes were alive, only her fear-widened, aching eyes that were focused on something that moved, there ahead of her in the phantasmal sand, something that crawled slowly toward her with loathsome life.

It was movement only, at first, and the lengthening shadow of a mesquite bush. Then an arm writhed into the lunar luminance, a long, shudderingly emaciated arm, livid and ghastly. It lifted inches from the ground, dropped, and the tentacular, fleshless fingers of its hand hooked into the dirt, dug deep, pulled, pulled head and body after it, out of the shadow.

A head! But it was a gargoylesque mask, livid, hatchet-edged, sunken-socketed. The head of a thing long dead, of a woman long dead, crawling out from the shadow on her belly, crawling with slow malevolence toward the staring, motionless Ann.

Bedraggled, grey hair was stringy about that dreadful countenance. Clearly in the moonglow Ann saw saliva drool from between lips drawn back to reveal blued and toothless gums. In the awful visage there was no expression, no sign of human intelligence, so that that which slithered toward her seemed a soulless, imbecile thing, utterly brainless. But then the dragging, prostrate body came fully out into such light as there was, and a vagrant beam struck deep into the abysmal pits under the livid brow, and red hate stared out at Ann.

Power over her limbs came back to the girl in that moment, power to whirl, to run from the inexorable advance of that crawling, hateful, mindless thing. Sand spurted from beneath her feet. She plunged back up the slope down which she had come with hope and relief flaring within her. A queer low wail rose from behind her. . . .

Abruptly the hillcrest before her changed form, took on an outline that halted her in her tracks and wrenched a groan of ineffable fear from her parched throat. For another crawling creature seethed over the ridge, rustled slowly through the sand! Another gargoyle face peered at her with mad hate, the face of a man this time, pitted and scarred and with its flesh sloughed away as though the owner had been rejected from a nameless grave! . . .

CHAPTER THREE

The Whip

THE horror slithered fearsomely down with a dread leisureliness that told how sure it was of its prey, how certain it was that it had cut her off. The woman behind, the man ahead—and Ann knew, knew without looking, without daring to look, that more of the crawling things were closing in on her from all sides, that they had enclosed her in a ring from which there was no escape!

Terror was a living thing in her breast, a thing that tore upward to her throat and burst from her mouth, in a piercing, shrill shriek she had not willed. Again she screamed. . . .

A shout from below whirled her around, a deep-throated shout that somehow she knew had responded to her outcry. The woman who crawled was nearer, fearfully nearer, though Ann had been certain she had outsped the creature's slow advance. But beyond her, whence the resonant shout came again, a second oblong of light broke the black expanse of the barracks, an opened door—and in it was framed a tall thin figure that stood there peering out.

That *stood!* The girl's whirling brain seized on that fact to distinguish the newcomer from the ringing grey creepers who closed about to capture her for an unguessable fate. *He was erect!*

"Help!" she shrieked. "Help!"

The man's head jerked to her. Though he was only a slim black silhouette against the saffron luminance, Ann knew he must see her plainly. "Help!" she cried again.

He was motionless, and the woman was crawling always closer, and behind her Ann could hear the approach of the snaking man as sand sifted away from beneath his crawling advance. Oh, Mother of Mercy! "Help! Save me!"

An ululation of sound burst over the desert, a long-drawn crescendo filled with threat, with unspeakable menace. It stabbed the girl's brain with new terror, chilled her, rocked her with a veritable apotheosis of fear. It rose to an apex of quivering sound, cut short—and the silence that followed it was aquake with the awful recollection. . . .

Good Lord! Ann came up out of the bottomless sea of horror into which that cry had plunged her and was startlingly aware that the desert crawlers no longer advanced upon her, that they were gone, completely gone as though they had been figments of her own distorted imaginings! Oh, Mother of Mercy! Was that truly what they had been? She shuddered at the appalling thought. They had seemed real, so real, and now they were vanished. Was she . . . ?

No! She would not even phrase that question to herself. They had been real, too real. And there was covert enough for them to have hidden now, covert enough in the black pools of shadow cast by mesquite and cactus, in the rolling, uneven terrain. That's what it was, of course. They were hiding . . . .

Let it be enough that they no longer slid toward her, that their dreadful bodies writhed no longer toward her, that their skinny arms no longer reached for her with soul-shattering menace.

The man in the doorway beckoned to her. Had the strange outcry that had banished the grey creepers come from him? Ann started to him—froze once more. Who was he? What was he? Why was he here in this camp from which terror had driven all others? What mastery did he hold over the crawling people? Was he one of them? Fear flamed within her. She whipped around to run away, to run back to Bob . . . .

But slowly she turned back. Bob was injured, dying perhaps. Down there was water for Bob, help for him. She must go down there, whatever the peril, to get it for him. She had promised him to return with help.

She drew a long breath into her tortured, aching lungs, and willed herself to move. Then she was running down the hill, through the sand, running the gauntlet of the weird creatures she knew must be all about her, though she could see no trace of them. She was running interminably while the very soul within her cringed with fear that this instant, or *this*, would bring the clutch of bony fingers at her ankle, would see a crawling, slimy creature spring up at her out of the very ground.

INCREDULOUSLY, Ann reached the open door, plunged through. She whipped around as it banged shut behind her, as the tall man rattled a bolt into its socket. She stood gasping, shuddering, as he turned to her—and smiled.

"Hello," the man said. "You're Mrs. Travers, I know. I'm Haldon Kane, your foreman. Where is Mr. Travers?"

Ann gasped, catching her breath. "He's out on the desert, hurt. We've got to get help to him, quickly. A truck came over the hill, driven by a maniac, and wrecked us, broke Bob's ankle. He's——"

"A truck. That must have been ours. Damn those fellows!" The oath ripped from between thin lips in a long, horse face. "When they've got their skins full of white mule they *are* a bunch of raving maniacs. I sent them down to Axton to get them away from here so you wouldn't have to hear their caterwauls your first night in camp, and that's what they've done."

"They—they looked scared to me." The explanation had been too pat. "As if they were running away from something."

"Sure they were," Kane responded smoothly. "Running away from the beatings I'd promised them if they were here when you and Mr. Travers arrived."

A dark suit, complete with coat and vest and white collar, clothed his slender frame. Ann could not quite picture him victorious in a hand-to-hand tussle with the stalwarts of the truck. "But we oughtn't to leave Mr. Travers alone any longer than necessary," he said. "I'll jump in the flivver and fetch him."

"You have a car! How lucky! Come on." Ann started to the door. "He was delirious when I left him. We've got to get to him quickly."

Kane was somehow in her way, though he had not seemed to move. "It won't take the two of us, Mrs. Travers. Hadn't you better stay here and get things ready? Put up water to heat on the range?" He gestured vaguely toward the end of a long door-walled corridor that appeared to bisect the barracks. "Tear up some sheets into bandages and so on? From what you tell me he's going to need plenty of attention, and we ought to be ready to act quickly."

"But I can't stay here alone." Panic flared up in Ann once more. "Those awful creatures——"

"Won't bother you here!" The smile was wiped from the foreman's face, and momentarily a grim ferocity came into it that made the narrow countenance with its pointed chin somehow Satanic. "Not here. . . ."

His insistence seemed somehow sinister. "I'm going with you," the girl gulped. "I won't stay away from Bob that long."

She tried to shove past him. But his hand was on her arm, his long-fingered, bony hand. It stopped her. His black, glittering eyes took hers, were gimlets of black flame boring into her brain.

"I said you are safe in here. I'll go bond for that. But if you put one foot over this threshold—" Kane's voice dropped to an ominous, fearful whisper —"I could not protect you if I were the devil himself. The moon and the desert have spawned evil, prowling things out there, and they have scented you, and they are waiting for you.

"It will do your Bob no good if I save him and he wakes up to find you—what you will be when they get through with you."

Shudders of icy dread shook Ann's slender frame. Kane whipped around, was through the door. Momentarily Ann was rigid, incapable of movement, and in that moment the door slammed behind him, footsteps pounded on hard sand, a motor roared. The girl fought her hand to the doorknob. The car she heard roared away. . . .

It was too late. He was gone, Kane was gone. And she was alone, alone in the hollow with—the foul spawn of the desert! Surging terror jerked her hand to the bolt, rattled it home. . . .

FOR a long time Ann remained in the grip of a nightmare paralysis, staring unseeingly at the rough-planed panels of the door. What was Kane? What was his power over the crawling horrors of the sands. . . ?

Or had he any such power? Was she sure, dead sure, that the eerie cry that had cleared them from her path had come from him? It had seemed sourceless, had seemed to invest the atmosphere from all directions at once. . . .

But when he returned—*if* he returned —he would bring Bob with him. She must get ready. . . .

The light here came from a lantern hanging on a hook beside the entrance. Ann lifted it off, turned to locate herself. The structure was hastily thrown together; the walls and partitions were of rough, unpainted lumber, joists and studding not covered. Angular shadows moved as she moved the lantern, slithered menacingly. The sharp odor of new-sawed wood stung her nostrils, mingled with the stench of man-sweat, the rubbery aroma of boots, the stench of machine-grease, of strong soap, of stale tobacco. The place was alive with the aura of occupancy, yet it was deathly silent.

Had Kane pointed to left or right when he spoke of heating water on the range? Ann could not remember. She would have to look. A curious reluctance slowed her movements as she reached for the driven nail serving as knob to the nearest door.

What was behind it? What would she find behind it? She pulled it open.

Light struck into a big room, showed an overturned table, cards strewn over the floor, a lumberjacket in a heap in the corner, a smashed chair. Chaos. Had a drink-maddened brawl done this, bearing out Kane's glib explanation of the flying truck? It might have, except for one thing. There was no smell of alcohol here, there were no flasks emptied or full, no glasses of any kind. . . .

The nape of Ann's neck prickled. Something *had* happened here. Something that had disrupted an orderly gathering into hasty, disorganized flight. *Something about which Haldon Kane had lied.*

But Bob would soon be here. Time later to investigate; now she must get a bed ready for him, hot water, bandages. A bed! Sheets to rip for bandages! None here. Maybe in this next room.

No. This was an office, the foreman's office. A rude desk told her that, a small safe with its door open. Here too were signs of panicky departure. Blueprints spilling from a rude cupboard in the corner, a pen stuck point down in the floor, ink blotching the place where it had stabbed. Papers disorderly on the desk, held down by—— What *was* it?

Ann took a step nearer, lifting her lantern to throw a stronger light. The black, slender thing coiled ominously on the table-top, ended in a thicker, wire-wound handle. It was a whip, a short-handled, cruel whip. A bull-whip such as she had seen mule-freighters use, in the borax mines on the journey here. But they had no mules here, no oxen. . . . The end of the lash trailed over the further edge of the desk, was hidden by it. Oddly fascinated, the girl circled till she could see it.

The long lash ended in a snapper, a barbed thing such as she had seen raise weals on the tough skin of a mule. This one glistened in the light. A drop formed, dripped off, splashed on the floor. It was a frayed disk of red on the planed board. It was a splotch of blood!

An iron band constricted Ann's temples, and the floor heaved under her feet.

CHAPTER FOUR

Where Horror Fed

FROM somewhere came a muffled roar. Ann's head jerked up. It was the sound of a motor laboring, pounding against the clogging desert sand. Kane was coming back. Had he found Bob? Was he bringing Bob back with him?

The girl whirled, her feet pounded wood. She reached the outer door, rattled the bolt free, grabbed for the knob, twisted it and pushed. . . .

The door would not open. Somehow it had jammed. The car sound was louder now, was right outside. Ann pushed again, threw her weight against the portal. It was immovable.

Good God! It hadn't jammed. It was locked! Locked from the outside!

The car didn't stop! Mother of Mercy, it hadn't stopped! It had passed; its noise was growing fainter, was dying down. Was it some other car than Kane's, perhaps? Or. . . ?

Ann beat small fists on the wood, pounded till her hands were bruised and bleeding. "Bob!" she screamed. "Bob!"

Something like a laugh answered her, a mocking laugh, muffled by wall and by distance. There was a window somewhere on this side of the structure, a window from which light had glowed. The frantic girl twisted away from the locked door, toward it.

Then she was at it, was peering out through glass. Her own face stared back

at her from blackness. The lantern glared behind it. The lantern! Of course! Its light was stronger than that outside, was making a mirror of the pane.

Whimpering, Ann smashed the lamp to the floor, reckless of fire. She could see through now, could see the desert spectral in the moonlight, could just see a dilapidated, open flivver plowing toward the gaunt timbers of the ghost town. Someone was hunched over the wheel, and beside him a body folded limp over the car side, its arms hanging down, its hands just touching the running-board. Bob!

The window was framed glass; its sash did not lift. The girl flailed at it with her bare hands. Glass splintered, crashed. Her fingers were bloody, her knuckles gashed. She plucked shards from their hold in the frame, uncaring. She lifted to the high sill, squirmed through. Jagged edges of broken glass caught at her, tore her frock. She dropped to the sand outside, sprawled. Then she exploded to her feet and was running toward the ruins of Deadhope.

Down there, where those skeleton timbers affronted the sky, nothing stirred. Nothing at all. While she had battered at the window the laboring car had vanished into nothingness as the crawlers had vanished. She could see it no longer, could no longer hear it. But she could see the tracks it had left in the desert, long tracks reaching clear into the mazed shadows of the skeleton village. She could follow them. Staggering, stumbling, reeling, she could follow them to where Bob had been taken.

The soft sand sifted from beneath her flying feet, gave no footing. Even through her desperation, her frenzy of anxiety for her husband, her soul-sapping fear for him and for herself, the feeling of eerie unreality flooded back on her that first had manifested itself when she awoke in the car to see a world flooded by ghostly moonlight. The naked timbers ahead seemed to retreat as she ran, as if she were spurning a treadmill beneath her, an eternally wheeling treadmill on which she would run forever and make no headway. Pain strapped her leg muscles, stabbed her bursting lungs. Yet somehow she seemed no nearer her goal. No nearer . . .

THE pallid desert all about her was blotched by shadows that weirdly were other than shadows. The sands shimmered like water under the moonlight, like water furrowed by the wind, swirling into a whirlpool. Ann gasped, halted her headlong rush, her heels digging into the silt, her eyes staring. There was a circular, wide wallow here where the desert had been plowed up, torn, trampled by some terrific struggle. As though some great beast—or some man —had fought here long and unavailingly against a ravening something that had dragged him down at last.

Yes, here was the mark of shod feet and here—blood-darkened—the depression his body had made when it had come down. The shifting sand had kept the shape of the impact because it had been wetted—wetted red by life-fluid spurting from severed veins. And from this spot a long furrow started to run along with the tire-tracks Ann followed! Vividly, as if the tragedy were being reënacted before her pulsing eyes, the girl could see what had made it: the gore-bathed corpse pouring blood; the slimy, crawling things dragging their victim to their lair. . . .

The record was plainly written—too plainly—in the sand. No wonder they had fled in crazed terror from this dire hollow, the half-mad men in the truck.

No wonder they had not dared to stop when Bob——

Bob! Oh, God! He was somewhere in there, somewhere in the ruined town ahead to which the crawlers had dragged their prey! Ann's larynx clamped on a scream, and she was running once more, was following the twin tracks of the flivver in which Bob's limp body had been, was following the blood-darkened furrow that gibbered at her an awful promise of what it was to which her lover had been taken.

On and on, endlessly, she ran, till— suddenly—barred shadows fell across her and she leapt aside, panting. . . .

It was only the shadow of a tumbledown house, stripped of its siding. Others clustered around, the rotted skeletons of a vanished town, the fleshless bones of Deadhope! But where was the flivver? Where was Bob?

The girl reeled, paused, gasping for breath. She staggered against a rotting beam, clung to it, gagging, retching. Her heart pounded against her heaving ribs as though it would break through the thin confining wall of her chest. She lifted a hand to her breast to still it, felt paper rustle under her hand. Paper! The formulae of Bob's process. Bob's secret.

Bob's secret! Dizzy, nauseated, afraid, the thought pounded into Ann's brain. BOB'S SECRET. *She must keep it safe.* She glanced around with eyes crafty, not wholly sane. No one was in sight. The jumbled beams against which she leaned screened her from observation. Here were two that made a cross, an *inverted cross,* and beneath them was another that lay close to the ground so that there was only a slit beneath it. Ann clawed at her bosom, clawed out the precious envelope, shoved it under that beam. There was no sign of digging to betray that cache, but the envelope was out of sight and it was marked by a sign she would not forget. The sign of the inverted cross. *The sign of Satan.*

The momentary rest somewhat restored her. She could breathe again and her vision had cleared. There were the tracks, the rutted tracks of the car that had carried her Bob, winding among the strewn timbers of the ghost town. And there, still marching with them, was the grim furrow dug by that which had been dragged here. Ann's eyes followed that grisly spoor, probed a pool of shadow, some fifty feet ahead, to which it led.

It wasn't a shadow! It was a grey-black shapeless mound in the barred moonglow, a mound that heaved restlessly, a mound that was animate with gruesome life. Through the desert hush sounds came clearly to Ann, smacking sounds, low whimperings, *the scrape of a gnawing tooth on bone.* That gruesome shape was feeding! *On what?*

A hand squeezed Ann's heart, and an awful fear sheathed her with quivering cold. The furrow of the dragged corpse led straight to that squirming pile, and the tracks of the car in which Bob had been brought here! *What was it that composed that grisly meal?*

Sound rasped through the girl's cramped larynx. A whine, a whimper—it was not a word. It was not anything one could have recognized as human speech. But perhaps *He* understood it, He to whom that prayer of a woman's tortured soul was spoken. Perhaps He knew that the racked brain of the devoted wife was saying, over and over: "God! Dear God! It isn't Bob. It isn't. It can't be. Please, God, don't let it be Bob."

PERHAPS He heard and touched that loathly tumulus with His finger. Perhaps Ann's sob of agony and dread reached the ghastly feeders. At any rate, the heaving mass split apart. Grey, earth-hugging forms slithered away from it, like satiated vermin from their putrid feast, slithered through the sand, out of range of Ann's vision. She did not see where they went, saw nothing but the motionless something to which her burning gaze clung, that which they had left behind. A nausea retched her stomach, but she could not see—she could not be certain what it was at which she stared.

She could not be certain, and she had to be. She pushed herself away from the beam against which she leaned, took a reeling step toward—toward the motionless, awfully motionless *debris* ahead. Her legs, water-weak, buckled, and she tumbled headlong into the sand.

She moaned, and then was crawling toward *it*, was shoving palms down into gritty, cutting sand, was lifting herself on breaking arms, dragging herself onward little by little. And all the while the dread question grew in her shaken mind like a bubble blown in acid, burst so that she did not know why she crawled, and grew again.

Time was a grey nothingness that flowed over her. The anguish of her ripped hands, of her torn knees, was a pulsing torment she did not feel. She was mumbling, "Not Bob. God. Not Bob," and she did not know what it was she said nor why she said it. But she kept going, eternally, hitching through the sand, dragging the agony of her body and her soul to a destination she had forgotten but that she knew she must reach.

The pallid desert must have pitied her then, the desert and the shadows that moved on its spectral breast and were not shadows. Even They must have pitied her, the leprous-faced horrors that crawled —or did They think her one of them, this tatter-clothed, crawling woman with the contorted features of dementia and the eyes glowing red with madness? At any rate they let her pass unscathed until her out-reaching hand fell upon something that was not sand, something that rolled and left a red, wet stain on the sand where it had lain.

The clammy, shuddersome feel of the thing upon which Ann's hand had fallen shocked her back to reason. To reason and the flooding horror of her search. She shoved up on extended arms, arching her back; she looked dazedly about her.

Madness pulsed in her once more as she stared at that which the crawlers had left—at tattered, gnawed flesh; at a torso from whose ribs meat hung in frayed strips, at a skull that had been scraped quite clean so that the grinning bone glowed whitely in the lunar rays. And everywhere on the pitiful remnants that once had been human were the marks of teeth, of *human teeth!*

But even through the swirling blackness that mounted in her brain, the gibbering question still screamed its query. *Who was it?* Bob? Was it Bob? How could she tell? How could she tell when there was no face left on this, no skin?

Whimpering, Ann looked hopelessly down at that upon which her hand still rested. It was a bone that had been torn loose, a thigh-bone. Hanging to it by a shred of ligament was the long calf-bone, bits of flesh still adhering, and the foot was quite untouched. The foot! The *right* foot!

Ann remembered. It was Bob's *right* ankle that had been broken!

And this—right ankle was—whole!

Oh, God! Oh, thank God!

Something gave way within Ann and she slid down and down into weltering, merciful blackness.

SOMEONE was shaking her. Someone was whispering, "Mrs. Travers. Mrs. Travers. Wake up."

Someone was bending over her. Ann's eyes came open, and she saw Kane's narrow face in the moonlight, its lips writhing. Somehow she was on her feet. Bone crunched under her heel, but she did not notice it. Her hands shot out, gripped the lapels of Kane's coat.

"Where is Bob?" she shrilled. "What have you done with him?"

Strong fingers clutched her wrists, tore them away. "Come out of here," Kane said. "Quickly."

A howl sliced across the words, a howl of animal threat. Arms went around her and lifted her, cradled her. The man was running, breathing hard, was plunging through the vague moonlight that glowed around them. Ann twisted around in the arms that carried her, saw Kane's face above her, sharper, more Satanic than ever as its eyes slitted dangerously, as lips curled away from dull-white, huge teeth in a narrow mouth.

She beat at his breast with futile thrusts. "Where's Bob?"

He carried her across the silvered desert, carried her toward the black bulk of the barracks. "I don't—know," he gritted. "I don't know."

Ann squirmed, fighting to get free. The grip of his arms was unrelenting, inescapable. "You lie," she spat at him. "What have you done with him?"

"I'm not lying," the man grunted. "He wasn't there when I found the wreck. He was gone."

Fury was a red flame swirling in Ann's brain. "You lie," she screeched again. "You've got him somewhere in there, somewhere in Deadhope. I saw your flivver pass the house and I saw him in it."

"My—flivver?" The nostrils of his tremendous hooked nose flared, and white spots showed in the thin-drawn skin on either side of it. "Not mine. I have no flivver. "Look, this is my car."

They had reached the entrance to the barracks. A car puffed before it, the engine running. It was an old Dodge sedan! A Dodge! A sedan! But the car Ann had seen dart past and vanish into the barred shadows of the ghost town had been a Model T. It had been a touring car in which Kane had brought back Bob's horribly limp body. . . .

Wait! She had not seen the driver clearly. Was it Kane? She could not be certain. Oh, God! She *was not* certain it had been Kane.

"He was gone when I got there," Haldon Kane said again. Ann had ceased struggling. He set her down. But he had to support her as they took the few further steps to the barracks door, so weak she was from exhaustion, from terror and wild anxiety. "I found the overturned roadster, the cushions by its side on which he had lain. But no one. No one living . . ."

There was a curious emphasis on the last word. Ann twisted to him. "Living! Then there was . . ."

A veil dropped across the glitter of his eyes. His free hand made a curious gesture, as if he were pushing something away from him, something revolting. "Never mind that." His lips seemed to move not at all. "It isn't—important." Then, "Mr. Travers was not there. But I don't understand—you said you saw him in a flivver, saw someone taking him down to the old town?"

"Yes." The monosyllable hissed from between Ann's compressed lips, as she fought to expel a grisly speculation from the maelstrom of her mind. "I heard it, saw it. But it disappeared down there —as though it were—something unreal." They had reached the barracks door. She

twisted to Kane, fear of the crawlers forgotten in a greater fear. "But you must have seen it, too! It had to pass you."

"No." A muscle twitched in his hollow cheek. "No. I saw nothing. Nothing passed me." The response dripped dully into a crystal sphere of heatlessness that seemed suddenly to enclose the girl. "Nothing. No one."

A shadow moved out in the desert, sand slithered. Kane's pupils flickered to it. His hand darted to the doorknob—and the portal swung open effortlessly. But it had been locked—locked—minutes before!

He shouldered Ann through, came into the dark hallway himself and had the barrier shut in one smooth flow of movement. Red worms of fear crawled in his eyes.

"That's better," he breathed. A pale, eerie luminance sifted in through the window Ann had smashed, flowed over him, showed a toothy smile that was palpably forced on his narrow face. "Better. But where's the lantern?"

Ann jerked a pointing hand to it, where it had guttered out. "I—dropped it."

Kane flashed a curious glance at her, then at the lantern. From that to the smashed window. "Have to get that fixed," he snapped. "At once."

Then he was gone!

THE girl was startled. Then she realized that as she automatically had followed the direction of his glance he had soundlessly taken the one necessary step into the foreman's office, had closed its door. She heard his footsteps moving about, heard the rasp of a pulled-out drawer, heard a dull thud as if something heavy had dropped. Then there was no sound in there, no sound at all. . . .

Minutes dragged past as Ann stared

with widened eyes at the blank wood. Coils seemed to tighten about her, gelid coils of nameless dread. Certainty grew upon her that something had happened to Kane in there—something that all the time he had feared. It was her fault. *Hers!* In breaking the window to gain exit she had breached his defences, had made a way for something to enter— something that had lurked in the darkness of that room. . . .

She backed, inch by slow inch, till she felt the outer door pressing against her. Her hand lifted behind her, her fingers found and closed about the knob. She turned it, pushed, her apprehensive gaze still fixed ahead.

A faint breath of air stirred in through the slitted opening she had made, and with it came a vague, hissing sound. The whispering voice of the desert? *Or the sound of the crawlers, closing in?* Panic scorched her breast, was a living flame in her brain. She pulled to the door, shot its bolt with shaking, bloodless fingers. Fearful, horribly fearful as she was of what *might* lie in the secret silence of the room from whose entrance her gaze had never wavered, she was more terrified still of the creeping things she *knew* prowled the sands. She dared not go out there again. She dared not stay here, not knowing with what peril she was housed.

Ann whimpered, far back in her throat. She could not remain forever rigid in the grip of an icy fear. She must—do something—or in minutes she would—go mad.

There was no sound in the darkly brooding barracks. No movement. There couldn't be anything, living, in there. She must know what had happened to Kane. At all costs she must know. Or—give herself over to gibbering madness.

She forced unwilling limbs across the narrow corridor. Its nail-handle was hot to her frigid clutch. The door came creakingly open. Her body blocked light from the obscurity within, but something lumped on the floor ahead, a shapeless something that was fearfully still. Ann fought herself over that dread threshold, into the gloom. . . .

A shadow came alive, swooped down on her, engulfed her! Not a shadow, but cloth, black cloth enveloping her, smothering her, clamping her threshing arms, her flailing legs, clamping tight and holding her immobile. She was being lifted from her feet, was being carried off. And through the thick, blinding folds of the shrouding fabric a laugh sounded, a hollow mocking laugh, *the laugh that she had heard while a battered flivver had chugged past with Bob, with her limp and broken husband.*

CHAPTER FIVE

Despair Underground

ANN could fight no longer. Bruised, battered, her soft flesh torn, her brain a whirl of agony and terror, she sagged, strengthless, flaccid. Consciousness shrank to a minute spark in the vast, dark limbo of her fear. Terror piled on terror, fear on fear, had brought her at last to that ultimate point where her distracted mind must find refuge within an enclave of numbed, despairing acceptance of horror or be wholly shattered.

She was only dimly aware that the arms encircling the bundle they had made of her were so powerful that they handled her weight with utter ease. Only vaguely did she feel shambling, level progress. It did not matter now what became of her, now that Bob was dead. . . .

But she did not *know* that Bob was dead. Perhaps he was still alive. Perhaps she was being taken to him now, to the place where he had been taken. Hope stirred within her—a faint thread of pitiful hope that again she might be near him, might see his face, might for an instant press her lips to his dear mouth before she died. But *was* it to death she was being borne? To merciful death?

And once more she was awake to ineffable fear, to gruelling terror. If that which was carrying her off, human or ghoul, desired only death of her, he could easily have killed her in the same unguarded moment that he had overcome her. he had not. *Why?*

Neither this searing, dreadful query nor the faint hope that preceded it was destined yet to be answered. Quite suddenly Ann felt herself deposited on some soft, high pallet. A slow chuckle came muted to her ears, and the shambling footfalls faded away. Then silence enfolded her once more, and helpless dread.

The girl lay lax, straining to catch some murmur of sound. She heard only the *pud, pud* of her own pulse. Had her captor gone off? Was whatever doom that lay in store for her postponed?

Ann chanced tentative movement, held her breath as she waited for its effect. Nothing happened. Strangely, this was more frightening than a heavy-handed rebuke, a threatening voice, would have been. She was alone. He had left her alone. How sure he must be of his power to have done that, of the impossibility of her rescue!

Rescue! Who was there to rescue her? Kane? Haldon Kane lay dead on the office floor. She had seen him, had seen in the gloom a mound of blacker black that must have been he, lying lifeless.

Even in her extremity of dread, Ann found time to regret her suspicions of the man, her certainty that it had been he who had vanished with Bob into the ghost town, that he was the master of the creepers. She realized now that the crawling fear she had felt in his presence had been the contagion of *his* fear. The man had been afraid, had been as terror-stricken as those who had careened in mad flight from this doomed hollow in the desert. But he had remained, faithful to his charge—had remained here to guard the mine for herself and Bob and had met the death he feared in doing so.

WHAT was that sound? During interminable minutes Ann had tossed, had struggled unavailingly to free herself of the muffling fabric which held her rigid, had twisted, jerked, fought until sheer exhaustion had forced her to quit. Then for an endless time she had lain quiescent, gathering strength to struggle again. . . .

It was close at hand—the slow slither of a heavy body through sand, the almost imperceptible hiss of labored breathing. It came closer, and Ann was quivering, the cold sweat of terror dewing her forehead, her breasts aching with its agony. They had her at last, the crawlers, the belly-creeping, snaking Things with the form of humans and the dead eyes of the damned. At last they had come for her, and she was helpless to escape them.

A hand prodded her, fumbled along the fabric within which she was muffled. Ann drew in breath through the constricted cords of her throat. The sound it made was a screeching, sharp-edged squeal.

"Hush," a muted voice hissed warningly. "Hush."

Fever ran hotly through Ann's veins, exploded within her skull. Good—Lord! Who was it that warned her to silence? Whose hands were they that groped down her flanks, that pulled, tugged at the lashings about her ankles? Bob's? Oh, Merciful God! Could it be Bob, escaped somehow, come somehow to find her, to release her from terror? . . .

The bag pulled up over her ankles, her knees, stripped up over her torso, caught momentarily under her chin and then was entirely gone. Ann squirmed, twisted about, gasped. Closed her lips on the glad "Bob!" that had almost escaped them.

This wasn't Bob's face, this gaunt, long countenance silhouetted against dim moon-glow in a broken-arched aperture across which a shattered beam sprawled. It—wasn't—Bob's. Hope seeped out of her, almost life itself.

"Oh!" she gulped. "I thought it was my husband.".

"Quiet," Kane breathed. "Quiet, Mrs. Travers, or we may be heard." His lips were paler, tighter, his eyes more narrowly slitted, more piercing. A curious excitement danced in them. "I've taken an awful chance tracing you here. We're both in terrible danger and you must not make it worse."

"What is it? Who is it that's doing all this? What terrible things are happening here?" Pushing herself up, Ann whispered the questions. "I won't move till I know."

"For God's sake!" he groaned, his pupils flicking into the darkness beyond her. "If it is known that I am still alive, that I have freed you . . ." His gesture finished the sentence. "We've got to get out of here." His skin was fish-belly grey with—was it fear . . . ? "Come. Hurry."

The urgency of his speech, his evident terror, got through to Ann. Once more he had risked his life to save her. She had no right to impede him now. And yet . . .

"Can you walk?" His left arm reached for her. Odd how long and slender his hand was, how it clawed vulture-like. Odd that his right should be concealed behind his back. *What was it he hid from her?*

Ann avoided his grasp. He had fought for her, sided with her. He was her only hope for safety She must be mad indeed to shudder with revulsion from his touch as though he were something unclean.

"I can walk," she muttered. "You needn't help me."

"Go ahead, then." He turned toward the radiance-silvered opening, pointed with a preternaturally long, straight finger. "I'll follow."

A tocsin of alarm sounded deep within Ann at the thought of letting him get behind her. But she could not refuse. She slid by him, shrinking; she almost reached the light.

"Wait!" Kane spat. "Wait."

Ann twisted. "What . . . ?" she gasped. "What is it?"

He was startlingly close, towered gauntly gigantic above her. "We may not get through." His voice was a husked whisper. "If you have anything you wouldn't want found, any—papers, for instance, give them to me. I'll hide them here."

"Papers!" the girl blurted. "I——" She bit off the words. Good Lord! Why should he ask that now? Her mouth was suddenly dry. "I—I don't know what you're talking about." *How would he know that she carried any papers unless he had wrung the information from Bob?* "What do you mean?"

THERE was a subtle change in Kane's face. Through their slits his eyes were ablaze with a strange eagerness; the long lines from their corners to his strangely pointed chin had deepened. "Travers was bringing out the formulae for his new process. They weren't in the luggage in your car, and——" He checked himself, tried again. "And . . ."

"And he didn't have them on him!" Ann almost shrieked the accusation. "You've searched him! It *was* you that brought him in." She leaped at him, her hooked fingers clawing at his saturnine eyes. "What have you done with him?"

Kane's hidden hand leaped into view. In mid-spring Ann saw the whip in it, butt reversed. The wire-wound handle crashed across the side of her head, sent her down.

She sprawled, half-stunned, and Kane bent to her. His whip hand pinned her to the ground; the other was on her thighs, was scrabbling frantically over her body, was violating the privacy of her breasts. "Where are they?" he snarled. "Where are they?"

"Where you can't get them," Ann mouthed. "Murderer!"

His countenance now was utterly Satanic. "You've hidden them, damn you," he spat. "You've hidden them."

"Yes." There was nothing left to her now but defiance. "Yes. I've hidden them where you'll never find them."

His hands gripped her shoulders, shook her, worried her as a terrier a rat. "Tell me where they are," he snarled. "Where are they?"

"I'll—never—tell," Ann said as he shook her. "You can—kill me—and I won't—tell."

"You'll tell!" Kane surged erect. The whip in his hand lashed up, swished above his head. "You'll tell." It whistled down, coiling, writhing like a thing alive.

Screaming, Ann rolled from under just as it pounded down on the spot where she had been. Dust spurted as the snapper at the lash's end dug dirt. Kane snarled once more and jerked his terrible weapon up again.

Terror exploded in Ann, blasted her to her feet in a lightning-swift splurge of effort that had its impetus from something other than her will. The snakelike lash whipped around her legs, seared from her a shriek of purest agony. It jerked,

swept her footing from under her. The girl crashed down. The whip jerked free and curled above Kane's head for another blow. Savagely his arm arced down.

But the lash did not descend. It tautened, jerked the whip butt from Kane's hand. The button-like snapper had caught in some inequality of the dark roof. A bestial snarl spat from Kane's twisted mouth; he whirled savagely and snatched at the thong as it swung from some hidden fastening. It pendulumed, avoided his first rage-blinded grab. Ann writhed away into the darkness, pitched over the edge of a steep incline.

Somehow she was on her feet. An animal bellow from behind catapulted her into hurtling speed. Footsteps pounded behind her. The descent pitched steeply and now she was more falling than running. Her footing was no longer sliding sand. It was a flooring of small stones that rolled beneath her, that threw her suddenly sidewise.

One flailing arm struck a wall; she gathered herself for the crash of her body against it. That crash never came and she was really falling now. She pounded down on—on something alive that squealed, that slid out from under her and scuttered away in the darkness!

The rattling thump of pursuit pounded above her. Passed. Ann lay in pitch darkness, dazed by the shock of her fall, quivering from the stinging torment of the whip blows, shuddering with revulsion at the cold and clammy feel of that upon which she had thumped down, retching with terror at the prospect of Kane's return. He must soon realize that she had avoided him by tumbling into some side passage off the lightless tunnel. He would come back to seek her. And he would find her there helpless to escape his fury. She was done, completely exhausted. She could flee no further.

But his pounding footsteps kept on, faded into distance, into silence. Slow, timorous hope began to grow in the dizzy turmoil of the girl's mind, matured into certainty. Her blood ran a little more warmly; strength commenced to seep back, and the ability to think.

But thought brought despair blacker than the Stygian gloom in which she lay. Bob was dead, undoubtedly he was dead. Kane had only half lied when he had said he had found nothing alive at the wreck. He had *left* nothing alive! It was Bob's corpse that had slumped over the side of his flivver, Bob's corpse he had hidden somewhere here. Somewhere in this underground maze that must be the workings of the old mine. Somewhere . . .

A noise cut off thought. A tiny noise, sourceless, almost inaudible. A sensation of movement rather than of sound, of furtive movement paralyzingly near. There it was again! The flicker of a breath. A moan so low that only in the breathless hush of the underground could it have been heard.

The knowledge that she was not alone, that something alive was here in the dark with her, brought no fear to Ann. She was beyond fear. She was beyond emotion. With the conviction that her husband, her lover, was dead, she too seemed to have died. Only her body was left—her aching, torn body—and her senses. But something like a dull, dazed curiosity made her strain to locate that sound, made her wonder what it was that produced it.

The low moan came again, firmed into a word. A name! *Her* name! "Ann." And then, "Oh, Ann. I'm so sick. So sick."

"Bob!" The girl screamed into reverberating darkness. "Bob! Where are you? Oh, God! Where are you?"

CHAPTER SIX

The Crawlers Close In

"ANN!" The voice was so weak, so terribly weak. "I thought—you would never—come back." There was no longer delirium in Bob's voice, but evidently he was unaware he was no longer beside the wreck in the desert.

Ann managed speech. "Where are you, Bob? It's so dark I can't see you." Then he didn't know what was happening. He didn't know that anything was happening. "Keep on calling."

Pangs of excruciating agony rewarded the girl's effort to turn, to get going toward him.

"Ann. Here I am." It didn't matter. Nothing mattered except that Bob was alive, that Bob was restored to her. "I'm here, Ann." She gritted her teeth, choked to silence a scream of anguish, twisted over on hands and knees. "Come to me, Ann."

"I'm coming, dear. I'm coming as fast as I can." There was nothing in her tone to betray the network of fiery pain that meshed her body. "But it's so dark I can't see you. Keep calling, Bob. . . ."

There was torture in Bob's accents, torment to match her own. "I've been calling for hours, Ann. Hours." Sharp stones across which she crept cut her knees. Her hands were sticky with the blood oozing from their gashed palms. "Why is it so dark, darling? Where are the stars?"

Ann's arm reached out for another torturous advance, rasped against vertical stone. An iron band constricted about her temples, and a sudden fear tightened her scalp. Her other hand found the rock-face. She squatted, felt wildly to left and right, groped above her head. Apprehension firmed to certainty. This was a wall, a wall of stone right across her path. But Bob's voice came from right ahead, from beyond that wall!

"Are you coming, Ann?" It sounded clearly, apparently unmuffled by anything intervening!

"Just a minute, dear. I'm resting." Bob was hurt, weakened by the awful fever that had swamped his mind in delirium. On no account must he be frightened. "I must rest, I'm awfully tired." It took indomitable courage, steel-nerved grit to keep out of her call the despair that knotted her stomach, the panic that twisted her breast.

Ann found projections in the rock-face before her, gripped them and dragged herself erect while all her maltreated body screamed protest. Leaning against the stone, she groped above her head, high as she could reach. The barrier was still there, the barrier from beyond which Bob's voice still sounded with uncanny clearness. "Ann!"

From the unholy dark that clamped almost tangible oppression around her, madness once more gibbered its mopping threat at the tormented girl. This wasn't real! It couldn't be real! Her ears told her that Bob was right here, right in front of her, so near that she had only to reach out a hand to touch him—but that reaching hand found only cold, damp, immovable stone.

But what was this? Her fingers, clawing sidewise, touched something cylindrical, greasy. A candle! Great God! A candle stuck in a niche. And a match next to it. A single match! Light!

Ann clutched the candle, the match. She was shaking, trembling as with an ague. By striking this match, by touching its flame to the wick of this candle, she would be able to see again. To see what it was that barred her way to Bob! But there was only one match. One only. And her hands were ripped, bleeding, numb with cold and weakness. . . .

THE universe itself stood by with bated breath as Ann licked a finger and held it up to discover if any draft wandered here to blow out the precious flame in the moment of its birth, as she felt with a quivering hand for a dry spot on the rock before her, as she placed the head of the match against one that she found and rubbed it slowly across the rough surface.

Phosphorous spluttered, flared. The girl's whole soul was in her eyes as she watched that tiny flare, as she watched the blue spark ignite the splinter of wood. Her heart missed a beat as the glow flickered, pounded wildly when it grew stronger again and became a robust flame she dared move the all-important inch to the charred fiber of the wick. And no detonation that meant the collapse of a city's wall ever fired a besieger's heart with greater exultation than the ignition of that candle-end did hers.

Light guttered, steadied, drove back darkness. It revealed a chamber hollowed out of rock by human hands, human tools. It showed, some ten feet high in the farther wall, the aperture through which she had tumbled into this artificial cavern. Below this, and to one side, the growing illumination fell across a great mound of burlap bags, some of which had burst to spill forth jagged fragments of ore. The burlap of which the bags were fashioned was new and fresh! How could that be when the mine had not been worked for decades?

"Ann! I can see your light." Bob's cry struck across the wild surmise springing to the girl's consciousness. "Ann!"

She turned. There was the rocky wall touch-had told her about, unbroken. And always, as though he were right here in front of her, she could hear Bob. "Ann! You're almost here. What are you waiting for?"

It was nightmarish, fantastic. "Ann!"

Then she saw where the voice was coming from. Above her, right above her, there was another break in the surface of the rock, an arched opening like the one through which she had so fortuitously entered, except that it was barely two feet high and not much more across. It gaped blackly at her, and the stone that edged it was slightly blacker for inches than the rest of the wall, and from it Bob's whimper came as though out of an old-fashioned speaking tube. "Please come to me, dear. Please hurry."

A speaking tube. That's what it was! A tube, the orifice of a small tunnel boring into rock! And somewhere within it, not far away, Bob lay, weak and sick, and in need of her! The thought sloughed exhaustion and pain from Ann like a discarded garment. She got a foot on an out-jutting knob of rock, lifted, slid her candle into the hole she could just reach, got her fingers onto its edge and was scrambling, was lifting herself up that sheer rock-face. She had one knee up, another, was squirming into the narrow tunnel.

"Coming, Bob," she said. "I'm coming now." She had to snake through here on her stomach, for the roof of the passage was not high enough even for her to lift to hands and knees. But Bob was somewhere in there, and even had the tunnel been narrower still she would somehow have squeezed through.

The flickering luminance of the candle Ann pushed ahead of her showed damp-blackened stone, slimy, scummed over by the blanched small fungi of the regions where the sun never reaches. Stalactites ripped long gashes in her clothing, tore her skin. Ahead there was the scutter of the eyeless creatures of the dark. But here and there Ann saw the mark of a pickaxe, a tooled groove, and knew she was not the first human to crawl through this tight gallery, knew that it was man-formed, man-driven through the bowels of the earth, knew that it was the old mine through which she crept. But . . .

The ground slanted upward, beneath her, the tunnel opened out. "Ann!" Bob's face was suddenly before her, pallid, bloodless, Bob's body recumbent on the same auto cushions that so long ago—years, it seemed—she had dragged from the crumpled remains of their car.

"Bob! My dear! My dearest!" she had her arms around him, was kissing him. "My sweet."

His hand came up, feebly, stroked her face. "Ann! I've been dreaming—the most horrible . . . Good Lord! . . . Where is this? What place is this. I thought . . ."

"Don't think, Bob. Don't think. Things have happened, all kinds of things. But everything's all right now. I have you back and everything must be all right."

"But, Ann——Holy Jumping Jehosaphat—*what's that?*"

ANN twisted in the direction of his startled gaze, saw across the low, irregularly circular chamber where they were the orifices of a number of such tunnels as that through which she had come, saw a clawed, skeleton hand writhe from one of them, an emaciated arm. And it was followed by a face!

The face looked at her, broke into a loathsome grin. That is, the livid gash that was its mouth widened to expose rotted, black teeth in a grimace that might have been intended for a grin. But there was no humor in the concave, grey countenance above it, no humor in the blank, imbecile eyes. There was only menace, lewd menace that brought back all the horror of that dreadful night and multiplied it a thousand-fold.

Breath hissed from Bob's lips, close against her face, and Ann felt his body stiffen to the rigidity of terror. That same terror ran molten through her own frame. . . .

The Thing moved gruesomely, and a sound came from it, a chattering, mindless howl, hollow and horrible. It echoed— No! It was being repeated from the other openings into this low, flat chamber, and from them came the rustling dry rasp of fabric dragged along stone. Skeleton fingers clutched the edge of a second hole. . . .

Realization burst like black flame in Ann's skull. They were closing in! The loathsome crawlers were closing in on her and on Bob! *On Bob!*

Breath gusted from her throat in a shriek the more poignant because it was soundless. Ann threw herself over the prostrate form of her husband to blanket him, to shield him from the obscene menace closing inexorably in. Her hand struck the candle, struck the light from it. Blackness swept down, blanking out the monstrous faces peering in, blanking out the grotesque half-human masks and the reptilian, snaking arms that writhed out of the rock in a constricting circle of doom. But it did not quench the slithering noises of the crawlers' coming, their voiceless husked cries, the pungent, fetid odor of their foul bodies.

Bob's cheek against hers was icy cold. Ann hitched to cover him more completely, to cover him with her own quivering flesh from the Things that came slowly nearer, nearer. . . . Perhaps they would be satisfied with her. Perhaps possession of her would sate them. Perhaps she yet might save him from them.

It was feeling, not thought, that curdled in her brain with this last thread of hope, and reason gibbered to her how futile it was. They would take her, and they would take him, and there was utterly no hope for either.

Something touched her outstretched, bare arm, slithered gruesomely down its

length. Ann's skin crawled to the bloodless, lusting touch. A fleshless hand fastened about her ankle. . . .

Rock grated, thunderously. The darkness paled suddenly to the color-drained, spectral luminance of moonlight. For one reason-devastating moment Ann was aware of a grotesque, leprous mask thrust close against her face, of lecherous eyes in which hell-fire glowed. Then an enormous, batlike shadow fell across the twisted, prone form behind it, fell across her. Shrill, horrible sound burst like a tornado in the confined space—the piercing, weird ululation that had answered her cry for help and banished the crawlers when first she had glimpsed them. It crescendoed to its blasphemous apex of soul-shattering threat, held that topmost note till Ann knew that in another instant it would blast reason from her brain and leave here forever mad. . . .

Abruptly it ended. The nerve-racked girl was aware that the crawlers had pulled away, that they were writhing on ground-scraping bellies to their holes, that they were sliding into them like so many rats. Above her, someone chuckled.

Ann rolled, thanksgiving bursting in her heart, trembling on her lips, rolled over to see who it was that twice had saved her from the fearful threat of the crawlers. Who was this unknown, unseen friend that alone in the weltering horror of Deadhope had aided her?

Gaunt, black and gigantic in the silting moonglow, Haldon Kane loomed above her. In his Luciferean countenance huge teeth showed, grinning with demoniac triumph, and about that head of Satan his black whip whistled and writhed!

"You," Ann sobbed. "You!"

THE whip-lash writhed down, flicked her chin, lifted again. The dextrous play of Kane's thin wrist kept it in hissing, omnious motion. "Of course," he snarled. "You didn't think you could get away from me, in this place whose every nook and cranny I know? After ten years one should be more familiar with even a maze like this than another who had known it for ten minutes."

"Ten years! But you haven't been here that long! Bob hired you only last week." Clutching at straws, Ann was trying to keep him in play, was desperately trying to stave off the final moment.

A mocking hideous laugh mingled with the whir of the whip. "Travers didn't hire me. I was here long ago, ever since it was deserted by fools who thought they must pay for labor to work it, who thought they must dig five times as much dirt as the thin vein occupied so that that labor might have place to stand at its work. . . . Who do you think I am?"

"You said—Haldon Kane, the——"

The circling whip-lash rippled in time to the chuckle that dripped from its wielder's mouth. "Kane is miles away from here, still running from the one sight I allowed him and his men of my pets. How do *you* like them?"

Ann shuddered, could not keep her eyes from the menace of the black thong snaking above her. "They—they're horrible. . . ." she whimpered. "They——"

"They're not pretty, but useful. I don't have to pay them, you know, and their food costs little. They find it themselves. . . ."

"They find food—in this desert? How. . . ." A gruesome speculation formed in Ann's mind, added a new horror to that which encompassed her, was answered by the grinning fiend.

"There were more of them when I brought them here. Many more. And it was not disease that killed them. Do you understand?" Hell itself quivered in his sardonic smile. "Queer," he mused. "How simply this State can be persuaded to farm out its convicts to anyone who will

engage to board and clothe them. It saves the taxpayers money, you see, especially if the contractor engages also to guard them himself. And then—even guards are not necessary when a simple inoculation will make the prisoners amenable, very amenable to orders from one who has a brain. . . ."

His voice trailed away, leaving behind it a slimy smear of horror, then came again. "But they're hungry. My pets are hungry now." Again that slow, Satanic smile and the whip's hissing. "Shall I let them feed?" His slitted eyes flickered to Bob's pallid figure, came back to her and seemed to strip the clothes from her in one lewd glance. "In the presence of such juicy morsels I have already had quite a little difficulty restraining them."

Nausea retched bitterness into Ann's throat at the ultimate horror he implied. "No. Oh God, no!" she whimpered. "Kill us but don't let——" Terror choked her.

"Perhaps I may. Perhaps I may even let you—and Travers—live. . . . Your husband's formulae—what did you do with them?"

The man was no longer smiling, but his whip seemed to chuckle as somehow he managed to evoke a rattling sound from the snapper at its end. The choice he offered was clear.

Ann's lips twitched. Gelid fingers clutched her throat. She contrived to squeeze out speech. "I'll show you. Promise to let us go and I'll show you."

"Get up, and take me to where you have hidden them." The whip stopped its eternal whir, floated down to his side, hung there, tense and ready. "Then, if you will sign this mine over to me I will—let you live."

"And Bob?"

"And your husband. I swear it."

Ann had to drag herself up by his leg, had to hold onto his arm, while the nausea of repugnance retched her, or she could not have remained standing. Her head came above the roof of the chamber, and she saw that the desert stretched, away from it, shimmering in the moonlight. Something like a trapdoor fashioned of rock lay to one side. When that was in place there would be no sign of what lay below.

"Come," the man who was not Kane said. "I don't know how long my pets can restrain themselves."

The skeleton town was to one side, silhouetted against a moon across whose face luminous clouds drifted. "Over there," Ann husked.

ANN stumbled over to the spot, with the man close behind her. Here were the beams in the form of an inverted cross, below them the other beneath which she had slid the envelope. Ann managed to stoop over, to slide her hand into the recess. . . .

A cold chill took her. There was nothing there! Oh God! The envelope was not there, the envelope that was to ransom Bob from horror!

"Well?"

She turned haunted, lifeless eyes to her tormenter. Her lips moved soundlessly.

He needed no words to understand. Livid fury leaped in o his eyes. His lash surged up. Ann shrank against the stripped framework of timber, horror staring from her twisted face.

"You've tricked me!" the man screamed. "You've dared to trick me!" The black thong spat at her, spat across her face. "I'll flay you alive."

Agony seared through to Ann's brain. Her body was a shell of ice enclosing agony, seething with terror. The whip hissed up, stopped.

"No. That's too good for you," the man squealed. "*They* shall have you!" His chest swelled, and an ululation burst

from between his colorless, writhing lips —a sound somehow like the warning cry she had heard twice before, but somehow different, somehow more horrible.

They were coming! Past the quivering, passion-shaken figure of the fiend she could see them squirming up out of the hole where Bob still was. Verminous grey shadows in the silver of the moon-bathed desert, spectral shadows of uttermost horror from a living grave, they were crawling loathesomely toward her.

"*Take her!*" their master shrieked. His long left hand jerked a pointing finger across his quivering body, his whip curled above his head, lashing air, hissing a song of doom. "Take her! Her flesh is sweet, her blood is warm."

They slithered along the sand, coming fast now, faster than ever before they had moved. Ann could see their drooling mouths now, their devastated faces, their mindless eyes in which glowed the fires of damnation. "*Take her!*" the maddened voice shrilled again, and grey talons writhed out, grey hands gripped the hem of her dress.

She held on to the splintered timbers behind her, she kicked out at them with her small feet. But they were dragging her down. They were dragging her down to their seething, foul mouths.

And most horrible of all was the silence with which they attacked her, and the spectral glow of the moon on their contorted forms, more horrible even than the crackling of the man's whip, and the shrillness of his mad voice as he screamed, "*Take her!*"

The grip of Ann's hands on the beams behind her was torn away. She was on her knees. Twisting, she grabbed again at the shattered timbers, still frantically fighting, still desperately struggling against the inevitable horror that tore at her. A fanged tooth sank into her thigh, ripped. She jerked convulsively.

Above her there was a grinding crash! Light was blotted out. Cataclysmic sound burst all about her. Behind her there was a thunderous crash, a high-pitched scream of agony. Dust was in her nostrils, her eyes. It choked and blinded her. Coughing, spluttering, she flailed out frenzied arms, struck wood close on either side, wood above her.

Her knees, her legs were queerly wet. But hands no longer plucked at her, teeth no longer ripped her flesh. And there was no longer a shrill voice in her ears, keening, "Take her."

The dust settled. Upheld by shattered timbers, Ann moaned. Her brain cleared. Silvery light splotched shadow around her, and slowly she became aware that she was penned in a pyramidal space of shattered, jagged timbers, that beneath her the ground was soaked, muddy with blood, that behind her there were small whimperings, tiny noises of infinite suffering. The whimperings faded at last to silence. Her bewildered mind struggled with these things, and realization finally dawned on her. That last, hopeless grab of hers, that last frenzied clutch, somehow had seized upon the key beam of a precariously balanced heap of timbers. It had collapsed, and missing her, by some miracle had fallen upon and crushed the crawlers behind her, and their master. . . .

A miracle? Perhaps. And then again . . . *"Oh God!"* Ann sobbed. *"Oh God, I thank Thee."* Perhaps she was right. Perhaps He in whose sight no sparrow's fall is unnoted . . .

THE sun may have warmed them to courage again, the men whom the crawlers had routed from Deadhope and sent careening away in marrow-melting fear. At any rate, it was they, bristling with automatics and borrowed rifles, who returned, when that desert sun was already blazing high in the sky, to dig Ann out from under the blood-spattered beams, and fetch her again delirious husband from the strange pit where he lay. They carried them to the room prepared for them in the bunkhouse and aided them with rude surgery till a doctor and nurse could be summoned from Axton to take over the job.

But it was not till a week later that Ann came sufficiently out from the shadows to talk to Bob. "It's all like a horrible nightmare," she said. "I still don't understand what it was all about."

"We've pieced it together from what we've been able to find here, and the things he said to you, and what little was known about him." Travers' mouth was still lined with pain, his eyes somber. "The man's real name was Grandon Rolfe. He knew your Uncle Horvay in the old days, knew that his silver vein had petered out till it was unprofitable to work the mine.

"After Deadhope was abandoned he moved in. He got convicts from the prison camp at Pimento, got them out here and made imbeciles of them with an injection extracted from loco weed, that grows wild all through this desert. Then he worked the mine with them, starving them and whipping them into submission. With free labor, with no cost for equipment, it still could be made to pay. . . ."

"But why did they crawl like that?"

"Because to further save expense and time, he excavated only the narrow vein of silver ore and made them work on their bellies, like snakes crawling in their burrows, till they no longer were able to walk erect."

"Oh, horrible——"

"Not more horrible than some coal mines of which I know, in this country and abroad, where the miners work stooped over all day long, and tiny children are used for any task that requires quickness of movement. Greed inspires horrible things, my dear, and it is only in degree that Rolfe was worse than a great many highly-respected industrialists.

"However, he knew the jig was up when our men came in. He stopped operations, covered over all signs of them, and pretending to be a friendly neighbor, wormed out of them the reason for their activity, my discovery of the new process. He made up his mind to get hold of that and——"

"And his twisted brain conceived the idea of using his crawling idiots to scare them away, and then to frighten the process out of us."

"Yes. It was only your bravery that defeated him, my dear."

"Not bravery, Bob. I was scared to death. But all your work, all your hopes would have been ruined." Then a new thought leaped to her brain, stinging it with anxiety. "Bob! The envelope. The papers with your formulae. They're gone!"

"No, dear. They had only slipped into a little hole farther back than you could reach. I have them." His hand reached across the space between their beds, found hers. An electric circuit seemed to close. Its current tingled between them, made them one. "I don't deserve you, Ann."

"Silly," Ann said dreamily. "Some day I shall go through worse things than that for you. . . ."

Bob's eyes shone. "You mean. . . ?"

"I think so— Oh Bob, I love you so much!"

THE END

THE CAT GODDESS

By E. Hoffmann Price

Out of the measureless crypt of Time, Frazier called Sekhmet, Queen of the Sunrise, Queen of Lions. But the price he paid for his daring was dear; the toll of the outraged gods was heavy. . .

Who thirsts more for blood than the lion of the desert, and whose essence is more fiery than flame?—Siret az-Zayd.

"THE gods of old Egypt were real," declared Frazier. "I have contemplated their perfection, and I have finally devised to see them face to face. I will command them, and they will appear, unveiled."

It was too outrageous to challenge; yet Frazier had the unfortunate gift of succeeding in what he attempted, and I feared that he was right.

His body lived in the *Vieux Carré* of New Orleans, but Frazier's self wandered in far-off, fabled cities, in Irem of the Thousand Pillars, in Kara Korum of the Black Sands. His nervous, erratic gestures, the forward thrust of his head, and the unnaturally prominent whites of his eyes, curiously staring, hinted that his Asiatic quest of subterranean Agharti had not been entirely in vain. It would have been better if he had been lost in one of the caverns that lead to Agharti.

"The passing of centuries has starved the gods," Frazier continued. "They lived on the emanations from the minds of uncounted worshipers, even as your body thrives on material foods. That leads inevitably to my next contention: that when sufficient of our human race pay homage to what are considered abstract qualities, that very act of worship sets up a cosmic vibration which causes primordial thought-substance to concentrate, producing a vortex which is the birth of a god—an intangible, but living entity."

Frazier paused, regarded me fixedly with his dark brown, curiously staring eyes. He glanced about the high-ceilinged, sparsely furnished room, and continued: "Carver, I have finally devised a ritual which will re-create and revive such a vortex. Tonight you will witness the rebirth—perhaps I should say the resurrection—of a deity."

He turned toward a table—one of the three pieces of furniture in a room almost as barren as an anchorite's cell—and picked up a scroll, which he thrust at me. It was a scrap of yellow, silk damask scarcely more than a foot long. It was inscribed in Kufic characters, angular, archaic script which is conceded to be the first of written Arabic. One end was still attached to the rod on which the entire manuscript was once rolled. That rod, I noted, was of dark, heavy wood, and each end of it was adorned with the head of a lioness carved exquisitely of agate. It was ancient beyond reckoning, and uncounted furtive fingerings had softened the sharp incisions of the engraver's tools; yet the vermillion and black tracery of the Kufic script was scarcely dimmed, despite the interlineations and marginal notes that trembling hands had later added.

"Someone cut it," I observed, indicating the clean, sharp edge of the free end.

Frazier's curse was volcanic. Then he added: "But I fooled the vandal! By pure logic, I have recovered the missing text, and have transcribed it for use. Its last owner was Maimun, the Persian heretic and necromancer. With all his learning, he vainly spent a lifetime of trying to recover the lost lines. But I resurrected them from the grave of time."

The triumphant glitter of his eyes forbade doubt; yet he sensed my unspoken question. "Read it," he commanded. "Aloud."

Modern Arabic is a task, and that archaic script was baffling; but I tried it. "*Ya malikatu 's-sabhh! Ya malikatu 's-sab'a*—O Queen of the Sunrise! Queen of Lions—" I stopped short. The succeeding phrases were an abomination—a shocking blasphemy. Frazier, however, misunderstood my hesitation, and snatched the scroll away.

"Rather difficult," he grudgingly conceded. "And you didn't do badly—but that's not the way they pronounced it, centuries ago. Listen carefully."

Frazier's usual speaking voice was dry, uninflected and colorless; his reading was a revelation, and an unpleasant one. He chanted the lines compellingly in sonorous utterance. He gave the consonants a peculiar quality, curiously blending and shading the vowels in a manner foreign to any Arabic spoken today. There were gutturals that seemed to emerge from his diaphragm. I distinctly felt the seasoned wood of the floor vibrate as he intoned certain sounds.

It was nerve-wrenching; it was devastating; yet I sat there, listening and unable to protest. Mystery and terror and fascination lurked between the syllables of that stupefying chant. The cigar stump that I had at first clenched between my teeth finally dropped from my lips. I understood what he was saying; but it was like the rumble of drums rather than the enunciation of any language. Frazier was addressing the innermost fibre of the soul. He was weaving a diabolical harmony that was rapidly approaching a crescendo of a magnificent blasphemy.

AND then the hollowness of that empty room began to echo so that Frazier's voice was followed by a rumbling as of distant, antiphonal responses. Finally the antiphone and Frazier's chanting set up interference beats so that a third voice began whispering and hissing; spectral serpents were awakening to greet a phantom sun.

God! It was awful, that surging sorcery. The air became tense and electrical. It was as though I were sitting before a veil, which though baffling my eyes, could nevertheless not keep me from *feeling* what was denied to vision.

Out of the dim dusk of that barren room gleamed the disc of a hammered bronze temple-gong. Its insidious, sympathetic whispering for an instant distracted my unwilling attention. I realized that I was shivering violently, and that perspiration was streaming down my cheeks, and that my body was becoming numbed from the futile effort of nerve and fibre to resist that damnable resonance; that that realization shocked me into the effort to fight off the advancing

paralysis. I seized the mallet and struck with all my strength. The shuddering, crashing vibration stabbed into that rumbling chant. The brazen outcry tore into the abysmal muttering and dismaying echoes.

Frazier ceased intoning. His face was a rigid, pallid mask from which his eyes stared wider than ever. Then his glance shifted to the still faintly humming gong. A thin smile of understanding displaced his first flare of wrath.

"Carver," he said, "I have reached the uttermost pinnacle of Egyptian magic. You witnessed the power of the opening lines of Maimun's scroll. By a careful study of the tone-quality of each syllable, by noting the rhythm pattern of the lines, I have resurrected from oblivion, if not the actual original invocation, then at least their vibratory equivalent. I have restored what some fanatic enemy of learning destroyed. You heard the beginning—wait until you hear the conclusion!"

"Someone," I retorted, "should have conferred a benefit on humanity by entirely destroying that damned scroll! Throw it into the grate before you read it too often."

"The basis of fear is usually ignorance," Frazier snapped. His remark was singularly irritating in view of the perceptible tremor of his hand as he abstractedly fingered the scroll.

"Then suppose you explain the logic of it," I objected. "Though I doubt that any explanation can make that accursed text any more acceptable to one's nerves."

"It naturally would be disturbing," Frazier began. "But the principle of it is simple enough. The effect, by the way, is practically independent of the literal meaning of the words, although of course their symbolism enters into the pattern. The power of the reading lies mainly in the fact that the Semitic languages— Hebraic, Arabic, Aramaic, Amharric—*in their purity* are fundamental, and based on primal vibrations. Thus intoning them sets up a sympathetic resonance with the master chord of the cosmos. And that is the heart of all magic, of all the so-called thaumaturgy, which really is not wonder-working at all, but rather a perfect harmony with the elemental structure of creation.

"This scrap of a scroll gave me the key so that by pure logic I was able to restore the lost text. And having done that, there remains but the ultimate proof: that of evoking the old gods and regarding them face to face."

I feared more than ever that Frazier was right. The idea was too monstrous to be an unfounded fancy. I knew that Frazier had the occultist's intuition, and the relentlessly mathematical mind of the scientist: and that both were welded to an immobile stubborness.

With the rigorous perfection of the calculus he had deduced a basic law, and by inhumanly keen imagination had restored what someone had wisely destroyed. There was no longer any doubt that he would use his awesome knowledge to the uttermost and conjure out of the ashes of dead centuries an all-consuming mist of flame. The unveiling of a god exceeded the daring of Egyptian wonder-workers, but Frazier would not swerve from his course.

"Throw the accursed thing away," I urged nevertheless. "Those first few lines —good God, man, I didn't know whether I was freezing or burning, or being torn asunder on the rack. If that was but the beginning, then the end must be utter destruction."

Frazier shook his head. "I'm going to try it to a finish. That's why I called you. I need an assistant."

I LEAPED to my feet, seized my hat, and jammed it well down over my ears. Listening had been bad enough; assisting—! "If you think I'm going to dabble with insanity, you're mistaken! Forget it. Or get someone else."

"Suit yourself," Frazier retorted almost tartly. "I know it's deadly. That's why I want you to stand by, just outside the circle of influence, so you can intervene if it gets out of my control. But if you won't, why, then I'll have to take my chances. Mighty good of you to have dropped in anyway, Carver."

He turned toward a door which I had never seen opened, despite my somewhat frequent visits during a period of several years. I was quite content with his casual dismissal, but as his fingers closed on the doorknob, I seized him by the shoulder and whirled him about. "If I can be of any value as a spectator, all right! But I won't participate in the ritual," I compromised.

"That's better, Carver. I knew you'd not fail me in a pinch. Just wait here a moment—I'll be back presently."

The door closed behind Frazier. I paced up and down the long room, and to distract my uneasy anticipation, I finally stepped to one of the barred French windows that opened into a small Moorish patio about which the house was built. A glance sufficed to explain why the doors which opened from the street into the courtyard had been chained shut and locked for the past few months; why Frazier had cut a new entrance into the formerly unbroken facade of that massive old building. A young lioness was stalking majestically down the walk that led toward the mistily spraying fountain in the center of the patio.

Frazier owned the entire building, and was thus at liberty to humor his unusual fancy in pets; but I sensed, and at first without any semblance of conscious logic, that the lioness was not an exotic whim but a part of Frazier's experiment in

Egyptian magic. And then I recalled the opening line of Maimun's scroll: "Queen of the Sunrise . . . Queen of Lions. . . ."

She was lithe and tawny, and harmless seeming: no more than a monstrously overgrown cat. She paused midway to the fountain, looked toward the barred window, and for a moment regarded me with impassive, topaz eyes that reflected the disdainful condescension of all felines for humanity. A cat-lover would have been tempted to reach between the bars and stroke the sleek, well-fed beast; but I had no such inclination, particularly with the unpleasant recollection of the ritual chant, and the premonition of what was to come.

The click of the latch at my left broke into my somber speculations. Frazier had returned. He was bare-footed, and wore a white linen tunic. The flowing garment was awkwardly draped, but despite his somewhat ungainly figure, he was oddly impressive standing framed against the shifting gloom of the room beyond.

"I see you've been admiring Malika," he remarked, abruptly gesturing toward the barred window. Then, sensing my unspoken inquiry, he continued: "She is the symbol of Sekhmet, the entity we are invoking. If Sekhmet is to materialize, she must appropriate some of the etheric double of some living creature—very much as spirit materializations at a séance are effected by the use of the medium's etheric double. Such a loan of vital force is harmful; I propose to avoid that danger by having in the vicinity an animal whose occult harmony with Sekhmet is so close that our own etheric doubles will not be taken."

"Then you won't have that beast in the room?" I demanded, ready then and there to leave Frazier to his own devices. Malika, I judged, was a pet; and while lions are neither as treacherous as leopards nor as innately savage as tigers, the heaviest

veneer of domestication would vanish at the reading of that terrific scroll.

"Lord, no!" laughed Frazier. "The courtyard is quite close enough!"

He stepped toward the threshold. I followed him, instead of knocking him senseless and tossing that accursed scroll of Maimun into the grate. A short passageway opened into an elliptical room with a vaulted ceiling. The floor was black, and the curved walls a dead white. Concentric with the floor was a circle laid off in line; ranged at equal intervals along the perimeter were seven green, basalt pedestals. Six of them were occupied by female human figures, each with the head of a lioness, and each rigid right hand grasped a *crux ansata*, the loop-handled cross of power. In the twilight that crept through slits in the dome, those female forms loomed monstrously, like great cats lurking at the mouth of a mountain pass. The treacherous light gave their blank, sightless eyes a disconcerting intentness that no sculpture should have. I thought again of that awesome incantation, and would have withdrawn had it not been the chance that I might yet intervene.

FOR a long moment, Frazier contemplated my wonder. Then he announced: "These are effigies of Sekhmet, the lady of lions, the flame crowned, the queen of the sunrise. For all those dreary centuries, she has cast sightless eyes toward the morning, and peered vainly across the shifting wastes. She has been awaiting one who would release her from the bondage of oblivion.

"I am that one! And she will occupy that vacant pedestal, manifest in her splendor!"

He believed it. He took my belief for granted. He made a circuit of the chamber, striking light to torches which projected from sconces on the wall; at each pause in his march, resinous, smoky, red flames sprang to life. The solemn, lion-headed figures in that shifting, sultry light became more ominous than before. No ritual was needed; those wavering flames seemed already to have endowed those seven presences with a faint pulsing of vitality. A premonitory chill shuddered up and down my spine, and the hair on the back of my neck began to ripple.

The air was tense with Frazier's purpose; I knew then that nothing could dissuade him from venturing into the darkness of Egyptian magic. I did not anticipate what to expect, but I knew that it would be dreadful: for it is blasphemous to think of looking at any god, eye to eye.

"All right, Frazier," I said after a long silence. "How am I to stand guard? I am acquainted with a few occult principles, but you've told me very little."

He stepped behind the vacant pedestal and at once returned with a long, wooden, brass-bound trumpet that could not have been shorter than seven feet.

"Halt the ritual by blowing a blast on this horn," Frazier said, handing me the instrument. "The counter-vibrations will destroy the resonance of the chant. I have spent several months in experimenting, at each trial venturing further, but always stopping short of complete harmony with the master chord. I know that I am right —but I did not dare take the final step without an assistant. And while I am prepared to meet and overcome the various perils, the least miscalculation on my part would be fatal without your intervention. You, however, will be safe enough if you remain within the pentacle I have inscribed outside the circle of Sekhmet."

"But what is the danger?" I demanded. "How will I know when to interrupt?"

"Sekhmet will appear as a beautiful woman with topaz eyes," he explained. "She is represented with the head of a lioness only to symbolize her nature rather than to portray her. You will recognize her!

"And the grave danger will not be Sekhmet, but those others who may accompany her—malignant presences evoked by the under and overtones of the vibrations set up. Therein lies the great peril—but that is the chance I must take.

"Take your post; then blow a blast on the horn. It's not difficult, but you have to get the knack."

I stepped into the small pentacle Frazier had drawn on the floor near the only exit of the circular room and raised the long trumpet to my lips. My first few efforts were futile; but I persisted until, without warning, the gaping, wooden throat of that ancient instrument roared to life. That bestial, savage bellowing echoed and thundered like the challenge of a prehistoric monster; the very floor quivered as the earth shudders at the charge of uncounted horsemen.

I saw Frazier's gesture of protest, but could not hear his voice until an appreciable though brief interval after I had lowered that vibrant tube of wood from my lips. Then I heard Malika snarling in the patio. The roaring blast seemingly had shaken her feline nerves; but it had given Frazier renewed assurance.

"Perfect!" he approved. "Just the counter-vibration we may need. But don't sound off until I signal—keep your balance, and pay no attention to elementals or other alarming manifestations. The pentagram will be your safeguard. And on your life, don't leave it, *no matter what happens!*"

AFTER what I had heard that evening, Frazier's ominous injunction could add little to my increasing apprehension. I watched in silence as he took four small tripod-censers from the foot of the vacant pedestal and placed them on the circumference of the circle, at the cardinal points of the compass, the positions of which had been marked with appropriate symbols. With one of the redly flaring torches, he ignited the kindling beneath the charcoal and lumps of olibanum and myrrh in each censer. Frazier seemed utterly to ignore my presence; then, seeing the pallor of his tense features and the intentness of his staring eyes, I knew that there would be no further instructions.

Frazier had committed himself. He was hemmed in by those somber, unhuman green basalt figures, veiled by the low-hanging, bluish fumes that now poured from the copper censers. And as Frazier, scroll in hand, began making ceremonious, ritual gestures and genuflections, it seemed that he had already entered an alien space and single-handed was defying eternity.

I was looking at a man who knew that the gods are but the solidified dreams of mankind. Fear stood for a moment beside me in that protecting pentagram; then as Frazier began to read the scroll of Maimun, I knew that whatever gods might hear would be numbed beyond wrath.

His voice was thundering like a sea of fire lashing against brazen cliffs. What I had heard before was but a dim, pale echo of the terror that now poured forth. It was not the volume of his utterance, but rather its trenchant quality, that thrust and stabbed my taut nerves and made each fiber of muscle resonate as a goblet rings to a plucked violin string. Deep gutturals rumbled in the background of that soul-searching blasphemy which had baffled Maimun, the master necromancer; strange vowels struck rolling harmonies; and the measured rhythm was the warp on which that penetrant pattern was woven.

"Daughter of the Fire Mist! Lady of Lions! Your body's splendor feeds the weeds of ruin's garden, and the worms of time have gnawed your lotus breasts!"

He was chanting now in a dialect so ancient that I could not understand a word, but I felt the sense of the absolute sound. Frazier was enticing a goddess from the grave of eternity.

"Shade of a shadow! Bird without feathers! Arise from Amenti and gaze once more upon the dawn! The gate is open and the path is clear. . . ."

The censer fumes had become a swirling veil tinged by the red glare of scarcely distinguishable torches. The heavy sweetness of myrrh and the resinous fragrance of olibanum were stifling; but in that vortex of writhing smoke, Frazier still gestured and chanted, until the vault at last echoed with fierce rumblings and hissing whispers. The reverberations now beat like sledges on many anvils, and separate surges of sound stabbed into the web like flashes of lightning across a black firmament. I wondered why the vault did not collapse from the terrific impact of those satanically timed vibration-assaults—and then, for the first time, I understood why the walls were elliptical, and the dome an ellipsoid.

Frazier stood at one focus of the curve, and the vacant pedestal was at the other; thus the vibration harmony that was rendering and wrenching me to numbness was but the ghost of what was concentrating on a single point of that green basalt block, the focus of the elliptical dome. That one spot was receiving uncounted myriads of impacts that I could not sense, and the dome endured only because every emanation from Frazier's focal point was reflected and not absorbed.

I turned toward the vacant pedestal to note the effect of that concentration of force—and terror held my gaze. Frazier's lips were not moving. He has ceased chanting; yet that awful surge and thunder was swelling in volume! He had called forces from beyond the veil, and invisible presences were sustaining what he had set in motion.

Unseen powers were chanting, and they were changing the rhythm, conducting a sorcery of their own. Dead gods, revived by the scroll of Maimun, were stirring and rustling and murmuring, and the smoke-laden air became palpable, oppressively dense; yet each laboriously drawn breath was a draught of drugged wine. The vault had become an enclave that Frazier and his resurrected gods had stolen from eternity.

DIM shapes crowded the periphery of Frazier's circle. Some were polycephalous forms which, though vaguely resembling men, had closer kinship to beasts; others were lordly, towering human forms whose menacing gestures contradicted their benignant faces. They were living, yet a shifting, wavering flux of shadow substance; but momentarily their density increased until I could scarcely distinguish Frazier's white-robed form and fanatic eyes. Yet though they were gaining in power, they could not break across the occult barrier to execute their threats.

Suddenly the shadow shapes disintegrated and their substance began to spin in a whirling vortex that transcended space and shape and confining limits of the vault. For a moment, I thought that Frazier had exorcised them; then I perceived in the center of the vortex, clear and substantial and distinct from the mist whorls, a pure radiance that took form as the head and shoulders of a bearded man of majestic face and stern, dark eyes. His lips moved but the Presence emanated thought rather than audible speech.

"Beware!" warned those unspoken, battering waves of will. "You are seeking to resurrect an ancient evil and an archaic lust. Break that forbidden rhythm before

it destroys you. Who thirsts more for blood than the lioness of the desert, and whose essence is more fiery than flame?"

But Frazier defiantly advanced to the very edge of his circle, making gestures of power, matching will against will, and fearlessness against warning. He seemed no longer to be Frazier, but rather Lucifer stalking across hell's flame-lashed deserts. And at each conquering gesture and each bold pace, the lordly Presence became more unsubstantial, until his radiance subsided into the grey swirling of the stifling-sweet, oily mists.

The torches were now blanketed by the resurgent, living fog that had come from beyond the borders of time and space; yet the vault was not in darkness, nor had the self-sustained waves of vibration diminished. Tongues of bluish flames danced in halos about the lioness heads of Sekhmet, and the green basalt monsters became luminous and unsubstantial as the form-fluent shapes that once more crowded against the circle, wrathful and clamoring. Thin threads and streamers of multicolored light pulsed and throbbed in a slender spindle of radiance which centered on the seventh and vacant pedestal.

Frazier was winning. The unseen sustainers of Maimun's magic were battering down the resisting shapes that vainly assaulted the impregnable circle. And as the besiegers slowly disintegrated into wisps of vapor, a fresh wonder evolved. The space within the circle now seemed not to be a plane, but rather a gateway into hyperspace; the ellipsoidal dome, by some uncanny distortion, had become a paraboloid of infinite sweep instead of a closed curve, so that it now had but a single focus; thus instead of merely reflecting the vibrant surges of Maimun's archaic chant, it was drawing energy from beyond terrestrial dimensions and concentrating it on the green basalt pedestal.

As I watched the incredible calculus of

the higher sorcery, I saw that that seventh pedestal was no longer vacant. The slender spindle of light was swelling and throbbing under the fierce blasts of cosmic energy stolen from beyond space; in that murderous glow, I saw the figure of a woman of incredible loveliness blossoming out on the block of basalt. The imperious sweetness, of her fine, scarlet lips, and the delicate, cardioid outline on her face, and thin, high-bridged, haughty nose were a beauty lost in the wonder of her eyes. They were slanting, greenish-topaz, and phosphorescent as those of a lioness crouching in the darkness. Sekhmet had materialized in beauty that was a corrosive sweetness and a burning wonder.

Maimun's forbidden magic had succeeded—but it was not yet complete! As she stood there, smiling at Frazier and extending inviting, slender arms that were banded with circlets of hammered gold, a leaping flame crackled along the perimeter of the circle; and as my eyes recovered from the glare, I saw that the effigies of Sekhmet were no longer solid basalt, but plastic, fluent radiance that pulsed with life. The sightless, staring, sculptured eyes glowed now feline and phosphorescent, in rivalry of those of the very Lady of Lions!

The hammering waves of vital force from unplumbed abysses of superspace had blasted the atoms of those carven images into new orders and had imparted stolen life into lifeless stone. The infinite sweep of the now paraboloidal vault rang and howled and thundered as a forge in which black-faced, sweating gods shaped worlds out of incandescent, primordial substance. The ritual which had resurrected Sekhmet from the memories of long-dead worshipers had infused life into all that was within the circle of its influence. The very floor was writhing and undulating as though it were sentient as those fearsome, lioness-headed forms.

All the terror and awe that had been before were nothing compared to that which accompanied that instant of transformation. I knew that I was looking into a corridor of some archaeaval hell; I knew that doom was closing in on Frazier in his moment of triumph; and I knew, also, that it was time to lift that long, wooden trumpet to my lips and blow a lung-rending blast to shatter the wizardy of dead Maimun, blow until blood vessels burst, until that unnaturally curved and distorted vault collapsed—anything at all to halt the divine wrath that was closing in on Frazier.

THEY had arisen from their green-glowing thrones, those six beast-headed women. They were stalking toward the center like great cats slinking to the kill; yet something compelling forced them to stealth. If Frazier could but draw his glance from the phosphorescent eyes of wondrous Sekhmet—if Frazier could ignore her curved crimson smile and the invitation of her amber-hued arms—if Frazier would turn and with a word of power repel those green-flaming monsters evoked of dead stone. . . .

In my extreme horror, I forgot Frazier's orders. I could not wait for him to give me the signal. I raised the blasting trumpet to my lips. Then I knew that Frazier was doomed. The substance of the very air in that anteroom of destruction had changed. That dense, drugged, oily air was too thick for the lung-filling inhalation and sudden explosion needed to blow the shattering note. I realized then that my breathing had subsided to a scarcely perceptible flutter. In self defense, my body had rebelled and refused to take in more than the faintest ripple of that unnaturally vital atmosphere. It was as though I had tried to inhale a viscous liquid. That one forced draught in my lungs burned and seared, made my senses reel from overstimulation.

And yet those six monstrous effigies were moving with infinite stealth. They were tensing their bodies to keep them fluent and poised while waiting as for a signal to close in, waiting for some unseen restrait to be removed.

Sekhmet's eyes and arms invited. She made formal gestures, statuesque yet inexpressibly graceful. Frazier, facing her phosphorescent splendor, had begun his advance toward the pedestal. I could hear no speech, yet I knew from Sekhmet's gestures and the motion of her lips and the alluring arch of her brows that she was urging him to join her on the pedestal, and walk with her along the shimmering pathway of multicolored radiance that led back into the uttermost abysses of eternity whence she had just emerged. Sekhmet was accepting him, and Frazier, moving as in a dream, completed another pace.

Then I understood why those six awful figures of animated stone were waiting. They could not harm him until he had committed the ultimate blasphemy. Frazier's wizardry had permitted him to look at a goddess unveiled, but for him to touch her was forbidden. Frazier knew best of all that while men may evoke gods from the dust of time, no man may become one with what he has created. Yet Frazier persisted in his advance.

I knew that he would make no signal to me now. Again I raised the trumpet. I forced a searing, corrosive inhalation into my lungs, but before I could blow a blast, the burning, acute agony made me cough. And though my senses swam, I caught the poison sweet, mocking smile of Sekhmet and knew that she was betraying Frazier to a doom.

"Who thirsts more for blood than the lioness of the desert, and whose essence is more fiery than flame?"

The Presence had warned Frazier, and Frazier was persisting. He was now within arm's reach of that enthralling loveliness and her divine radiance. The six monsters leaned forward, and their teeth gleamed.

One hope remained. Frazier had warned me to remain within the shelter of my pentacle. I knew not what savage entities lurked in the mist banks and perverted spatial vistas of that warped corridor of doom. I knew not what consuming flames might calcine me if I ventured from the protecting pentagram; but that one chance I could not decline. Frazier and his learning must be preserved, and I saw a way. In my desperation I had recollected what I had forgotten in the terror loosed by the reading of Maimun's scroll.

They were so intently watching Frazier that they would perhaps be unaware of my move. I leaped from the pentagram— not toward the circle, but toward the passageway leading to the adjoining room, only a few yards away, but uncounted eternities distant. As I cleared the threshold, I saw from a fleeting glimpse over my shoulder that Frazier's hand had not yet touched the slender, glittering fingers of flame-shrouded Sekhmet. . . .

I plunged into gloom, unbroken save by the dim glow of the dying embers of the grate. The sullen light was reflected from a great disc of beaten bronze. Its note had broken the spell of Frazier's tentative reading of the scroll—and that was the last chance! Great waves of drugged fumes had followed me down the passageway; but before the increasing concentration could overcome me, I found the mallet and hammered the five-foot disc to a fury of brazen reverberation, striking until it seemed that all creation would collapse at that roaring thunder.

Yet even as I struck, I heard above that earth-shaking clang a savage snarling, a deep-throated roaring, and a high-pitched, suddenly stifled cry of mortal terror. Then came an abrupt silence, unbroken save by the hissing and humming of the still-vibrant bronze.

A choked, gurgling cough told me that Frazier lived. I dropped the mallet and retraced my steps. The air in the vault still reeked, but only from censer fumes. The torches flared redly, and were no longer masked by writhing mists; and the six sculptured figures sat stiffly on their thrones of basalt. The vortex of power had been shattered by the jarring dissonance of the brazen gong. I had thwarted the concentration of evil that had kept me from blowing the trumpet; yet I had lost my race against Frazier's doom.

HE lay sprawled at the foot of the vacant pedestal. I ventured into the circle and saw that Frazier's body, stripped of all but a few shreds of linen tunic, was hideously mangled by feline teeth. He stirred, feebly gestured toward the six basalt colossi I had seen so terribly animated, and muttered unintelligibly. There was but one conclusion that I could draw, and that was as incredible as it was inescapable: yet I could not deny the evidence that remained after the passing of the hell glamour. . . .

Blood—fresh blood—still dripped from the now immobile jaws of those green statues, and trickled down to stain their cold, sculptured breasts. Frazier strove to explain; but I could not understand his dying mutterings, and I was glad that I could not understand.

A surge of revulsion drove me from that blood-splashed vault. In the adjoining room, I snapped the switch that controlled the lights which hung over the courtyard. I hoped, for the sake of sanity, to see Malika licking fresh blood from her dripping jaws so that I could tell myself, and others, that the blood that stained the six statues had spurted upward from wounds inflicted by Malika's wrath. There was no way, of course, in which she could have passed iron bars and two feet of masonry—yet that was more acceptable than the knowledge I could not deny.

I saw Malika: but she was dead, her body wracked and tormented, and emaciated so that only tawny skin was stretched over bones. I remembered Frazier's preliminary explanations, and knew that the vital force of the powerful beast had been stolen—drained to furnish the link between the material plane and whatever hyper-dimensional hell had disgorged Sekhmet and her attendant furies.

"Who thirsts more for blood than the lioness of the desert, and whose essence is more fiery than flame?"

Frazier knows, and so do I. And when I visit a certain museum, I refuse to pass down a majestic hall where lioness-headed Sekhmet peers past the cream-hued bulwarks of masonry that confine her—looks across time and space and beyond the savage crags of anicent Egypt: for I have seen flesh torn by green basalt jaws, and I know that in some enclave of forbidden space, a woman with greenish-topaz, phosphorescent eyes licks fine, scarlet lips as her six companions smile reminiscently.

DEATH TAKES A BRIDE!

By Nat Schachner
(Author of "Thirst of the Ancients," etc.)

DAN TURNER knew positively now that they were being followed. Stealthy feet were padding through the woods, keeping even pace with theirs. The footfalls ceased when he stopped, suddenly, on the pretense of letting Cora rest; they took up their surreptitious pursuit when Dan and Cora went on again.

He fought to keep his voice steady as he urged his bride of a few hours to greater haste. Poor Cora! Their honeymoon had started with disaster. Some two miles back, their car lay abandoned with a smashed rear-axle, broken by an unseen boulder in a deep puddle of water.

"I know you're tired, honey," he whispered, careful to keep his voice low, "but there *must* be a village somewhere along this road."

Thin trickles of moonlight pierced the thick overhanging branches. They made a pallid blob of Cora's lovely face, muted the honey color of her smooth, thick hair as it peeped from under a black, *cloche* hat.

She flogged her weary limbs to greater speed, stumbling over the rutted lane. She clung with a desperate grip to her husband's sturdy, reassuring arm.

"Dan!" Her voice, breathing out of the dimly revealed darkness, was throaty with suppressed fear. "There's something—

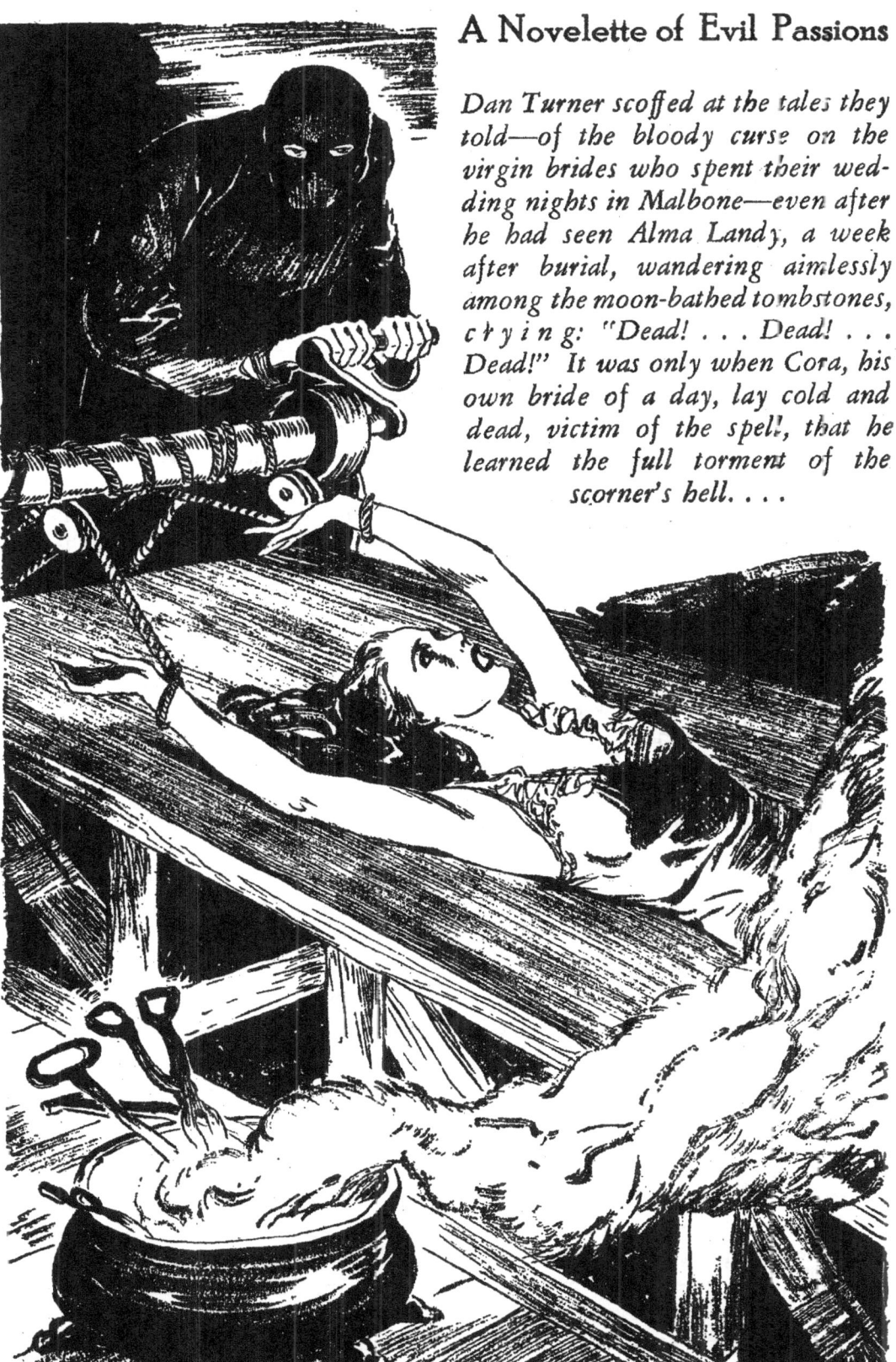

A Novelette of Evil Passions

Dan Turner scoffed at the tales they told—of the bloody curse on the virgin brides who spent their wedding nights in Malbone—even after he had seen Alma Landy, a week after burial, wandering aimlessly among the moon-bathed tombstones, crying: "Dead! . . . Dead! . . . Dead!" It was only when Cora, his own bride of a day, lay cold and dead, victim of the spell, that he learned the full torment of the scorner's hell. . . .

in those woods—following us. I—I'm afraid!"

Unconsciously, he accelerated his pace. He had hoped desperately that Cora would not hear. If only he had a gun, he would not feel so terribly helpless, with the girl he adored acting as a bait to whatever foul thing it was that glided like a sinuous serpent through the trees.

But he strove to put reassuring heartiness into his words when he answered. "Nonsense, Cora. You're just imagining things. It's—it's only the rustle of the wind over dried leaves." Then, with an explosive gasp of relief that was far more genuine, he cried:

"Look, darling, we're out of the woods! There's a clearing ahead. We'll find houses, people, help!"

Thank God! He had not realized how jittery he had been in that darkling, hemmed-in lane. Now let whatever it was dare to show itself in the revealing moonlight. He was not afraid any more.

The trees widened before their breathless progress, and then, suddenly, they were on an upland clearing. Cora shrank against her husband with a startled, "Oh!" Her slender form, snug in a mud-splashed traveling suit, trembled with apprehension. For a moment, Dan's spine was a rigid, ice-covered ramrod.

A dead moon flooded an eerie village of the dead with frozen light. White-glowing, phosphorescent teeth seemed to jut from the gaping maw of some monstrous beast. A dank, miasmic vapor swirled low over broken, weather-worn tombstones. It ebbed away momentarily to disclose the flaunting marble of a new stone and the turned earth of a freshly-made grave under which an unquiet body had not yet had time to find surcease and rest. Then the haze billowed away in a solid, clinging sheet again.

Dan exhaled his withheld breath and laughed shakily. The laugh sounded hollow and strained even to himself. "It's only a cemetery, Cora. No one there can harm you. They've been peacefully dead a long time."

Cora's shriek gashed through the deathly silence like a saber thrust. Her terror-strong fingers gripped desperately on her husband's arm; her face was a ghastly blur of fear.

"Oh, God! Dan, look!"

Dan spun on his heel, peering in the direction Cora pointed, rigid as if in a vise. Merciful Heavens! For a moment he swayed in sheer, unbelieving horror. His skin was a strangling encasement, squeezing his body until he could not breathe. Leaping blood roared and pounded in his ear drums. What in the name of God was that?

The ghastly exhalation of cemetery dew had lifted. And with it, seeming to rise from the unplumbed depths of the fresh-covered grave itself, like an evil incarnation, was a white-clad figure like a resurrected corpse!

THE pallid moonlight swathed the eerie apparition in an aura of moldering phosphorescence, emphasizing in fiendish detail the long, trailing dress that seemed to merge into the plucking grave beneath. Icy horror whistled through Dan's veins, jerked the breath from his stiffened lips. Cora's limbs were numb with terror, her eyes wide and staring.

The apparition was dressed in a bridal gown! A corpse-bride had risen from her rendezvous with death!

How long they stood in frozen immobility Dan was never to know. Nightmare paralysis held their fainting limbs rooted to the ground for a timeless eternity.

Then the Thing that was the bride of Death seemed to flow toward them. Its face, dim beneath a filmy, frozen veil, was ghastly white, its eyes black, burning pits in a hell of agony. It lifted its corpse-white arm, pointed with accusing finger directly at the fear-rooted pair.

"Dead! Dead! Dead!" Like hammer blows the dreadful, toneless accents fell on their reeling senses. Then the arm swung down, and a shrieking, bubbling laugh came from its throat. It rose in soulless horror until air and earth and sky were a welter of demoniac sound, piercing their ears with unbearable agony. Still shrieking, still laughing with the dreadful emptiness of the grave, the white-swathed creature flowed without seeming motion —closer, ever closer!

Something snapped inside Dan, released him from his gripping panic. He caught his fainting wife by the arm; he jerked her along the muddy road with all the force of his jittering muscles. They ran, headlong, blindly, up the winding road, up to the brow of the hill, panting, breath spasmodic in their nostrils, goaded on to draining new spurts by the ceaseless, hideous laughter that swelled out behind them.

At the top of the slope, the road dipped sharply, down into a cupped valley. It was like a saucer bowl, bright and clear-etched under the white mockery of the moon. Cubes of solid blackness were scattered through the frost-white fields, clustered in ominous, serpentine masses along the central dip of the road. No light broke the grim, looming bulks, no stir of motion anywhere showed that life pervaded the sheeted valley.

Dan and Cora flung themselves down the sloping lane with desperate, racing feet. As they dipped over the bulge of the hill, the unhuman shrieking choked off abruptly, as if a skeleton hand had thrust out of the grave to drag back its escaped occupant. Silence blanketed the earth, broken only by the thud of their feet, the stertorous whistling of their tortured lungs.

Dan caught his wife just as she stumbled in blind, fainting weariness. Man-

hood, reason, came back with the cessation of that dreadful laugh. He felt ashamed of himself for having run, yet . . . what terrible warning for them did that bride of the grave portend? Why had the lurking presence pursued them through the woods until they reached its home in the village of the dead?

He shivered, tried to speak lightly. The broken gaspings of his spent energy made the effort a hollow japery: "You've married a brave husband, Cora," he said with a tight grin. "Imagine running away like that from some poor lunatic of a girl who happens to roam the fields at night."

Cora tottered with fatigue. Her sweet, finely chiseled face was pale as death, and fear brooded in the dark blue depths of her eyes. A shudder went rippling down her slender form.

"She was no creature of this earth, Dan," she whispered. "She came from the grave—to warn me. Don't you see? She was a—a bride too! Oh Dan," she wailed and clung to him, "I'm terribly afraid! I know something dreadful is going to happen!"

He stroked her arm tenderly. Even through the tweed cloth of her coat it was icy cold. "Please!" he begged. "Don't give way to nerves. There's nothing to be alarmed about. We're almost in the village. We'll find someone to fix our car. We'll go on, and forget about it all."

But inside, he knew instinctively that they were not through, that Cora's premonitions were correct. The wind of impending evil moaned through his body, and stifled the beating of his heart.

THE first house of the straggling street loomed in front of them. Its two squat stories crouched low to the ground like a stretched-out, tense cat motionless before a mouse-hole. A single, yellow streamer of light glared out at them like a baleful eye. It was deathly silent under the frosty moon.

Dan forced cheerfulness. "Here we are, dear," he said. "Looks like a hotel. That means our troubles are over."

Cora shrank back. She stared at the sprawling house with the fixity of a somnambulist. "Dan, dearest," she cried. "I feel something evil in there, something that is reaching out, dragging me down!"

Her husband said half-angrily: "Now you *are* giving way to your nerves! It's a commonplace country hotel with normal, usual people inside." He himself had felt the same stealthy flow of malign influence emanating from the house, but because he was a man—and a practical, hard-headed engineer to boot—he refused to yield to his shrieking instincts. Besides, a stealthy glance down the single, darkened street of the village had shown no other signs of life.

He rapped boldly on the door. A thin edge of yellow light knifed from under the door-sill. The abrupt knocking made thudding reverberations in a cavernous interior. A confused mutter of voices stilled suddenly. Deep, breathless silence lay like a pall, as if the inmates were crouching inside, waiting . . . waiting. . . !

Cora cried out again: "Let's go on, Dan! To the next village, anywhere. . . !"

Because he felt the same half-angry, inward urge, he pounded again, furiously. "Open the door!" he shouted.

This time there was movement. From inside came the sound of a slow, dragging shuffle. The door opened wide slowly, complaining stridently on its ungreased hinges.

Deep, yellow radiance flooded out into the night, scattering the silver phosphorescence of the moon. A man stood silhouetted in the doorway, peering out at them with shaded eyes.

"What ye want, strangers?" he demanded. His voice was deep and harshly forbidding.

"We want to get in," Dan answered angrily. He resented the man's tone, the fact that he blocked the entrance with his huge body. He was not afraid of anything mortal, anything formed of flesh and blood. Not like the shadowy Thing of the cemetery that. . . . He forced himself back to the business at hand. "Our car broke down about three miles back. We'd like to have it fixed, and incidentally, to get something to eat. This is a hotel, isn't it?"

"Yeah," the man growled, after a perceptible pause. "Ye might call this a hotel; leastwise as much as ye kin find in Malbone. But thar ain't no one kin fix your car till mornin'. Jeff, the mechanic, don't live in the village." And still the big man made no move to get out of the way.

Cora clung to her husband, whispering very low: "Please Dan, let's go on. I don't like his looks."

But Dan snarled in his throat, like a thoroughbred meeting a strange, hostile dog. Very deliberately he moved forward.

"Come on, Cora," he whipped over his shoulder. "The gentleman's inviting us in."

Their unwilling host stepped back just in time to avoid being shoved out of the way. Dan followed into the room. His strong, reassuring grip held Cora tight.

The other man stood to one side, legs astraddle, rocklike, smoldering fury in his small, red eyes. He was a huge man and his face was craggy and dour. Flaming red hair made an uncouth thatch over beetling brows. His nose was red from much drinking. His great hands hung at his sides, clenched and knotted with veins. Red hairs made a furry surface of their backs.

Dan glanced swiftly around the room. It was low-ceilinged and timbered, dark with years of smoke and soot. The floor was strewn with dirty sawdust and there were several rickety round tables with straight-backed chairs set about them. At the farther end of the room was a shabby bar, cracked and filthy, with a fly-specked mirror behind it, flanked by a row of dirty, lusterless bottles and glasses.

A MAN sat in a corner, elbows propped on a table. A half-emptied glass of stale, flat beer stood in front of him. He stared at the intruders with sullen, glowering eyes. His frowsy face was dark with stubble, and black hair hung in a low mop over a sloping forehead.

"Ain't many nights you're lucky like this, Silas Benton, is there?" he said rustily, fingering his glass with dirty fingers and sidling his glance sidewise at Cora. The girl looked around the unattractive interior with a little shudder of repulsion. She pressed close to Dan for protection, like a timid, helpless creature.

"Shut your mouth, Mose Landy!" Benton growled. He turned to Dan, while his red eyes slithered covetously over the girl. "As long as ye're here, might's well take care of ye," he said ungraciously. "Kin give you supper."

"That's swell," Dan said with a heartiness he was far from feeling.

Benton seemed to be cook, waiter, and owner all in one. Long minutes passed before the thick, greasy food was slopped on thicker, greasier plates. The butter was rancid and the coffee tasted strangely bitter. Cora nibbled hesitantly at moldy bread and sipped the coffee. Dan was hungry, but even his strong stomach could not down much of the food.

While they were eating, the man called Landy hunched over his beer, watching them covertly from under his black, limp hair. He did not speak.

Dan shoved the last plate away with relief, looked up at Benton. The landlord seemed like a huge, red gorilla, bent slightly forward as if ready to drop on all fours.

"Have you a place for us to sleep tonight, until that mechanic of yours can get on the job?"

Benton let his reddish eyes shift to Landy. "Yeah," he said hesitantly, "I got a room, but . . ."

"But what?" Dan asked sharply as the man stopped.

"Well ye see, your wife mightn't like it. Last week a young gal, she died in that there room."

Cora lifted her lovely head. "Oh, the poor thing!" she breathed sympathetically. "What was the matter with her?"

Benton scratched his head and looked at Landy again. "Ain't rightly known," he confessed. "She jes' up and died, like."

The dark, frowsy man unfolded himself slowly from his chair. He was tall and lanky when he stood up. "Whyn't yuh tell folks the truth, Silas Benton?" he demanded harshly. He turned slowly to Cora. His eyes glowered stormily. "There was a curse on her." His gaze flickered, softened, and went hard again. "She was a brave gal, Alma was. She heerd of the curse that lay on Malbone, yet she fought agin it. She always said, with a toss of her pretty, little head: 'Mose, I ain't givin' in to this here superstition. The other poor gals, they all died natural-like, just like Missus Olmstead, millionaire Olmstead's wife, up there on the hill. It was just happenstance it was always on their weddin' nights. The man what marries me,' says she, 'has gotta marry in Malbone, an' nowhere else. I'll show 'em there ain't anything in that curse!' "

"Yeah," Benton interrupted savagely. "Bein' as how you're tryin' to spoil trade for me, ye mought's well tell the rest. Alma, she died on her weddin' night, like t'others, right in that spare room of mine upstairs. It's still fixed up, with the trimmings an' everything, like it was when she died, ain't it, Mose?" He started to chuckle unpleasantly, while Dan felt a strange tightening sensation in his brain.

"Shut up!" Landy shouted furiously. "Course it is. I'm paying you for it, ain't I?" He swung on Cora, who shrank back with a little cry from his twitching, dis-torted countenance. "She was Alma Landy—my wife—that night, an' she died! Like all the others. I begged her not to do it; I begged her to come to the big town and marry me there; but she just laughed. An'—an'—" he was fum-bling blindly for words, "now she's gone, and all I got's beer, an' Benton's rotgut, tuh drown my thinkin' in!"

Cora forgot her fears, moved with wom-anly sympathy toward him. But he was gone, slamming the outer door behind him with a crash.

Benton pointed significantly to his own fiery pate. "He's a bit cracked since it happened, but you ain't got no call to worry. The curse holds only for a wed-din' night."

Dan sucked his breath in sharply. Mag-gots of dread started crawling in his brain. Drumming fingers played a devil's tattoo up and down his spine. Words burst in panting jerks from Cora's fear-stiffened lips:

"Why—why—it's our wedding night too!"

BENTON'S jaw sagged. His mouth gaped liked a slimy pit, disclosing blackened stumps of teeth. Dan arose. He would not stay in this place any long-er. Better to take Cora out into the night, to trudge wearily to the next village, than . . . .

The door swung open with a gust of air. A man stamped noisily into the room, shaking himself all over like a terrier which had scrambled out of a pool of water. He was small and wiry, and he carried a professional bag.

"Hello, Benton!" he greeted. "Just got through with Ma Hendricks, and thought I'd step in for a drink. Lord knows I need one. But the youngster's a fine, healthy, squalling boy, so I suppose it's . . . . Hello!" The doctor's bright, snap-ping eyes and little trim Vandyke turned toward the young couple. "I see you've got visitors tonight."

He stuck out his hand in friendly fash-ion. "I'm Dr. Edward Corwin, the only médico for miles around. I bring them into the world and usher them out. Stay-ing for the night, I hope?"

"Well," Dan hesitated. After all, it was hard, in the presence of this bustling man of science, to confess dread of an old woman's superstition. "I'm Dan Tur-ner, and this is my wife, Cora. But—you see—that is—"

"Mose Landy scared 'em off with his wild talk of curses laid on Malbone," the landlord interjected venomously.

The doctor swerved on them. His eyes were unfathomably bright. "Poor Mose," he said softly. "Of course, he's a bit mad. But then Alma was a fine girl. You see, it all started when Marian Olmstead died three years ago. It was her wed-ding night, up there on the hill, in the French château that Richard Olmstead had transported brick for brick, from France. Olmstead's been nearly crazy from grief ever since. He loved Marian very much. There was a curse, he said, on the château, and he had brought it back to Malbone. The natives embroidered on the tale, and made it a legend to apply to any virgin on her wedding night." He stopped, seemed to weigh his words care-fully. "There *have* been several deaths since, under similar circumstances. Un-fortunate coincidences, you understand, not worthy of an intelligent man's be-lief. But no one, except Alma, has dared marry in Malbone for months."

Cora cried out wildly: "This is *my*

wedding night, too, and I won't stay." She shivered as if with ague; her eyes glittered with strange lights.

Dan felt the doctor's slightly amused eyes on him. Some secret spring in him quivered in response to his wife's terror, but being a man, he dared not confess his dread. He looked steadily at Benton, the landlord, averting his eyes from Cora.

"Please prepare the room," he said. "My wife and I are sleeping here tonight."

"Oh!" Cora put her hand to her mouth, gulped, and said nothing more. Dan felt as though he had struck her brutally with his fist. He wanted to take her in his arms, and beg forgiveness; he wanted to tell her that they would leave this very instant. But the landlord's heavy feet were already clumping up the stairs, and Dr. Corwin smiled quietly:

"Nothing like meeting a man of sense, sir," he said. "And as for your charming wife, a little nightcap would help soothe her nerves." He went behind the bar, pulled out a bottle, filled three glasses with deft fingers.

"My own private stock that I keep handy. It's a Napoleon brandy, very old and very pale. Here's luck to the newly-weds."

He handed Cora a glass with a little bow, gave one to Dan, took one for himself. They clinked and drank. Dan smacked his lips. It was real cognac. It warmed his insides; he saw Cora flush a bit and lose the haunted look in her shadowed eyes.

Benton was clumping downstairs again, when the sound of an automobile careening down the road roared in their ears. It came to a grinding halt before the hotel; brakes squealed; a steel door slammed, and someone catapulted into the room. He was a haggard, gaunt-faced man with burning, bulging eyes in which mad little lights crawled. His clothes, though spat-

tered with mud and disheveled as if they had been slept in, bore the unmistakable stamp of Saville Row and English tailoring.

THE man glared fiercely at Dr. Corwin. He seemed to see no one else in the room. "She's gone away again, Corwin," he wailed. His lean, clawed hands fluttered like reeds in a gale. "She's left me, like she always does."

Corwin spoke to him soothingly: "Now, now, Mr. Olmstead, please be calm. Explain yourself. *Who* is gone; *who* left you?"

The millionaire shouted insanely: "Don't be a fool, Corwin! I mean Marian, of course—my wife. Every time I try to hold her, to keep her with me, she slips away. This time she's gone—for good!"

His head dropped suddenly in his hands. Great dry sobs racked his gaunt frame.

Cora swayed to her husband. "Oh, my God!" she murmured. Dan felt his scalp freeze to his skull. Dr. Corwin said Mrs. Olmstead had died three years before; Landy and Benton had corroborated it. Yet here was Olmstead, speaking of her as if she were alive, as if she had run away.

The doctor's eyes snapped warning to their shocked senses. He walked over to the sobbing man, laid his hand on his shoulder. "All right, Mr. Olmstead. I'll find Marian for you. Come; we'll search for her together!"

The millionaire raised his head eagerly. He seemed like a man reprieved from Hell. "You mean that, Corwin?" he cried. "You'll find her . . .?"

"Of course I shall," the doctor assured him, pushing him gently through the door. He turned, shrugged his shoulders slightly to the couple. "I've got to humor the poor fellow," he stage-whispered. "He has some queer delusions."

Then he was gone. A moment later

they heard the motor of the automobile roar into vibrant life; then the grinding of gears, and the slither of sand beneath turning wheels.

Benton, the landlord, paused at the foot of the stairs. His red eyes slid past Dan and Cora, stared with poisonous intensity at the closed portal through which Olmstead and Corwin had departed. His craggy, red-mottled face was twisted in hate.

He caught Dan's surprised glance on him, and a veil dropped over his eyes. "Yuhr room is ready, mister," he muttered.

Cora leaned heavily on her husband. She yawned. "I—I feel sleepy, Dan, dearest," she confessed.

Slowly they went up the creaking steps. A single Delco bulb made dim illumination in the hall. At the farther end, to the left, was an open door.

Benton grumbled: "That's your room. The other doors just lead into spare rooms with old junk an' the like. Ain't had much call for roomers since . . . ." He checked himself. "Good night! Hope ye enjoy your weddin' night in Alma Landy's bed." And he withdrew, silent now, like a cat, in his tread, chuckling and mumbling to himself.

Dan stared around. Tiny, prickling feet seemed to have made a playground of his skin. In this very room, a young girl had died on her honeymoon night. And he had been fool enough to bring Cora to this rendezvous with death, simply because he had been afraid of a stranger's scorn.

It was pathetic, that room, yet subtly ominous. The old-fashioned four-poster bed was covered with a garish, red, rayon coverlet; the vanity bureau was brave with cheap, ornate toilet articles, in flowered imitation ivory—the very things to delight the heart of a country girl. Nothing had been touched since that fatal night;

even the palpably new, lace nightgown hung pathetically on a hook near the bed.

Dan shivered and started slowly to undress. He wished the night were gone already, that they were far away from Malbone, with the morning sun clear and shining with ghost-dispersing rays. Cora was unaccountably quiet. She yawned again and sat heavily on the bed. Her tweed coat was off and she fumbled with clumsy-seeming fingers at the hooks of her dress.

"Tired, darling?" Dan asked tenderly. Her lovely face had dark shadows on it. Her eyelids drooped. "I—I don't know. . . ." she started, and then her voice trailed off.

DAN looked up quickly from his chair. He was unlacing a shoe. It was then that he saw the framed picture on the vanity. It stood at an angle, away from the door, and the dim-burning Delco bulb in the nearer corner barely illuminated it. There was something familiar about the young girl whose photograph it was, something familiar about her. . . .

Dan stood up quickly. He forgot about Cora's tiredness. He forgot everything but one pulsing thought. He must see that picture at close range; he must rid himself of that terrible suspicion before it grew on him.

In one bound he was at the vanity, had swept the frame into a violently trembling hand. Cora jerked her sleepy head erect. There was a puzzled, strained look on her face, as if she were savoring some nauseous concoction.

Dan's breath came in whistling gasps. His hand seemed frozen to the picture, yet it burned, like searing hell-fire, in his grasp. Stark, ravening horror exploded in his brain. His limbs seemed poured into an unyielding mold. "Merciful God!" he whispered through locked teeth, over and over again.

Cora forced herself from her stupor. The pallor of her face had deepened; there seemed to be no blood behind its translucent white.

"What—what's happened, Dan?"

His eyes burned into the picture. "This —this—!" he mouthed thickly.

It was a quite innocuous photograph. A young girl, fairly pretty, with sweet, somewhat irregular features and wide, dark eyes, dressed in a long trailing bridal gown and a veil to match. Evidently Alma Landy had posed before an itinerant photographer on her wedding morning, blushing with happiness, not realizing then the doom that was soon to overtake her.

"This girl—Alma Landy—" Dan said slowly, "who has been dead and buried for a week, is the Thing we saw in the cemetery!"

The light from the single bulb seemed suddenly shadowed over with leering, glowering shapes. The room swirled with stealthy movement. Unnamable Things closed in on two terrified mortals, baleful eyes gloating with horrid expectation.

Dan could feel the slow motion of his sluggish blood as it forced its way reluctantly through his clabbered veins. His head was sizes too small for his bursting brain. It was impossible—it was incredible—yet he knew his eyes had not deceived him. The dead girl had risen from her new-made grave, had cried out in unhuman accents: "Dead! dead!" She had writhed with strange, unearthly laughter. God in Heaven! He felt his overtaxed brain slipping, going mad. . . .

He whirled feverishly on his wife. The damning picture dropped with a thud from nerveless fingers. "Cora!" he cried, "Dress again! We must get out of this place. Now, this very minute! Do you hear?" He stopped abruptly. "Good God, Cora! What's the matter?"

His wife was swaying slowly. Her hand clutched spasmodically at her bosom; her breath came in loud, sucking gulps; there was strained agony on her clammy face. "Water, for the love of God!" she moaned. "I'm burning up, inside. Water!"

She sank across the bed, her limbs twitching and writhing.

"Cora!" Dan's shout was almost a scream. He raced to her side, jerked her face around. "Cora, darling, what ails you? Don't—don't! Cora, I implore you—!" His voice was a blur of tears.

Cora's eyes were dark with pain, unseeing; her bosom rose and fell with the thudding rapidity of a trip-hammer, she clutched at her heart as if she would tear it out. "Water, please!" The words issued barely audible from her pain-twisted lips.

Dan sprang up. "Of course! At once, immediately! Wait for me! I'll get you water, everything!"

*　*　*

His voice was an anguished wail as he flung himself out of the thick-shadowed room, raced with insane speed down the hall, cleared the narrow staircase in two breakneck bounds, smashed through the taproom. The blood seemed to spurt like a millrace from every pore, his ears roared with crashing thunder; his brain was a molten furnace.

His blindly stumbling feet lashed at the bar; his trembling hands fumbled over the glasses and bottles. Glass crashed to the floor with explosive sounds.

"Say, what's goin' on in here?"

It was Benton's voice, harsh, demanding. Dan turned his fear-frozen face toward the landlord. "My wife," he whispered—funny how his voice had failed him, "she's sick. She wants water. But don't think . . . ."

Benton jerked toward the bar. His

reddish, crag-hard features were masked with terror. "God, another one!" he stammered.

He snatched up a bottle, yelled: "Come on!" and was bounding up the stairs. Dan raced after. The water would bring her to—he was sure of that—yet dreadful fear climbed the stairs with him.

They burst into the bridal room with a thunder of noise. But no answering sounds greeted them. The air was thick with mocking presences. The prone figure on the bed was still.

"Cora!" The cry was a bayonet thrust through the silence. Dan hurled himself toward the bed, caught a still shoulder, shook it frantically. His wife's dear, pale head bobbed with the motion, fell back limply. Her eyes stared without focus at him, at the walls of the room, whichever way her body was turned. They refused to close.

The landlord sucked his breath in noisily. His red hair bristled, his bulbous nose twitched. He stared at the useless bottle in his hairy hand.

"I'm afeared, Mr. Turner, it ain't no use. The curse of Malbone—it's laid on her, too."

Dan jumped to his feet. His eyes glared, his face was that of an old man. "It can't be," he panted. "She's alive, man! She just—just fainted. Get a doctor, quick, do you hear?"

Benton backed away from him as from a crazed maniac. "Sure," he agreed hurriedly. "I'll get Doc Corwin on the 'phone this minute."

Out in the hall, he lifted the receiver, turned the crank three times. There was low-voiced conversation while Dan clung close to his wife's body, gulping great sobs.

DR. CORWIN put his stethoscope away, straightened up, and said gravely:

"There's no question about it, Mr. Turner. Your poor wife is dead. Heart's stopped, eyes turned up, limbs already setting in rigor mortis."

Dan listened dully. He had known it all the half hour it took Corwin to get there, even though his reeling mind had refused to admit it.

In a blur, he heard Corwin give directions to Benton, the landlord, for laying out the body; tearless, moveless, he had seen the poor remains of the girl he loved taken out of the room by men who seemed to have appeared from nowhere. Without knowing that he had seen, he noted the quick sidelong glance the red haired landlord had thrown him as he departed with the body. Dr. Corwin was trying to console him. Still in a haze, he heard the meaningless words. Then they suddenly made sense, pierced the aching void of his mind.

"Of course, as a man of science," the doctor was saying carefully, "I don't believe in the efficacy of a curse, or in ghostly apparitions. But the death of your wife, following on the strange and unaccountable deaths of every other woman who married and spent her honeymoon night in Malbone, that is—since Marian Olmstead collapsed in her husband's arms —well—" he laughed a bit sheepishly, "it does begin to lend color to legend. But then again, it may be some new type of virulent disease. It may be your wife handled some article of Alma Landy's, and was immediately infected. I would suggest," he went on gravely, "that your wife be buried at once, in order that the infection, if that's what it is, may not spread."

Dan raised his haggard face. He glared at the doctor. "I won't permit it!" he shouted. "Not in that cemetery—not in that—!" He stopped short, suddenly.

Corwin had misunderstood his broken words. The doctor shrugged. "I understand," he nodded. "You have a plot near the city, where . . . ."

But Dan had jerked to his feet. He had forgotten. Cora's death had driven every other thought out of his head. His hand shot out and gripped the little doctor's shoulder in a death-like clutch. Alarm sprang into Corwin's eyes. Words were tumbling hot, stammeringly from Dan.

"That cemetery, Doctor!" he exclaimed. "There's something hideously wrong up there."

Corwin thrust off his hand, came up standing. "What do you mean?"

"I mean—I saw Alma Landy coming out of her grave, dressed in her bridal gown!" A twitch of fear made a spasm across his suffering mouth. "It was just before we came down into the village. . . ."

The doctor stared into his eyes as if to detect symptoms of madness.

"I'm not crazy," Dan expostulated earnestly. "We both saw her, Cora and I. Would to God I had taken that warning; Cora wanted to flee this place! But I, fool that I was . . . ." He broke off, choked and went on again. "I saw her photograph up in the room. I couldn't have been mistaken."

Bright pinpoints of flame narrowed Corwin's eyes. He exhaled slowly. "So *that's* it, eh?" he said, very low. "I've suspected every now and then. . . ." He interrupted himself, laid his hand on Dan's arm. "Listen, Turner, I'm going up to the cemetery now. Do you want to come with me?"

Dan steadied himself, every muscle tense and hard. "Yes," he said quietly. "Poor Cora is dead, but perhaps we can see to it that no one else ever dies from the curse."

"Good!"

They went down into the bar. Benton was nowhere in sight; the men who had laid out Cora's body were gone. The stillness of the grave overlaid the house, segregating it from the rest of the world. A light still burned dimly over the bar.

CORWIN jerked to a halt and gave a startled little cry. Dan staggered as if he had been struck. Words stuck in his throat, refused to come out. Only strangled sounds forced their way through.

The doctor said wildly: "Where is your wife's body? This is where she was, in that coffin. I saw them put her there, I swear it!"

There was no question about it; the coffin was empty. The plain pine casket yawned like an open grave, but its occupant was fled. Cora's body had disappeared!

Dan reeled with nauseating horror. Almighty God! Wasn't it enough that his wife of one day had died wretchedly, almost in his arms, without this dreadful vanishment? Was she also to become one of the undead, ghastly corpses who walked the fields and howled hideously to a death-cold moon? Horrid scraps of medieval lore churned in his frozen brain: young girls who died and sought living prey with white, tearing teeth; who sucked the blood . . . .

Dan groaned and raced around the room, knocking tables and chairs into confusion and ruin. There was no sign of the pallid body anywhere. Corwin's face was a tight mask. His eyes snapped. "The pattern is fitting together," he rapped out tensely. "We've got no time to lose. Come on!"

Blindly, with leering fear gibbering in his skull, Dan followed the doctor into the moon-flooded valley. A roadster of expensive make stood in the road. They climbed in.

Like a startled whippet, the car roared up the hill road, mocking the echoes with its flight. Cold fury enveloped Dan. His hands balled into fists, his teeth gritted.

"Faster!" The single word whipped into the screaming wind. Ghosts, devils out of Hell, vampires, nothing could stop him now! Whatever dread ghouls had taken Cora's body—for whatever nefarious purpose—a grim, grief-maddened man had to reckon with now. The thoughts of Alma Landy's bridal corpse, wandering aimlessly and whimpering in the night, flayed him like raking spurs in gashed flanks.

Corwin accelerated the machine. "Got a gun?" he yelled over the roar of the motor, the howl of the wind.

Dan looked down at his fists, and shook his head.

"That's a pity," the doctor shouted. "But I have one."

The long road fled beneath them. They mounted the brow of the hill and screeched to a halt beside the abode of the dead. They flung themselves out, staring.

The white, clammy mist still lay like a corpse-shroud on the gruesome ground. Grey headstones glimmered with pale phosphorescence through the hoary smoke. Farther along the crest of the hill, grim battlements rose, silhouetted blackly against a low-hanging moon. Without being told, Dan knew it was the transported château of the millionaire, Olmstead.

He heard the doctor's low gasp and whirled.

Dim through the mist, rising from behind the headstone of Alma Landy's grave, was a shapeless figure. Evidently it had not seen them, for it crouched over the piled-up earth. Its long, clawed arms rose and fell like pistons. Something broad and dull of hue made regular thudding sounds in the soft loam. A whining, whimpering noise emanated from the engrossed creature.

Dan growled in his throat. Icy sweat trickled down his spine. Ancestral fears raised the hair at the back of his neck, made his heart a pounding, lashing dynamo. What manner of beast was this Thing that delved feverishly at the dead of night in new-dug graves?

Corwin moved away like an eerie shadow through the moving haze. Dan shook off his clamping terror, lunged after the doctor. His knee crashed into a sunken gravestone. A sharp, involuntary yell rasped from his throat.

The dim-seen ghoul started up violently. The instrument in its hand dropped with a clang of metal against bare stone. It whirled and black eyes glared hideously at them.

Orange flame stabbed the fog at Dan's side, and a shattering roar crashed in his ears. The figure leaped sideways into the enveloping vapors, just as another bullet smashed viciously through the night. A hideous, cackling laugh floated back over the cemetery. Then both sound and form vanished abruptly.

Dr. Corwin pocketed his pistol regretfully. "Missed him both times," he breathed. "I'm getting old."

But Dan had seen something. It was incredible, hideous in its implications. He whirled on his companion, breathing rapidly. "Do you know who that ghoul was?" he asked.

Corwin shook his head. "No. Why?"

"I recognized him when he looked up. I couldn't ever mistake those eyes, or that mop of hair. *It was Mose Landy!*"

The doctor's body jerked as if he had been shot. He caught Dan's arm with surprising strength. "Are you sure?" he hissed between tight teeth.

"Positive!"

Corwin released his grip. His eyes narrowed. He nodded his head. "That explains things! Alma brought several thousand dollars with her. Mose did away with her, kept the money. Now he's afraid of an investigation, and came here to snatch the body." The doctor started to run. "Come on. Let's see what he's done."

A moment later, they stood in amazed silence before the grave. It had not yet been opened. Only a few shovelfuls of dirt had been turned over. The discarded spade lay where it had fallen.

Corwin snuffed the air like a bird dog. "That means we got here in time," he declared exultantly. "Mose intended to *bury* a body, not to remove one! God knows what hideous uses he can have for the newly dead. Perhaps he dragged your wife's body up here also, and we scared him away before he was able to conceal it."

Back and forth they tramped, seeking their gruesome evidence. Dan's thoughts whirled in a blaze of agony. Pray God he would find Cora's corpse before it was subjected to unspeakable atrocities. At least she should have the cold comfort of a quiet, unmutilated burial. As for Mose . . . his hands clenched tightly as if already they gripped that long, thin neck between them.

The doctor's sudden call broke the bitter spell of his reeling mind. "Here she is! Look!"

* * *

Dan dashed through the mist toward the bending figure. Dread tugged at his racing feet, tried to hold them back. He was ghastly afraid of what he would find. Perhaps Mose had already worked his mysterious atrocities on Cora!

He burst upon the stretched-out figure in an agony of mingled impatience and fear. He looked down with hazed eyes. The mist cleared as if icy water had been dashed over his head. He uttered a horrified exclamation.

The prone body was that of a girl, but

her head was a dreadful, gory thing. It had been battered into a shapeless pulp, under the impact of furious blows. A long, mud-covered, blood-soaked bridal dress clung in pathetic folds to her twisted limbs.

"Only a fiend could have vented his rage on a dead body like this," the doctor muttered somberly.

But Dan did not hear him. He bent over the poor, mangled corpse, fighting his shuddering repulsion. He sucked in breath with volcanic force. His limbs stiffened.

"Dr. Corwin," he cried in strained horror. "This is not my wife's body. It's Alma Landy. But this blood is fresh! Alma Landy was not . . . !"

A shadow fell menacingly across white headstone and ground. It was elongated, distorted, and something blurred was in its upraised hand.

Dan came up with a rush from his knees, whirled. At the same time he heard Corwin's voice, loud with warning:

"Look out, Turner!"

It was as if the sky had fallen with blinding force on the top of his head. He sagged, legs turned suddenly to jelly. As he crashed headlong to the ground, he heard, faintly, as from a great distance, the sounds of struggle, and Corwin's pistol emitting quick explosions. Then everything became silent and black as the grave.

CORA TURNER opened her eyes slowly. They did not seem to belong to her. Neither did her limbs. She felt strangely dissociated, as if each leg and arm were floating independently in space, buoyant in a warm, vaporous mass. Her head was light and hollow, and her skull seemed an expanding sphere in which her thoughts turned constantly without volition.

Was she dead, perhaps? The thought

did not shock or surprise her. She remembered the past vaguely—that long dead past when she was alive, a human being with warm emotions and mortal fears. It seemed eternities ago.

The bridal chamber, her sudden sickness, the anguished face of her husband. Poor Dan! Was he still alive, or was he also in this limbo of forgotten things, floating in midstream alongside of her?

Then there was the queer look on Benton's face as he had stared down, water bottle in hand; the grave decision with which the doctor had pronounced her dead; her slow floating trip down into the narrow confines of the coffin, while she lay frozen, immobile. She had wanted to laugh loud into the startled faces of those strange humans who had carried her. *They* had thought her dead. She had laughed at that—inwardly. In truth they were mere shadows, while *she* . . . .

Then she could remember no more, until now, as her eyes were slowly, volitionlessly opening. She stared around with a puzzled frown. She was not in boundless space. She was within the strait confinement of four somber walls. Blackness crowded all around her, streaked with leaping, frozen fires. Deep red they were, straining through the impenetrable murk, yet curiously immobile, as if they were painted on a dead-black background.

A blood-red glow, seemingly sourceless, pervaded the place, bathed her limbs in eerie light. She looked down and saw her body. It was whole, not scattered and floating, as she had thought; and it was reclining on a soft, red-covered couch.

Her eyes turned again, as if on frictionless bearings. Against the wall farthest from her, a brazier cast up purplish flames. They were alive, those flames, not frozen like the ones on the walls. They sputtered and cast an eerie radiance, they danced and leaped with fiendish glee. Iron tongs and curious pincers shimmered with white-hot incandescence in the shallow, blazing dish. Her eyes kept on turning. They fastened on a strange device that seemed riveted to the floor. It was an oblong, ebon frame, with a fixed, black bar at one end and a bar on rollers at the other. Pulleys, ropes and levers made a complicated array.

Something stirred within her. She felt her eyes go wide. Her limbs seemed to float back from the outer space, to coalesce with a dull thud. Her body was suddenly heavy, compact; gelid, loathsome things seemed to pound with thumping tread inside her skull. Had she not been dead, she would have been sure she was mortally afraid.

A black figure that had been invisible against its ebon background flowed forward into the range of her straining sight. It was tall, enveloped in a dun, light-quenching shroud. A hooded cowl covered its head. It had narrow slits through which gleaming, fierce eyes burned into her very deadness, shriveling her soul with piercing heat.

A faint shriek wrenched from Cora's suddenly constricted throat. It hurt as it rasped its way out. A lump that had been lifeless and sodden within her bosom jerked piston-like with furious pumpings. Her heart? Then . . . then . . . she must be alive . . . she must be . . . !

TONELESS, hollow words issued from behind the muffling cowl. They sounded like the pronouncements of another world.

"Cora Turner! You are dead . . . dead . . . dead!"

There was a dreadful finality to that grim reiteration. Cora felt mad pulses beat with agonizing thunder through all her body. Surges of rushing pain swept over her in waves. Her skull, hitherto a vast empty universe, contracted until it squeezed her throbbing brain and her twisting thoughts, into a crushed, pulped mass. Even so had Alma Landy, a corpse arisen from her bridal grave, shrieked out: "Dead! Dead! Dead!"

"No! No!" Cora wailed. "I am not dead! I am alive—still alive! I feel pain; my heart is beating; I am afraid. Look!" she cried frantically, in mad attempt to convince herself, "I can move my limbs. The dead can not do that; they must lie in their graves, rigid, frozen!" Her eyes widened in ravening horror; they seemed forced out of their sockets.

For, in spite of straining muscles, in spite of fear-spurred willing, her limbs still lay stiff and unmoving on the couch. It was then that Cora realized that they had not budged from their position since she had awakened to awareness. Even her lips spilled out speech without motion.

The ebon figure said inexorably: "Cora Turner, you are dead! You died in Malbone ages ago. You died of a curse that first was laid on Marian Olmstead. Your corpse was placed in its straitened coffin, and buried beneath moldering earth. Obeying immutable laws, it has come at last to this limbo of the dead. You must not fight your doom. Never again will you live or breathe the air of humankind."

Cora felt hideous fear overwhelm her, freeze the pounding blood into gelid ice. Great God! Was it true what the shrouded being was saying; were such things possible? Her limbs were gripped in a nightmare mold; the coffin had been a damnable reality. Was then the evidence of her heart and her throbbing pulse but vain illusion?

Yes, yes, they must be! See, they had stopped now; she could not move or budge an inch. Her very thoughts slowed to a crawl, as if they were flies pushing gluey legs through an endless ocean of molasses. Soon they too would stop, and then. . . . She tried to shriek, and only the faintest of far-off noises issued.

"See," intoned the figure inexorably, "you realize it now. You will not struggle any longer against your doom. You are dead and your soul is ready to leave its worthless corpse untenanted."

For the first time, it seemed to her dazed, reluctant brain that there was a hint of warmth, of avid eagerness in that hitherto toneless, unhuman voice.

The dun figure glided to the brazier. He lifted his shrouded arm and a fine dust sprinkled downward into the glowing embers. At once a ghastly, violet light leaped in forked spires into the room, like the twin writhing horns of Satan. A violet haze spread slowly outward. The haze entered Cora's quivering nostrils, penetrated her sluggish dying brain. Her feeble thoughts blurred into a fainting drowsiness. She tried to close her eyes against the hooded figure, against the room and its devilish implements, but they were fixed in frozen wideness.

The black creature turned to face her. He lifted his arms high, and the ebon garments draped in sinister folds. The walls, the moveless flames, made a depthless background.

"Come down, O spirit of Marian!" he cried. "Descend from your empty tenements and enter the death-fixed, desireless body of this maid. Force out her reluctant, earthbound soul and breathe the infusion of your own warmth into her limbs." His voice rose to a mad screech, full-bodied, terrible.

"Do you hear me, bride of a single night? For years you have hovered in this place of haunts and vengeful ghosts; for years you have clamored ceaselessly for form and human substance once again; for years you have made a nightmare hell of my sleep, whispering urgently in my ear by day. I have furnished you with maidens one after another. I have plucked new-made brides from the very sides of gaping husbands; I have killed and tortured time and again in obedience to your commands, furnishing you with the bodies of virgin maids on their wedding nights, such even as you possessed that night three years ago. Yet you refuse my offerings always; you do not return to me. Why? With Alma Landy I thought I had succeeded; I thought I saw that quiver round her lips that only you possessed; then—somehow—she escaped from under my hands." His speech was insane now, wildly horrible.

"This time, my Marian, you must come!" He was tossing his hands in frantic motion. "This time . . . ah!" His voice muted to straining, frightened whisper. "This time—you—have—come! Forgive!"

TO CORA, suspended in a timeless void, it seemed in very truth that Marian had come. The haze before her terror-chilled eyes swirled in malignant spirals. Fetid presences seemed to stream from the depthless walls and join the mad rout of leaping vapors. Her fear-crazed brain sensed forms and shapes, and then—oh, God!—shadowy wisps of mist, horribly like slimy tentacles, unearthly violet in hue, groped toward her. Behind them, grinning, mocking, were the tremulous lineaments of a face— a woman's hate-filled face! Large saucers of smoke, pigmented like glaring eyes, poured venom into her shrinking, failing mind. The tentacles reached out—they were clawed in needle-like streamers—winding around her throat . . . Cora tried to shriek and could not. Her throat was in a tight, constricting noose, her body bathed by a sear of fire. Something was slipping from her . . . she was fainting, going far away while those frightful eyes poured into her body . . . *Help! . . . Help!*

Knock! Knock! Dull thudding of fate!

The dreadful phantasm seemed to rush away from her with a thin gibbering cry, and became, once more, a swirling of violet fumes from a purple-flawed brazier. The mad, screeching figure lowered its writhing arms with a jerk, cried out in sharp annoyed accents:

"Who's there?"

Cora's sense slowly returned. Her body was once more solid reality. A slow flow of warmth released her ice-bound blood, sent it pulsing sluggishly through unresisting veins. That voice! She recognized it now.

Richard Olmstead, the mad millionaire! Mad — insane from years of brooding about his wife, Marian, who had died mysteriously on her wedding night. But he was a human being, alive, not a devil or creature of the void!

Something creaked, like a panel sliding open stealthily. There came a thud of feet, the sound of a heavy body dragging laboriously over the floor. A voice spoke, panting from exertion; masked, yet somehow familiar. She had heard that voice before.

"Here he is! Had a hard time getting him—at the cemetery."

"Good!" Olmstead's shrouded figure faced to the left. "How about the other one?"

"Got away. Sorry, but. . . ."

The mad millionaire flung his arms up in a terrible, wrathful gesture. "Sorry!" he raged. "That means a lot, you fool. That other was more important than this blundering nincompoop. He knows more. He's dangerous, I tell you, to both of us, and you tell me you're sorry!"

"I couldn't help it," the other said defensively. "But I'll get him surely next time."

"You'd better," Olmstead declared ominously. "You've muddled enough as it is. I was just getting her into shape for

Marian's return—I felt her spirit hovering in the room—and you come knocking and pounding and scaring her away. Get that body over near the brazier!"

Cora tried frantically to move her head around. But the paralysis still held her. She was alive, she knew that now—but fear made a horrible seething hell of her brain. What more fiendish things were they going to do to her? Who was it they had captured out in the cemetery?

Another black-shrouded figure staggered across the room, carrying a dead, limp burden in his arms. He dumped it with a dull, cracking thud beside the avid saucer of fire. The flames flickered greedy tongues out toward the still, lifeless body.

Cora felt her lungs surge as a vast rush of air sucked through her throat—then out through suddenly unlocked lips again. A great quivering scream filled that chamber of death with frantic concussions of sound.

The pale, blood-streaked features of the fallen man, frozen in a deathlike mask, were the features of Dan, her husband!

The two shrouded figures whirled. Olmstead shrieked madly: "Dead! You are dead!"

CORA'S limbs were seething with released blood. Her skull was a battleground of crazed grief and pulsing horror.

"I am not dead!" she shrieked frantically. "I never was. You drugged me, you fiends! You . . . oh, God! What have you done with Dan? Dan!" she implored desperately, hopelessly. "Speak to me! Tell me you are not dead!"

She flung all her screaming will into her legs. They moved! They thrashed weakly to the floor; they lifted her from the couch. She swayed with strange weakness; the room swirled round and round.

In three quick strides, Olmstead was upon her, had lifted her feebly struggling form in arms imbued with the strength of the insane. "You see what you have done, you idiot!" he ground out at his hooded companion.

The other sneered. His voice was muffled by the close-drawn hood. "You're crazy, Olmstead. I told you the last time all your mumbojumbo won't help. Marian is dead, and the dead don't return. Not even for you. I admit you've paid me plenty for what I've done, but the game is reaching the end. The one who got away tonight knows too much."

Olmstead snarled and swung the girl like a sack of coal. "You've taken my money and laughed behind my back, eh?" he thundered. "You think I'm a rabid madman—that Marian hasn't been talking to me day and night?" His voice became a terrible screech. "Well, I'll show you, damn you! You'll go down on your knees in groveling terror when Marian appears in this girl's body. Maybe I've used the wrong methods, but the rack will do the work. By all the devils in hell, I'll twist and stretch every limb of her stubborn body until her soul will shriek with hideous pain and flee her tortured form. Then you'll see Marian coming . . . you'll see . . . you'll see. . .!"

He hurled Cora down on the oblong frame, tore with frantic haste at ropes and levers. Strong hemp gouged into her legs and arms; her head went back with a thud.

"You'll see . . . you'll see. . .!" he mouthed in senseless iteration. He swung with clawed, griping fingers at a lever. There was a creaking noise, the sound of rollers turning.

Cora let out a wild scream of pure, unending agony. White-hot swords slashed through every nerve and muscle in her body; every bone seemed torn shrieking out of its socket.

"What did I tell you?" the millionaire

yelled insanely. "She can't stand it! She'll get out and make room for Marian!"

The other figure stood a little to one side, watching. He said nothing, but his posture was one gigantic sneer of skepticism.

Olmstead swung the lever again. Another scream, wilder than the first, forced its way through Cora's bursting throat. Dear God! She couldn't stand this. The pain was beyond conceiving. She was a straining mass of stretched muscles, a bottomless pit of suffering. The clammy sweat crawled on her bloodless face; leering devils sat on her laboring bosom, crushed her with their infinite weight. God! If only she would faint, if only. . . . And still the bar twisted under the implacable strain of ropes and levers, and her racked, bound form strained further and further.

The cowl had fallen away from Olmstead's face. It was a glaring, insane mask. Maggots of madness crawled in his eyes . . . gnawing worms to which no human pity could appeal.

Another mighty heave and Cora's tortured soul flooded out in a great welling cry that racketed from wall to wall. Blood dripped in a fiery curtain before her pain-hazed eyes; there were millions of bones in her tormented body, and each was a blazing focus of torment. She tossed her head from side to side in convulsive jerks.

A dim-seen form, sprawled on the floor, seemed to be lifting, like a shadow crawling up a wall, like a denser exhalation of mist from the ground. Now she was delirious. Soon she would be dead. She shrieked again.

The hazy figure seemed to stiffen under the impact of her cries. It rose up and up, swaying, tottering, forcing itself erect with fierce will.

Dan! Dan was risen from the dead, an avenging spirit, coming to rescue her from her bed of pain!

"Help, Dan, help!" she screamed.

Olmstead dropped the lever, whirled. The swaying form lurched forward, met the millionaire's mad rush with a bone-cracking thud.

The ropes slackened on Cora's limbs in blessed relief. A dull, strained ache succeeded the exquisite torture of dislocated limbs. The haze vanished from her eyes.

A furious struggle was taking place in the center of the room. She saw Dan's face, streaming blood, startlingly white against the red; she saw his fist lash out, sink thudding into Olmstead's body. In dreadful agony, she beheld the millionaire stagger, come back with a mad whirling rush, clawed fingers clamping viciously around her husband's throat. Deeper, deeper, sank those steel-hard fingers. Dan choked and gagged, and the death mask of his face turned a horrible, mottled blue. His own hands fluttered vainly, trying to tear those throttling sinews from his neck.

Olmstead gloated: "This time I'll kill you myself. Then your wife. Everyone dies!" He laughed and his wild laughter filled the room with an ecstacy of madness.

"Dan, don't let him kill you!" Cora wailed. She thrashed against her ropes, heedless of the pangs darting through her wrenched system. Forgotten now were her own sufferings as she witnessed the man she loved being choked to death horribly. Her brain was a rocketing shower of stars. She would kill that madman with her own slender hands . . . if only she were free!

Dan seemed to hear her frenzied thrashings. He caught Olmstead around his waist, strained until his face gorged with suffused blood; heaved with all the dying strength of his pain-racked body.

There was a surprised howl, and the mad millionaire, fingers ripping from his victim's throat, went sailing through the misty air, to land with a horrible, crunching thud against the farther wall. He fell into a limp huddle of black, shrouding garments, out of which lolled a hideous, foam-flecked head.

Dan straightened slowly. Blood dripped from raking gashes in his throat; his face was still a queer, mottled mixture of red and ghastly blue. He had difficulty in sucking in enough air for his bursting lungs. The room swam in dizzying circles. But he tottered toward the rack, arms outstretched.

"Dan! Look out!" Cora's anguished warning pierced the veil over his eyes, brought him to a halt. The millionaire's companion, hooded and shrouded, was pointing the muzzle of a wicked-looking gun at his heart.

"Thanks, Turner," the masked figure mocked from within the muffling swathings of his hood. "You've saved me a lot of trouble. I intended to kill Olmstead anyway. He was a madman—a menace to society, as well as to me. It was getting too dangerous, catering to his fiendish delusions, even though I milked him for plenty. Now I can kill you, your wife, and everyone will think you fought it all out between yourselves. No one will suspect me."

His finger, hidden beneath black folds, pushed against the cloth. Dan knew that death was crouching to spring at him. A dull rage enveloped him. He heard Cora's despairing shriek. He lunged forward, hopelessly, knowing he could not reach the masked murderer before the bullet would tear through tissues and pulsing heart. Poor Cora!

A gun crashed with dreadful sound. Dan's shrinking flesh, in midleap, awaited the smashing impact of lead against bone,

the blinding light, the enveloping blanket of death.

But nothing happened! His weak spring brought him sprawling halfway across the chamber. The shrouded figure tottered; the gun fell to the floor with a thud; a groan issued from unsealed lips. Then the man in black pitched headlong to the ground, arms spread-eagled and stiff.

Dan shook his head dazedly. What had happened? Why wasn't he dead, instead of the outstretched man? Cora was crying hysterically on the rack. Painfully, he went to her. Poor darling, she must be released; she must be hurried to Dr. Corwin for treatment; she. . . .

"Got him just in time," a strange rough voice spoke. And still another grunted thickly: "Damn 'em both!"

Dan swayed around, and stared unbelievingly. From the black maw of the panel through which his inert body had been dragged, two men stepped. One held a still-smoking gun. They were Mose Landy, the bereaved husband, and Silas Benton, the red-haired inn-keeper of Malbone.

Landy said very bitterly: "I suspected Olmstead right away when Alma died right in my arms. He'd been cracked nigh three years an' he'd been talkin' pretty wildly. But I had no proof. Then, after I talked to you in Benton's Hotel, a funny thought struck me. It was crazy, but I wanted to test it out. I wanted to see if poor Alma's body actually was in her grave. I sneaked a shovel, an' was starting to dig when you came along. I had to run for it then." He shook his head mournfully, and a tear rolled down his frowzy cheek. "I ain't yet found out."

Dan said gently: "Your wife is—dead. I saw her body." He did not tell him that she had been killed only that night. There was no reason for further torturing the poor fellow. The blood oozing from her bashed head had still been warm and sticky when he had bent over her.

The frowzy man took a deep breath. "Let her rest in peace, poor thing," he said slowly. "Anyhow, what happened there in the cemetery gave me some more ideas. I hot-footed it back to Benton's. He heard my story, and he told me more things. So we determined to sneak into this here castle of Olmstead's. Close to here, we run into someone carrying a body. Just as Benton started to go for him, he disappeared, right into the ground."

"We waited a while an' followed him in. It's a tunnel, an'—well—you know the rest."

Dan nodded. "All except the identity of the fellow you shot."

Benton looked at him with a disgusted air. "Hell, that's easy!" he growled. He walked over to the shrouded corpse, ripped the cowl away. The thin ascetic face of Dr. Corwin stared sightlessly up at them. His Vandyke was still neat and dapper. . . .

Dan told Cora the rest as he held her tight in his arms. "It was easy for Corwin to play the game. Perhaps he first instilled the idea into Olmstead's cracking brain; perhaps not. But he could get to the brides easily enough. The drink he handed you was already drugged. There are certain Indian concoctions that give the appearance of death—a state of suspended animation. As a doctor, he could declare the young girls officially dead. He hired men to dig the bodies out of their graves, and bring them here. The effect of the drug was only temporary. Alma must have gotten away somehow, and in her tortured, semi-stupefied condition, wandered the countryside. Olmstead almost exposed the whole plot when he rushed down madly, to tell Corwin the news. Corwin went out with him, you remember. He must have collected his men, found Alma, and killed her. Evidently he did not have time to hide the body. Then he hurried back to his house, waiting for the call he was sure would come announcing your death. His men lurked outside, kidnaped you from the coffin when he signaled them. That must have been after I refused to bury you here."

Cora shuddered in his arms. "It was an awful nightmare."

Dan's lips went to hers. "We'll have to start celebrating our honeymoon all over again, dear," he said.

THE END

Stories by Masters of Weirdly Thrilling Tales Which Grip and Hold, from the First Word to the Last

—NAT SCHACHNER, ARTHUR LEO ZAGAT, JOHN KNOX, JAMES M. GOLDTHWAITE and others appear regularly in *TERROR TALES*

THE THIRSTY DEAD

By
Raymond
Whetstone

"It is good of you to pay a lonely old man a visit," the spiderlike creature quavered. But in the forest gloom the visitor could not see the thin smile of weird triumph, nor the row of pointed, eager teeth. . . .

I HAD seen him a number of times before, that little spiderlike old man, but never at such close range. Previously I had contented myself with peering through a spyglass at his house, squatting like a leprous toad in its setting of withered, dying maples. Sometimes he would come out on the porch, a tiny black figure, moving about restlessly as though he knew I was watching him, and at those times his appearance always aroused in me a strange, crawling feeling of dread. Nor was that feeling due entirely to the half fearsome whispers about him, hushed words more awful in their implications than in their actual meaning. Even from a distance I could tell there was something wrong with him—something almost unthinkable. Could it be that those ghastly hints about him were true?

Although he lived but a stone's throw from Willoughby, he never came to the village. Once a week Helga, his housekeeper, hobbled into the general store to buy supplies. She was a hideous old hag, with a perpetual sneer on her pock-marked face and a body bent and twisted like a solitary, wind-tortured tree. Needless to say, the villagers feared her almost as much as they feared her master. "She, too, has the evil eye," they would mutter darkly. "She, too, has given her soul to the devil!" And they would hastily make the sign of the cross every time they caught a glimpse of her.

I had gone out for a walk early that autumn afternoon, wishing to take a vacation from the novel I was writing. The forest-fires were beginning to blaze in the woods through which I passed. Crimson oaks vied with yellow maples in brilliance. Along the stream bank I followed flamed a scarlet line of cat-briers, while in the distance towered a single white ash whose leaves were turning a golden bronze. I strode along, exulting in this lavish display of beauty, filling my lungs with the clean sharp air, taking no thought of time.

Gradually the hours slipped by. The sun sank lower, winked out behind a violet line of hills. Darkness, impalpable as fine dust, sifted about me. Realizing how late it was getting, I started back toward Willoughby. I knew that my landlady, a motherly old creature, would become worried about me if I stayed away too long.

It was impossible for him to have known that I was coming. I had made no noise as I emerged from the woods. And yet he was waiting for me beside the road, a dusty lantern swinging from his arm. A cold wind seemed to blow through me as I caught sight of that misshapen figure and stared into those gleaming eyes.

"Well?" The word seemed to burst from my lips.

"My name's Moore—Philip Moore. You've probably heard of me." His voice had the reedy pitch of senility, unpleasant yet pathetic. "I—I was wondering whether you'd care to visit me this evening. My house is only a short distance away."

"I'm sorry, but I can't, Mr. Moore. It's getting late and I'm due at my boarding-house right now. Some other time, perhaps." I had drawn back sharply as he came closer to me. I'm not exactly squeamish about such things, but the very air about him seemed to reek with contamination. Then, too, that queer, unaccountable feeling that he was horribly abnormal—unhuman in some way—intensified my uneasiness. I began to walk away.

"Don't go. Please don't go." His bony fingers plucked at my sleeve, his thin face thrust close to mine. "Don't believe the awful things they've been saying about me," he quavered. "They're lies! Monstrous lies! You know I couldn't harm you, even if I wanted to. Look how weak and old I am. Be my guest, if only for an hour. I've been so lonely with nobody but that stupid housekeeper to talk to. It's such a little thing I'm asking of you —just an hour of your company. You— you'll do it, won't you?"

I hesitated, pity and curiosity struggling with my sense of dread and loathing. After all, what was there to be afraid of? The man didn't look capable of hurting a fly. And he was so eager for my companionship that I felt sorry for him. I knew what terrible things loneliness could do to one. Besides, I was anxious to see what that house of his looked like from the inside. There had been as many strange tales told about it as about its owner.

"Very well," I agreed reluctantly. "But I warn you, I can't stay more than an hour."

A light seemed to flash across his countenance, bringing every sharp feature into relief. I glimpsed two blazing hypnotic eyes, a hawklike nose with distended nostrils, and parchment-thin lips drawn back. . . . The effect was only momentary; but it turned the blood to ice in my veins.

"You will come, then?" he shrilled in triumph, like that of a deformed, incredibly ancient child. "You will come? Ah, my friend, how good you are to me! You are young . . . you have the joy of life in you—a joy that I have almost forgotten. Perhaps you will help me to taste the zest of life again—to grow young . . . Perhaps. . . ."

And even then I did not know. I did not understand what he meant. I followed him blindly, stupidly—as a sheep follows a butcher.

WE WENT up a winding path and through a weed-grown yard. Before us loomed the house, gloomy and forbidding, its dark windows staring vacantly like sightless eyes. Swiftly my host led the way across the rotting front porch and threw open a door. Air, dank and cold, rushed out, enveloping me like a suffocating blanket. I coughed once, felt irritated when the old man chuckled mirthlessly.

Revealed by the light from the lantern, the room we entered was dim and ghostly and seemed extraordinarily large. Many chairs and tables dotted the floor, while along one wall ran a massive fireplace flanked by empty shelves which once might have contained books. A film of dust lay over everything and cobwebs hung in festoons from windows and ceiling. The odor of decay was strong in my nostrils.

"I seldom use it," the old man whispered, evidently guessing what was in my mind. "I keep it closed, except when I entertain guests."

"And do you have many of them?" I could not help asking.

"You are the first . . . in a long time." Once more his face underwent that metamorphosis which had startled me so while we were along the road. I felt his hand on my arm, and I jerked away as though from the touch of reptilian scales.

"But I am forgetting my duties as a host." Slowly that gleam of obscene triumph went out of his eyes. Beyond a slight twitching of his mouth, his features were composed again. "Make yourself at home while I get some wood," he told me softly. "It's too chilly in here to do without a fire."

I sank into a chair, not realizing until that moment my overpowering fatigue. Setting the lantern on a nearby table, he glided across the floor and disappeared through a door in the other side of the room. I heard a feminine voice, quickly hushed by a muttered word or two from the old man. Then the door swung shut.

I was alone in that shadowy, mysterious room. Alone, and suddenly filled with a ghastly fear that choked the breath in my throat, squeezed my heart with its skeleton hands. I knew intuitively I was in horrible danger, knew I should escape while there was still time. Why I was so cold with terror I did not even try to discover. I only knew that this fear was real, almost a physical thing. Yet I couldn't. Some power—that weird sense of fatigue—stronger than my own will, kept me from moving, bound me as though by invisible chains to the chair in which I sat. Unable to help myself, I awaited whatever was to come.

The old man returned, carrying a heavy load of wood. Deftly he arranged the fuel in the fireplace, struck a match. Soon flames were darting up the black maw of the chimney and throwing waves of heat into the room. I leaned forward, forgetful of my fear, of that strange, heavy lassitude, my chilled body eagerly absorbing the warmth. I could feel the old man watching me, knew he was smiling, even though his face was in shadow.

For some time neither of us moved or said a word. Then the old man walked over to a tall cabinet that stood in one corner of the room and took out a worn violin case. Bringing it back to the fireplace, he opened the lid reverently. Inside on a bed of blue velvet lay a magnificent Stradivarius, its polished wood gleaming in the firelight. I gasped as I realized its value.

"It was Paganini's instrument—Paganini, the greatest violinist of all time!" The old man spoke dreamily, his eyes on the priceless thing in his hands. "He himself gave it to me before he died."

"Before he died?" I echoed in amazement. "But Paganini has been dead—for almost a hundred years!"

He paid no attention to my words. "Some say Paganini learned his technique from the devil," he went on, speaking more to himself than to me. "But who should know that better than I? Did not the same master teach us both?"

There was no doubt about it. The man was mad. Raving mad. Shuddering, I attempted to rise from my chair. But he motioned me to sit still. "I will play for you!" he cried fiercely. "I will play as Paganini might play—were he alive tonight!"

HOW can I tell of his music? How can one describe color to a blind man? The flame of his genius brought vital, throbbing life to the instrument in his hands. He swept his bow across the strings and a slow, seductive melody filled that shadow-haunted room. There was something hypnotic about its steady, unchanging rhythm—something which gave me a false sense of peace and security. Mesmerized by that clear stream of sound,

I leaned back, surrendering myself to an overpowering lassitude, a glorious crowd of visions pouring through my mind.

Gradually, almost imperceptibly, the music changed. A minor strain crept into it, defiling its purity. It was sinister and threatening now, a rushing flood of discordant sounds. The visions, too, were different. Hideous faces leered at me, clawed at me with fleshless hands. Grinning skulls floated around me, mouthing horrible obscenities. A screaming horde fought for a rotting shroud. That clear, limpid stream had become a foul muddy torrent from hell!

He had put down the violin and was slowly approaching me. Still under the spell of his diabolical music, unable to move a muscle, I saw the gloating look in his eyes, saw his lips writhe back from his sharp teeth. Saliva trickled from one corner of his mouth. . . .

"I have waited long . . . so long!" he mumbled, bending over me. "But now . . . now I can drink until I am satisfied!"

Then, like a ravenous beast he tore at my shirt, ripped it open. Clammy lips fastened on my throat, clung there. Pointed teeth sought my jugular vein! Sweat pricked through my skin as I strove to release myself from the awful paralysis which gripped me. It was useless. I could not so much as lift a finger to protect my body—*my soul*—from the malevolent Thing which had attacked me.

Suddenly Helga, the witchlike housekeeper, was in the room, her eyes blazing insanely, her skinny fist clutching a gleaming knife. "You child of Hell!" she shrieked. " Did you not promise to share him with me?" And a flood of vile curses spewed from her twisted mouth.

The Thing raised dripping jaws and lunged at her. Biting, clawing, they went down in a furious tangle of squirming bodies. Again and again Helga stabbed at the old man. But either she did not reach a vital spot or else he could not be harmed by an ordinary weapon, for the knife thrusts seemed to have no effect on him. The fight raged on, rendered more horrible by acts of sadistic hate.

And then—crowning horror—the room began to fill with weird and terrible shapes! I knew that hellish music had summoned them; knew, too, the reason for their coming. Vague and amorphous they were, twisting and curling, hardly more tangible than smoke or fog. But each one of them had a cruel, hungry mouth and eyes which were bright with blood lust! Slowly, inexorably, they drew nearer . . . ever nearer.

Sheer terror, then, must have snapped the invisible bond inside my brain. I was free, miraculously free, of the hypnotic spell which had held me a prisoner. Screaming like a lost soul, I raced for the door, flung it open. Behind me arose a fiendish clamor. I stumbled down the steps, the pack of hell-hounds close at my heels. A dozen yards away gurgled the little stream along which I had walked that afternoon. Desperately I strove to reach and cross it, to lose myself in the clean, dark, friendly woods beyond.

I was almost there when my foot caught in a root. I fell to the ground with stunning force. Before I could rise they were swarming over me, their slobbering ice-cold lips glued to my quivering flesh.

Merciful oblivion descended upon me, blotting out my horror and agony. . . .

* * *

I have been here for a long time now. The doctor pays me a visit every day. He is very patient and kind, but he keeps insisting that I had an attack of brain fever up there in the woods. He laughs at me when I tell him what actually happened. Damn him! Does he think he can fool me? Why can't he explain the unaccountable lengthening and sharpening of my canine teeth? Why does he turn his head away when I ask him what caused those wounds in my neck?

The nurse, too, is kind. She is a pretty girl with a long smooth throat in which a tiny pulse beats. That pulse fascinates me. I have an insane desire to press my mouth to it, to tear and rend —Oh, God! Oh, merciless God! Is there no hope? Is there nothing that can save me? Am I one of them already?

I am told that the old man and his housekeeper have disappeared. The house is no longer occupied. I can well believe that, for every night I can see their evil faces outside the window, gloating over me. Every night I can hear the hellish strains of the violin, calling to me, commanding me to come!

How can I fight against them any longer? I am so tired—so very tired. How long must I wait before I join them?

SIX DOORS To HORROR

By Arthur J. Burks

A Terror Novelette

*In that house where incense ling-
ered and men had died, the spirits
of FENG SHUI were still unap-
peased, Kwan Chiao said. And because his white friends did not
believe him, he took them there to
see. . . . Did he know, even then, of
the fearful things that were to sweep
up from the tomb, pausing not for
locked doors and walls—of the
fierce red wind that killed, and the
hideous dead who would not
die . . . ?*

K WAN CHIAO'S English was perfect. It should have been. He was
a graduate of Boston Tech, post-
graduate of Harvard, something else out
of Oxford. His friends had been told
that he spoke twelve Chinese dialects, but
this had to be taken on faith. His American dress was impeccable. Unless one
looked at his face it was difficult to believe that he was a Chinese.

His American friends were giving him
a going-away party. He was to leave for
China three days hence, there to take up
the work for which his education had
fitted him. His friends knew that he was
destined to become China's greatest archi-
tect. Of them all, his mind was the best
—and there were geniuses in that group
of young men and women, which included
Ann Tinney, beloved by them all, the
promised bride of Sam Crowther.

Kwan had the ancient and modern lore

of China at his fingertips. He was a brilliant raconteur. His black eyes sparkled when he talked. Beautiful women paid him the tribute of sighs. He was every inch a man. Race prejudice had no place in this enlightened group.

". . . and so," he was saying, "you know why my people revere their ancestors. It goes back to the dawn of time, to Pan K'u, the first man. That is why we bow down at our ancestral tablets. I can, with surety, trace my ancestry in an unbroken line for thirty-nine generations, to Kwan Kung, the Chinese God of War. I am what the world would call a brilliantly educated man. I say this without boasting, for you all know it is true. I am, you must know, of the best blood of China, blood of which China is proud. There have been kings and emperors among my ancestors, great artisans, great law-givers, sculptors, painters and writers, philosophers—but while I know your attitude towards the things of which I speak, I tell you all here and now, that I would not say, even in a whisper in the very depths of my soul, that I did not believe in *feng shui*, the 'science' of wind-and-water spirits.

"I have seen too many things. My ancestors have passed too many legends down to me. I love my father and my mother. I have a wife and children. I would not deny belief in these things we have mentioned, because I would be afraid that my loved ones would die horribly."

"Rot!" said Sam Crowther, whose huge right hand had been built by nature to throw forward passes half the length of a football field. "No enlightened person can possibly believe in the supernatural. That stuff went out with our grandparents. I dare to say what you don't dare to say, Chiao: that *feng shui* is a bunch of mahooey! I could, and would for a reasonable wager, go into the big-

gest Chinese graveyard and sleep on a grave—lulling myself to sleep with derisive laughter at the beliefs of your people. How could the dead possibly harm the living? And what.sort of ancestors would harm their own loved ones, left behind, even if they could?"

KWAN CHIAO lifted his own hand. It was smaller than that of Sam Crowther. It was more adapted to a baseball. It had hurled college teams to victory while stands cheered themselves hoarse for a pitcher whose name they couldn't even pronounce correctly.

"Please, Sam!" There was entreaty in his voice. "I think too much of you to allow you to talk like that. "There are things in Heaven and earth, Horatio . . .'"

"Yeah, I know all that, but . . . Look, Chiao, I'd make you a wager. Lead me to this *feng shui* business. If I can prove to you that it's baloney, maybe I'll be doing you a favor. You've got all the rest of our civilization tucked under that yellow skin of yours, why not let us cast out your superstitions, too?"

Kwan Chiao smiled patiently.

"Civilization? You forget yourself, Sam. My people were civilized when yours were swinging by their tails from the trees of the forest. Let's don't be insulting. I love you too much to be angry with your ignorance."

"But I'd make a wager . . ." persisted Sam Crowther.

"Cut it Sam," said Leon Plante. "Can't you see Chiao's in earnest?"

Kwan Chiao held up his hand again.

"Peace!" he said. "But I'm minded to make a little test if you're not afraid. A cousin of mine has a big home in Chinatown. He never lives in it. Nobody does. It's been shuttered since his father died, because——"

"I know why," jeered Sam Crowther. "Because they didn't plant the old boy with his head toward Mecca, or his feet to the sunrise and his head to the sunset or something. The *feng shui* in his burial wasn't right . . . ."

"Exactly!" said Kwan Chiao. "Laugh if you wish, but two days after his father was buried my cousin's wife died. The doctors—your kind of doctors, my friends—could find no reason why she should have died. But mark this: her eyes were wide open. Her face was set in a mask of terror. When they found her in bed her arms were lifted from the coverlets, palms toward the foot of the bed, as though at the last she had tried to fight off some intruder. There wasn't a mark on her, yet her face was black and her tongue protruded from between her teeth as though she had been strangled. Your doctors could not explain.

"Our wise old men shook their heads. All the rules of *feng shui* had not been followed. But my cousin still did not believe. Next night his oldest daughter— *seven years old*—hanged herself from the rafters of her bedrooms, and the same look of horror was in her face. Who ever heard of a seven-year-old girl hanging herself? My cousin fled from the place, but not before his firstborn, a son, had died in agony . . . ."

"I say, Chiao, that's putting it on thick," said Leon Plante. "I don't think——"

"I'm sorry, Leon," said Kwan Chiao. "I guess Sam razzed me too much. Let's talk of something more cheerful."

Sam Crowther now thrust out a belligerent jaw.

"Now, Chiao," he said, "I've got to face your music, your Chinese music, don't you see? You're a damned good talker. You've made us see things people were never meant to see. Where's this dump you're talking about? I'll spend a week in it, day and night. No use arguing, either. If you won't give me the keys I'll break in."

ANYONE who knew Sam Crowther knew that he meant exactly what he said. Nothing Kwan Chiao or Leon Plante or Ann Tinney could do would dissuade him, nothing they could say. Kwan Chiao, starting out the evening merely to entertain, had loosed a horror in a Park Avenue penthouse—had evoked a ghost which must be laid in Chinatown. A pall of gloom, of strange exotic terror, had settled over the group with Chiao's words. The three Americans looked at him with new eyes. He had become, this man with whom they had hobnobbed for four or five years, as alien as though he had come from another plant, or from beyond the grave. The thought struck the three almost at the same time.

And with the fine sensitivity of his race, Kwan Chiao got it, too.

His Western veneer seemed to fall from him on the instant. His smile faded, his face became immobile, expressionless. He rose to his feet as though he suddenly realized himself an intruder. He clasped his right hand over his left, bowed deeply from the waist.

"The home of this humble one," he said softly, "is open at all times to his friends. If they will deign to enter, their humble servant will defer his voyage to make them welcome."

"Oh, can it, Chiao!" snapped Leon. "Sam didn't mean any offense. Your yarn *did* give us a turn, but nothing has changed and we're all still the best of pals. Don't go Oriental on us. Let's *all* go to your dump and lay the ghost—and have a good laugh over the whole business."

"Where's the old man buried?" asked Sam Crowther.

"In a vault under the house, over a hundred feet underground," said Kwan

Chiao, "where he awaits ultimate return to China and burial in the land of his people."

"But the law!" gasped Leon Plante. "People aren't buried like that, not in New York City!"

"The law," said Kwan Chiao, "is often set at variance in Chinatown. Give me two hours to make my humble dwelling —which my cousin sold me for a song —ready for your visit. But, remembering all our ancient friendship, allow me one last word: go anywhere, do anything, believe or disbelieve anything you wish, but don't accept my mad invitation!"

"Put it like that," said Sam Crowther grimly, "and you couldn't keep me away. But I don't wish to let Ann in for anything. There's no reason why she should take a chance. . . . "

"Are you already doubting your own disbeliefs?" asked Kwan Chiao softly. "Are you afraid for her safety?"

"That's enough," said Ann Tinney. "When did I ever stay out of anything you three got into? It's wild, foolish, but wherever you boys go, there I go, too. Let's hear no more about it!"

CHAPTER TWO

Wind

THEY made a prank of it at first. They went all through the gorgeously furnished dwelling-place, which was a piece out of old China. Rich brocades were everywhere, silken hangings, drapes of imperial yellow and purple which had come from the storehouses of long dead kings and queens of the Celestial Kingdom by virtue of the miracles money could perform. The Kwans were fabulously wealthy.

The house was of three stories, near the juncture of Mott and Pell streets. In it were statuettes of jade on ornate shelves.

There were chairs which gave forth soft music when sat upon. There were clocks which looked like beetles, tables into whose ebony tops one could look as into deep block wells. There were lacquer screens inlaid with feathers. There were deep carpets on the floors.

And there was food for supper, twenty courses of it. Sam Crowther had gone moody on them, and it had been Leon Plante who had tried to get some spirit into the supper. Plante it had been who had insisted that they all dress in Chinese long gowns, with gorgeous robes for Ann Tinney and Gloria Gannet, her chum. There were two other men whom Crowther had brought in, psychics of some sort. Plante didn't like them.

The eyes of Kwan were bright as coals. He laughed often during the dinner. Plante looked at him sharply, detecting something unnatural in his laughter, a hidden note of growing fear. And Chiao looked often at his watch. The supper dragged on. The servants, recruited in Chinatown, moved with the silence of cats, bringing in delicious course after delicious course.

It was eleven-thirty when Kwan Chiao finally called all the servants in and curtly bade them depart for their homes. A silence settled in the vast, high-ceilinged room where the party had eaten. Kwan Chiao cleared his throat.

"I don't know how it will start, my friends," he said. "But that it will is as inevitable as sunrise tomorrow. I am afraid for us all, for myself as well as for you—for as long as I am in this house the danger hovers over me as well as over you. But I cannot desert my friends.

"This is a last warning. After twelve o'clock I cannot be responsible for you. I have done all I can to keep it out. Every door, save the door giving on the street, is barred and double-barred. The trap-door which leads down into the family crypt is in a back room. There are four rooms, with all their doors barred, between us and that trapdoor. Nothing living can reach us from there. There is one way out, one way in, which mortal beings can use. That is the street door. Let's all go out that way, now, before it is too late!"

"You can all go," rumbled Sam Crowther, "and welcome. I'm staying. I've gone too far to back out. But Ann, I wish you would go."

"Sam," said Ann Tinney, looking more ravishingly beautiful than ever in the gown which, even while it hid the gorgeous curves of her body, accentuated the beauty of her face and her almost unnaturally white hands, "I once quoted to you the words which passed between Ruth and Naomi. I meant them then. I mean them now. If you stay, I stay."

"I *have* to stay!" said Crowther.

It was then, perhaps, that the others understood more fully why Crowther had to stay—for his own peace of mind rather than for Ann's, because he was in deadly fear of fear itself!

"Five minutes left," said Kwan Chiao. There was an edge to his voice.

LEON PLANTE looked at him sharply. That edge to the voice of Kwan Chiao made Leon think of the Chinese music, discordant, alien, which they had heard from shops along Mott Street on the way here. Leon Plante looked at the faces of the others. A chill raced along his spine. Certain knowledge had come to him. Ann Tinney could not look to Sam Crowther, who had declared his love for her and been accepted, for protection—because, Leon Plante could see, Sam Crowther was thinking more of himself already. Gloria Gannet was a silly woman who giggled. In trouble she would be worse than useless. Kwan Chiao was a Chinese. Hitherto that had made no difference. Here, in

the heart of Chinatown, it made all the difference in the world.

"It's up to me!" said Leon Plante to himself. He looked at Ann Tinney. She met his eyes; and flushed scarlet. Plante flushed in his turn. For the first time since he had known Ann he had allowed her, inadvertently, to see in his eyes what he never would have spoken.

She was the one woman in his life, always would be, though she married Sam Crowther tomorrow. She had never been told, until Leon's grey eyes, steady, fearless and true, had told her now.

"Two minutes!" said Kwan Chiao.

There were four grandfather clocks in the great room. There were always many clocks in Chinese rooms. Their ticking seemed to be growing louder, more insistent. Leon Plante could feel menace in them. The clocks were trying to tell him something, were trying to tell all of them something. Their faces, in the gloom beyond reach of the cluster of incandescents on the ceiling, seemed suddenly to have eyes, noses, and mouths—and faces filled with frowns of warning. Louder the ticking of the clocks.

"One minute!" said Kwan Chiao. "You can still make it to the outer door!"

No one moved. The Gannet woman giggled, then broke off short when she realized how out of place her giggling was. The clocks *were* getting louder. Sam Crowther's eyes were wide as he stared at the white faces of the clocks, one after the other. Crowther's back was to Ann Tinney, as though he had forgotten her. His huge right hand gripped the arm of his chair.

"Don't be frightened," said the sing-song voice of Kwan Chiao, "when the clocks begin to strike midnight. They reverberate all through the house, but they are only clocks, after all. I'm sorry that the servants wound and set them. I just didn't tell them not to. . . ."

There was a buzzing sound in one of the clocks, that preparatory winding sound which some clocks have just prior to striking. Then it began to strike. It had struck three times when a second clock joined it. Now the sounds were so commingled that it was impossible to tell when the third clock broke in, or the fourth.

But Leon Plante was counting the chimes. He had counted to thirty, and the clocks all seemed to be still striking, each chime louder than the last. Even four clocks, set as closely together as careful servants could set them—then, *forty, fifty, sixty! seventy!* There was menace in the clocks now, the white faces actually seeming to reflect the haggard lineaments of some ghostly terror which possessed them.

Then, abruptly, while the party stared into one another's faces, the striking stopped, dead-still, and out of all the locked rooms, on all sides, came the echoes of the chimes. They seemed to race all through the deserted house, back to the kitchens, the back rooms—back even to *the* back room! And a cold chill raced along Leon Plante's spine as he noted where the chimes seemed to die away— far back in a certain room Kwan Chiao had mentioned, as though the chimes had been living things which had gone down the trapdoor, and were dying away with distance as they followed the steps down into the crypt of the Kwans, sending back their dying echoes from the bowels of the earth.

"Look!" screamed Sam Crowther. "The lights!"

ALL eyes were turned toward the cluster of ceiling lights. They were growing dim. Their startled eyes saw that the white faces of the clocks were vanishing into the creeping gloom that seemed to close on them from all sides.

"Quick!" said Kwan Chiao hoarsely. "Clasp hands, all of us! In order that, if one of us is tempted to flee into the dark, and bat his head against the walls, the others will restrain him."

They slid closer together, moving from chair to chair. They clasped hands, staring out of white faces into other white faces as the lights dimmed, slowly, inevitably—and went out.

And out of the far distance, from the same place where the chimes had vanished, down into the family crypt, came a rushing sound, like a growing wind that, feeding upon itself, grew and grew, rising to a whistling shriek!

Silence held the visitors as they listened to the wind. They heard it grow and grow, howling and shrieking, gathering strength. Then, as though it were entirely ready, they heard it rush toward them, sounding much as any other onrushing wind. But there was this difference. It came, for all its fury that spoke of volume, as though it were confined within a tiny area, rushing toward the room where the people waited. . . .

"There are four doors between us and the wind," came the voice of Kwan Chiao out of the opaque gloom.

They heard the first door wrench open with a crash, slam shut with a louder crash, which seemed to shake the building on its foundations! *They heard it being locked!* They heard the second door open, bang back, slam shut—shake the house. They heard the third door, louder, bang back, slam shut. *These too, then, were locked.*

They heard the fingers of the wind rip and tear at the only door left, the only door between themselves and whatever it was that came to them from the crypt of the Kwans. The door rattled, but held as though all the wills of all the people in the room battled to keep it from opening. They saw it bulge in the middle, *outward in the direction of the wind*—as though giant hands had seized the door-knob and pulled.

Leon Plante was the first to wonder why they could see the door bulge—the first to *see* why: that where there was space between the sides of the door and the jambs, space that was shaped like the space between bow and bowstring when the bow was bent under the pull of the archer, that space was filled throughout all of it, with rolling spinning flame which was the color of fresh blood! Blood with flecks of gold all through it.

Leon became conscious next that a man was shrieking as though he had gone mad—a man here, in this room with them.

The door opened at last, banged back, slammed shut, and locked itself. . . .

And the *red wind,* flecked with golden specks, spilled its horror into the room of the unbelievers.

CHAPTER THREE

Strange Judgment

THE names of the two psychics—whose real life work was the exposing of fake mediums, investigations of psychic phenomena—were Reynolds and DeCarre. As the red wind came into the room, filling it all with a soft radiance from which emanated a strange warmth, and an odor of fresh, soft earth, Reynolds rose to his feet, jerking his hands free of Gloria Gannet on his right, Sam Crowther on his left. Leon Plante, struck dumb and motionless by what he saw, stared at Reynolds.

Reynolds was holding something in his right hand. It was a crucifix which he had taken from inside the bosom of his shirt. He had reached for the crucifix, brought it forth so frantically that he had ripped the buttons off his shirt, twisted his necktie awry, and cut the skin of his neck, so that it bled. He yanked and snapped the string which held the crucifix.

In ordinary light the crucifix would have gleamed, golden yellow. But in the reddish light it was a crucifix of crimson. Reynolds' head was back. There was fearless determination in his face and eyes—his face that was beet red because of the red wind, his eyes that were like rubies in his red face. His lips were moving. To keep from going mad Leon Plante concentrated on the lips of Reynolds, strained his ears to catch the words the man was speaking as he held his crucifix toward the redder heart of the red wind which swirled in the room. Leon noticed that the faces of the others were red, and their hair, and even the yellow gowns which empresses and princesses had worn.

Reynolds was babbling, while the red wind flowed into every nook and cranny of the room, filling it from corner to corner, from floor to ceiling.

"Back, spawn of Satan!" he was crying. "Back to the grave whence you came! Back, I command you, whatever the faith you lived in—back to the grave, in the Name of the Sacred Trinity!"

Leon Plante shivered. Reynolds was invoking the ancient exorcism, using the ancient words which cast out demons and devils, striving to cast out this terror with fear of the Cross.

"Back, spawn of Satan! Back, O great Undead! In the Name of the Father, the Son, and the Holy Ghost, back to your grave and the cerements of the tomb!"

For a moment the sound of the wind seemed to dwindle away. Leon studied the red glow. It began to retreat from the corners, to draw back upon itself, to coalesce in the space before the locked door by which it had entered. A great hope began to grow in the heart of Leon Plante. He looked at the face of Ann Tinney. There was fear in it. Her right hand was clasped at her throat. Sam Crowther was a red man turned to stone.

His mouth hung open. His teeth, which showed as though he snarled, were red.

Then the wind sound began to mount again. The red stuff became a shapeless mass in the open space. The shapeless mass began to take shape, the shape of a cube, whose red was redder than the first red wind as it had entered, as though, growing together, compressing, the red itself had compressed, dyeing the whole a deeper red.

It became a rectangular column of red —in which the golden flecks swam thickly, seeming to be endowed with amazing speed which blurred their yellowness before the eyes. Leon Plante, irrelevantly, remembered that he had somehow lost contact with Kwan Chiao, and looked about for him. Behind him, near the door which gave to the street, was a red bundle.

A man sprawled there, inside the door, as though a savage blow had knocked him out of his chair. The man was Kwan Chiao, and he was motionless, supine, his red face and ruby eyes staring sightless at the ceiling. On his red forehead was a deeper red that moved, and took the shape and speed of a sliding trickle of blood. Something had struck Kwan Chiao a terrific blow on the head.

But there was no time to go to him.

L EON looked back at the column of red.

It was in motion now! It inched across the floor toward Reynolds. It crept forward, gaining speed as it crept. The eyes of Reynolds were big, and even through their hellish redness Leon Plante could see a look of doubt, of deadly fear. But Reynolds kept mouthing:

"Back, spawn of Satan! Back to your grave! Back!"

A man was still screaming. It was De-Carre, who sat in his seat with his mouth open. But his lips did not move. They merely hung open while shapeless, horrible sounds came out of the depths of his lungs.

The red column closed on Reynolds with a rush. It flowed over him, encircled him, covered him. Leon could see Reynolds in the midst of it, like a red shadow in another red shadow that was only a little less red—and Reynolds was still holding his crucifix aloft, his lips were still moving. But Leon could no longer hear the words of his desperate, frantic exorcism.

The column enfolded Reynolds, and Leon fancied he could hear vague, uncertain laughter come out of it. It was laughter that was alien, foreign, terrible. It sounded like the sing-song voices of many Chinese, laughing in unison as at a jest no foreigner could possibly understand.

Then the column flowed away from around Reynolds, back to the place where it had begun to form. And as though it had been the column which had held him up, Reynolds fell forward, struck the edge of the table, caromed off to the floor. His golden crucifix slid along the floor to strike in a corner and stop.

Instantly, as though its work were done, the red column began to fade out, to disintegrate, to erase itself. Simultaneously, keeping time to the fading of the red terror, the ceiling lights started to come on again. And when the lights were entirely on, the room was empty of the red wind. But they had not heard it roar away, back whence it had come.

At the door Kwan Chiao groaned, sat up, shaking his head. He rubbed his forehead with his right hand, looked at the blood which came off on his palm, muttered:

"I became mad with fear. I tried to run through the locked door. I batted my head against it. I deserved what I got."

But Leon Plante, his heart cold within him, was staring at the body of Reynolds, on the floor. Every other person in the room had returned to normal color—save that faces were pale, and that of Sam Crowther was bathed in sweat which clung to him in glistening beads—but the face of Reynolds was mottled with red, in splotches, as though he had suffered major burns all over it.

Leon Plante stepped forward, staggering a little, to look down at Reynolds. He stared down at him, then turned his head to look over his shoulder at Kwan Chiao. His voice sounded natural enough as he asked the question:

"Of what disease did your cousin's father die, Chiao?"

"Of smallpox, the red plague! Why?"

"Don't look, Ann!" said Plante sharply. "Nor you, Gloria! You men, come here!"

They gathered about the body of Reynolds; Crowther, Plante, Kwan and DeCarre, the latter now silent because Crowther, without explanation or excuse, had slapped him in the mouth so hard that his lips bled. Then they looked at each other, nodded their heads, licked dry lips. The corpse of Reynolds was the corpse of a man who had died of smallpox! Even laymen could tell that.

THE men stepped back. They were not afraid of smallpox, for it was a simple, somehow anti-climactic fact, that they had all been vaccinated. But they were afraid of what had taken Reynolds.

It was Crowther who remembered something, spoke hoarsely.

"The wind!" he said. "It came, roaring! It's faded out, but it didn't roar as it left! Why? *Because it's still here, in the room with us!*"

Crowther hurled himself at the street door, tugged at it with all his strength. Kwan spoke softly.

"It's no use, Sam," he said. "I tried to open it. It can't be done. I don't know how it's locked, or what locked it, but it can't be opened. We're prisoners here, as long as *they* elect to keep us!"

"They?" said DeCarre, his voice on the verge of an insane babble. "They? What do you mean by 'they'?"

Kwan Chiao was very calm, with the suddenly recalled fatalism of his race.

"By 'they' I mean one spirit, or many spirits. In each of us there are many 'theys'—the spirits, or parts of the spirits, of each of our ancestors, back to the beginning of time. To the dead all things are possible. Their spirits may appear everywhere at once, or in one place. Each spirit may be infinitely many, the many may be one. My cousin's father may be one, or he may be all the spirits of his ancestors. He came to us in what you call the red wind. I agree with Sam. *They, it,* are still here. . . ."

Kwan Chiao broke off short. DeCarre screamed again. Kwan Chiao paid him no heed.

"Sam!" Ann Tinney spoke for the first time. "They're here, his ancestors! I feel them. They're in this room, watching us! Sam, hold me closely—I'm deadly afraid!"

Leon Plante whirled and looked at her. She *was* afraid. She was clinging to Sam Crowther. But Crowther, without looking at her, shook off her clinging arms and stood free, his legs wide apart, as though he were prepared to do battle—not for her, not for anyone here except Sam Crowther himself. His clothing was black with perspiration.

Something indeed ghastly was happening to Crowther. He panted. His mouth hung open. His eyes were wide, unblinking. His shoulders bulged as though his mighty muscles sought to break the stout cloth of his clothing.

DeCarre kept on screaming: "The red wind is the blood of the last Kwan to die! The red wind is the blood of the last Kwan to die!"

"Damn you, Kwan Chiao!" said Crowther hoarsely. "It's a trick, a magician's trick. You've rigged this place to trick us!"

"You know it isn't true," said Kwan Chiao softly. There was a queer sing-song quality now to his English speech of which Leon Plante, who knew something of Mandarin, was instantly cognizant. His voice raced up and down along the four sounds which—at the very least—are given to every Mandarin word, to give them different meanings. "You know it isn't true," he repeated. "I would not trick those whom I love."

"Then we're all seeing and hearing what we think we hear, eh?" panted Sam Crowther. "And DeCarre has the right idea. The red column is the blood of your cousin's father. His soul is still red with the blood of his body which has not yet been absorbed by the elements. And the yellow flecks in the red? Ah, I know what they are! Shall I tell you, Chiao? Each fleck is the soul of one of your ancestors, and all are part of your relative's red soul. . . ."

LEON'S heart almost stood still as he listened to Sam Crowther. The man was going utterly mad. There was no mistaking the wild look in his eyes. Ann Tinney looked at him with her eyes wide, and a despairing wail burst from her lips.

"Sam! Sam!"

But Crowther didn't seem to hear her. Leon Plante's heart went out to her. He dared to do what he next did, to comfort her. He strode around the table, with an awesome sense of unreality, and touched her on the arm.

"Don't be fraid, Ann," he said softly. "Nothing will happen to you."

"I'm not afraid, except for *him!*" she answered. It brought a gulp to the throat of Leon Plante, and dropped a leaden weight on his heart. Ann Tinney so fully and completely belonged to Sam Crowther. But Leon loved her to the depths of his soul. He had just one wish—to serve her with all his power, and with all his love.

He dared to put his arm around her shoulders. She was taut as a bowstring for a minute or two. Then she relaxed for a split second against him. But even as his heart thrummed with happiness that she trusted him even this much, her eyes were fixed on Sam Crowther. Crowther was moving slowly forward, toward Kwan Chiao. He was sliding his feet forward, an inch at a time, like a tight-rope walker. His hands were coming forward, the palms wide, the fingers extended, separated from one another as though they had been talons. His eyes now were fixed on the throat of Kwan Chiao.

"Stop him, Leon!" moaned Ann Tinney. "Stop him, for the love of God!"

Leon Plante slid around the table, hurled himself at Sam Crowther. But in that same moment, Crowther sprang. He hurled himself at Kwan, his arm extended. Kwan stepped aside.

And what was Kwan Chiao saying. . . ?

"You have performed the ultimate sacrilege, Samuel, attacking a Kwan! Now there is nothing that can save you!"

If Sam Crowther heard he gave no sign.

His hands were lifting again—reaching for Kwan. Kwan Chiao did not move for a moment. He did not move until the great hands of Sam Crowther were in the very act of fastening themselves in his throat. Then he ducked—and Sam Crowther swung his great right hand. It struck Kwan Chiao on the shoulder, turned him completely over, crashing him to the floor ten feet from where he had been standing. Kwan tried to clamber to his feet.

Sam Crowther was inching toward him.

And out of nothingness came a sing-song collection of words which Leon Plante somehow understood:

"*Beware, unbeliever! Already is thy*

life forfeit. Would thee also forfeit thy soul?"

But Crowther was beyond hearing. He stooped as though to gather up Kwan Chiao, to clasp him in his bosom, to crush in his ribs with his great arms. Leon Plante jumped ahead of him, was hurled aside so savagely that he crashed full length against the door by which the red wind had entered. The door did not give in the slightest.

Kwan Chiao was on the point of eeling aside when the lights went out again—and out of the darkness the red wind began to grow again. It whispered at first, the whisper rising to a ghastly, horrific shriek. It seemed to be spinning, coalescing, gathering together. The red glow was becoming visible. The yellow flecks could be seen plainly. The red column, which Sam Crowther had been sure was still here in the room, was forming again. And as though it could not wait to form entirely, in all its formlessness it was advancing on Sam Crowther.

LEON PLANTE, his heart in his mouth, but daring anything for Ann Tinney, hurled himself straight into the red column. As though it had had hands with which to seize, and hold, and cast aside, the red column rejected Leon Plante, hurling him back. And then it was all about Sam Crowther as it had been around Reynolds.

The column was spinning so fast that it had lost its corners, and was a spinning cone, like a whirlwind or a cyclone, whose base was on the floor, whose crest was against the ceiling. But even as Leon Plante thought of this, it came to him that the base went on through the floor, down even to the level of the crypt of the Kwans, and that its crest reached aloft, on through the ceiling—as though there had been no ceiling at all—to the Chinese Heaven, wherever it might be.

Sam Crowther, red in the midst of the spinning cone, was screaming. He was lifted from his feet. He was being hurled toward the door by which the red wind had entered, so swiftly and savagely that it looked as though he would be dashed to bits.

His arms were flung wide. He spun on the axis of his own body like a top, like the cone which spun him in its midst.

But he didn't crash against the door.

The door opened as the cone touched it. It slammed back against the invisible wall beyond. The red wind, with Sam Crowther in its midst, left the room. The lights came on at once—the very second the door slammed shut. Leon Plante, wondering whence he gained the courage to do the things he did, hurried to the door, tested it.

It was locked, as Kwan Chiao had said all the doors were locked.

They all—those who were left—stood spellbound, listening to the successive opening of the next three doors, to their slamming shut, the clicking of their locks. The red wind was traveling, with Sam Crowther a prisoner, toward the trapdoor which led down into the crypt of the Kwans!

They heard the fourth door open—bang shut. *Then they heard a fifth door.* Its slamming was a *falling* slam as it opened back—and when it went shut it *fell* into place! And Ann Tinney moaned:

"The trapdoor to the crypt! They have taken Sam!"

Ann Tinney hurled herself at the first door. She beat on it with her fists until the knuckles were bleeding. Then she whirled on Leon Plante, staring wide-eyed.

"Leon, you love me! I saw it in your eyes tonight! Go after him, bring him back to me!"

For a space Leon stood, staring at her, and listening to the dying down of the wind, which was being swallowed by the earth as it went down the circular staircase into the crypt. Leon, irrelevantly, wondered if the staircase circled to the left, as the cone of the red wind spun. He looked about him. Then he stepped to Kwan Chiao.

"The keys, Chiao!" he said calmly. "The keys to the four doors—to the trapdoor, and to the casket of your relatives if need be. I am going after Sam Crowther."

"It is useless," said Kwan Chiao.

"If you stand in his way," said Ann Tinney, "I shall go myself. Listen!"

From somewhere deep in the bowels of the earth came a long-drawn scream —a wail of terror and despair. Leon knew it was the voice of Sam Crowther, coming out of the crypt.

It was at this point that they all heard, faint and far away, metallic and somehow horrible—*the loud banging shut of a sixth door!*

Kwan Chiao gave Leon Plante a ring of keys. Leon Plante, moving like a man in a nightmare—gripped by such fear as he had never known—fitted a key in the first lock. He put his shoulder to the door as the lock responded, and turned for a glance at Ann Tinney.

"Chiao," he said softly, "protect her, my friend, for the love of God!"

He shut the door behind him. He was in utter darkness. He turned the key in the lock before he started to feel his way through the ebony dark toward the second door.

CHAPTER FOUR

The Staircase

THE house seemed filled with vague presences. Leon could see nothing. He seemed to feel cold fingers touching the back of his neck. The floor creaked under his feet, and the walls cracked

around him. He could hear the fluttering of wings, smell a musty odor as of decaying cloth. . . .

Grim terror clutched at his heart. Fear such as he had never known before so numbed him that he did what he did like an automaton, without thinking. He found the knob of a second door, across the second room from the first, went through it—and so through to the last door—and into the room in whose floor was the trapdoor leading down to the crypt.

He dropped to his knees on the floor.

There was no carpet. He felt about with his fingers for the trapdoor. Out of the very floor came strange, awesome sounds. He heard a babbling voice which he recognized, in spite of its insane cadence, as that of Sam Crowther, coming from far below.

Leon Plante found the ring of the trapdoor, dragged himself to his feet, his knees bent as he gripped the ring. God, how he dreaded the opening of that door! What ghastly horrors would engulf him when it opened? Did he have the courage to go down into that ghastly place which even Kwan Chiao would not have visited?

He remembered the white fact of Ann Tinney, beseeching, heart-rending in its piteous appeal—and tugged at the ring.

The door opened easily—too easily. It slammed back. He lost his grip on the ring. The door slipped from his hand, crashed its weight on the floor of the black room. The house shook on its foundations. It shook as it had not shaken when the red wind had fled through its black confines.

Out of the black opening under him, which Leon could not see because the room itself was black to opacity, came the odor of stale incense, and a host of other smells.

And there was sound—sound which tugged and tore at the heart and throat of Leon Plante as with invisible but mighty fingers. The sound was the gurgling of water. It wasn't the gurgling of a mountain stream over clean white pebbles. It wasn't the swishing of rain through beautiful green leaves. It wasn't the rippling of the surface of some lovely lake.

The sound was a libidinous, horrible, oily gurgling. Just to listen to it was to think of many things, all of them horrible. One thought of a dank tarn surrounded by ghostly trees whose wood and leaves were of ebony, whose surface was dotted with the bloated faces of decaying corpses—corpses whose bloated hands and pudgy, fat fingers moved this way and that in the water as though seeking something loathesome on which to clutch—and bear to the thick dead lips for a ghoulish feasting.

One thought of a river of putrescence, floating through a cavern of utter blackness, bearing on its boiling bosom an endless army of naked dead—who spun and whirled and rolled with the eddies. . . .

THAT was the gurgling which came to Leon Plante out of the depths of the crypt, floating in an invisible, stinking spiral out of the bowels of the earth. Leon, making sure that the door could not rise and fall upon him, felt for the steps with feet which were trembling—and started down. Even as he started, the gurgling increased in volume. And the gurgling seemed to whisper, to moan, three certain words: "Wind-and-water . . . wind-and-water . . . wind-and-water . . ."

The spirits of wind and water were the spirits of *feng shui*. Already Leon and his friends had had experience with the wind. It had shown them abysmal depths of terror. What would the gurgling water, which sounded below in blackness, show to Leon Plante? And what, he asked himself as he began the slow descent, was happening to Ann Tinney back in that first room, while he went down into the crypt to find Sam Crowther?

He refused to think of that. Though the Chinese had never spoken of it, he knew of Kwan's hopeless love for Ann Tinney. Kwan would protect her with his life, to the end of all things, to the end of life.

She was safe, unless Kwan's protection failed, unless he were not strong enough.

Leon put down his foot, to the second step. It was solid under him. He walked down. He walked to the first turn of the spiral staircase. The gurgling, the horrible, obscene gurgling was mounting in volume. It seemed to be rising toward him. He could still hear the cries of Sam Crowther, and recognized in the mad tones something that filled him anew with terror. What he recognized was a sound as of snarling!

Then he all but cried out with terror.

He had taken another step. His foot had thrust deeply into water that was icy cold. It swirled about his foot when it was firmly set on the next step. He knew that the shaft around which the staircase ran was filled to this height with the swirling water—else how could his foot be immersed!

Yes, this much he knew—far below him still, he could hear the screams of Sam Crowther. The swirling water did not seem to still the sound, or even to muffle it.

Leon stood with both feet in the water, which swirled about his ankles, filling his shoes, and wondered what next to do. How was it that Sam Crowther still moved, and screamed, with all the many feet of water above his head? Leon knelt to touch the gurgling water with his right hand. It *was* water he touched, no doubt of that.

And then he screamed.

Something had floated against his hand. He felt of it. It was a dead face, cold, bloated—horrible. In spite of himself, with no command from his brain, his hand felt over the face, to the top of the head.

And there, damp, soggy with the waters, he found a queue coiled on the skull, thickly, tightly fastened to the skull from which the skin was scaling off in the water! And down from the ears of the face hung two strands of beard, and down from the upper lips two strands—and from the chin a single strand. And Leon knew the meaning of the beard of five strands—which was the beard of venerable wisdom.

To examine the corpse more closely, Leon stepped down another step, two more. It didn't matter now if he stepped deeper into the water.

But he didn't step deeper—for under his descending feet the water subsided down the stairs, falling away below him! And as the water fell away, withdrawing into the bowels of the earth as he went down, the face with the beard of venerable wisdom fell, too, following the surface of the water down!

DESPERATELY, because within him he could feel the spirit, the will of Ann Tinney, urging him on, Leon Plante followed the steps down. And ahead of him, now just beyond the reach of his feet, the gurgling water fell away from him, as though it led him down to the crypt of the Kwans.

He was conscious of a strange circumstance—though he had stepped in water with both shoes, water deep enough to reach his ankles, his ankles were not wet, and water did not slosh about inside his shoes!

Was the water ghostly, too, like the red wind, and the invisible presences in the room above?

Even as he asked this question of himself, he knew that he had reached the crypt of the Kwans, for ahead of him, a lambent ball of red fire, was a single eye of crimson which shed forth a radiance all its own. Below this, somber, grim, terrible, seeming to hint of the secrets of timeless eternity, reposed a casket on two pedestals of shining bronze. He watched the face of the five-strand beard touch the casket and blend into it, to invisibility!

The ball of fire seemed to hang suspended in space above the casket, as though it were a hideous taper to light the way into Purgatory for the Kwan who had cursed his son and died.

At this side of the casket a reddish-white figure, shaped somehow like Sam Crowther, did its genuflections under the ball of fire, and it was saying something:

"I believe! I believe! As proof that I believe, I go now to bring her whom you demand as concubine, that I may be further punished by watching her terror in your undead arms!"

Sam Crowther, as though he had heard whispered acquiescence beyond the power of Leon, fled up the stairs! He traveled with the speed of the wind. His face was utterly mad. Leon knew, with a certainty more certain even than death, that Sam Crowther fled to the room of the table and the forgotten feast, to capture Ann Tinney and bring her here, into the crypt— to be a bride of the dead.

Leon Plante, made brave by fear beyond reason, even beyond fear, whirled and raced up the stairway after Sam Crowther, calling out: "Sam! Sam! Come back! Come back!"

But he did not get far. For with a hiss and a rush, the gurgling water which he thought had reached into the nether regions under the crypt came back again, horribly gurgling. He could see it now, because of the crimson radiance. He looked down as it rose swiftly, to fill the shaft before he could ascend out of it.

But no, it did not do that.

Red tentacles of the water—red because the ghost of the departed Kwans was red

—reached out at him like the tentacles of a bleeding squid, and wrapped cold fingers about his ankles. He stopped and could not move—like a man in a nightmare who must run from some deadly danger, yet finds his feet rooted, moveless, while the danger flows toward him. More tentacles fastened on him—on his thighs, his hips, wrapped themselves about his waist.

"Sam!" His voice was a sob of utter despair. "Sam! Come back! Come back! You don't know what you're doing!"

IT WAS hours, it seemed, before he heard Sam Crowther returning. He heard his snarling voice, and with it another voice: "Sam, don't hold me so tightly! Sam, let me go! I am not afraid. I can walk. . . ."

It was the voice of Ann Tinney. Leon could sense her struggles in the arms of the mad Sam Crowther, as the big man carried her down the steps, while he himself waited, helpless, on the staircase. . . .

Then Leon Plante saw Sam Crowther coming down, holding the struggling Ann Tinney. The tableau was etched in red, because of the red light which hung like some evil globe above the casket. Leon Plante could see, hear, but could not move to aid the girl he loved because his body was held fast by the tentacles of the water. And that water seemed to have a spirit of its own, to be a sentient, all-encompassing being. . . .

Leon Plante stared at the figures coming down the stairs, and his mouth opened in a shriek he cut off short.

For he could see directly through the figure of Sam Crowther, to the walls of the staircase behind him, and the stairs of the steps he trod! Only Ann Tinney herself was real. He could not see through her. Her body blocked out everything behind it.

In God's name what had happened to Crowther? Now that Leon Plante looked

back, to when Crowther had been performing strange genuflections before the casket, he seemed as in a dream to remember having seen the casket through the faint, shadowy figure of Sam Crowther. Was this the astral entity of Sam Crowther? If so, where was Crowther himself? *Only the dead could escape their bodies!*

If this were the spirit of Crowther, wrenched from his fear-mad body, what had happened to the body of Crowther? Had the Kwans taken it for some weird purpose of their own? Were Ann Tinney, Leon Plante, Kwan Chiao, and the giggling Gannet also, in their turn, to lose their bodies to the sinister purposes of the Oriental dead?

Now, as Ann came closer, down the steps, her eyes wide as though frozen in a look of terror, the tentacles about Leon Plante's legs pulled him backward. It was as though he were being drawn toward the beak of some monstrous devil-fish, by that awful creature's tentacles. But he would have preferred the octopus to this.

The tentacles dragged him back so that his hands could not go to help the woman he loved.

Crowther and the girl stood at the top of the last wind in the stairs now, within sight of the casket. And there Crowther held her until her wild eyes could take in the casket, the red ball which hung suspended above it, and Leon Plante in a far corner, held tightly in the grip of the tentacles. Leon Plante stood on the floor of the crypt now, where he could see everything that transpired.

And Crowther, as Ann Tinney swooned, her head going back, came on down the steps with her body.

CROWTHER stopped before the casket. Then Leon Plante, still unable to move, though he fought at the tentacles until sweat poured from his body, was conscious of the music. It was wild, discordant music. It came from everywhere, below, aloft, from the ceiling, from deeper under the ground. Leon Plante thought back to many things Kwan Chiao had told him—about the great out of China's past, about the great ones who had been ancestors of Kwan Chiao. And he understood the meaning of the music —wild, discordant, the music of bells of different notes, of strange stringed instruments, and of the traditional flute of five notes.

The music was the sort which might have been played at a banquet given by some great Chinese general. It was a music of feasting, of happiness. But here, in this crypt, it was music of abysmal terror. And running through it, a thin thread, was a low lilting, bestial laughter, which came from nowhere, went nowhere —unless it came out of the casket and returned to the casket.

The music grew in volume, and now, out of the darkness on all sides, materializing as ghosts might materialize, came the musicians who played the different instruments. And through their bodies, as through the body of Crowther, Leon Plante could see details of the crypt, and the casket! The five musicians, then, were dead, and these were their ghosts which played upon ghostly instruments!

And they gathered about the casket of Kwan as though it were there that the feast would be held.

But it wasn't the ghosts themselves that frightened Leon Plante. It wasn't the weird music which made the short hair at the base of his skull rise and stand on end, the muscles of his stomach grow taut until he was sick with the tautness of it, the palms of his hands grow wet with sweat. It was the fact that the five musicians were the servants of Kwan Chiao— the five servants who, cat-footed, had served them all tonight in the supper room!

These were the five servants of Kwan whom, in sight and hearing of them all, Kwan Chiao had ordered to go back to their homes. Yet here they were, recognizable for all their faces and bodies were red from that whirling globe over the casket, making music at the casket toward which Sam Crowther, or his ghost—God knew what it was!—was bearing Ann Tinney.

Ann Tinney, recovering now, being jerked back from her swoon by the deadly fear which she must have taken into unconsciousness with her, was moaning, tugging at the ghostly garments of Sam Crowther.

"Sam!" she said. "Sam, what are you doing to me? How can you do this? Oh, you poor, mad child! Let us both waken and forget this horror! Where is your love for me that you would show me all this terror?"

And from the lips of the spirit of Sam Crowther came measured words that sounded like a snarl.

"What is love when a master demands a mate? Behold, O Kwan, I prove my new belief by bringing thee this woman thou saidst I would not bring because my love for her was greater than my belief in thee!"

But, watching the lips of Sam Crowther, Leon Plante had a strange feeling. It seemed to him that the words had not come from the lips of the Sam Crowther, but from the casket, out from under the lid of the casket which hid the ghastly face of a Kwan.

And now, as Leon Plante watched, that lid began to rise, as though pushed upward from inside by ghostly, ghastly hands! Slowly it rose, slower and slower. And finally it stood straight from the edge of the casket. The musicians played on. Leon could see the hands and arms of something, or somebody, pushing back against the casket lid.

Then the lid fell off with a reverberating bang, and that sound was the sound Leon had already heard, before ever he had quitted the supper room to come to this ghastly crypt—the sound he had mentally characterized then *as the sound of the sixth door!*

NOW, out of that casket, came a voice in thick, strange English.

"Give her to me, that the blood of my body shall be renewed. And when I have taken her, do you go back for her female companion—and after her bring, in this order, the faker DeCarre, and Leon Plante—and my kinsman, Kwan Chiao!"

"I hear and I obey! For I believe!" came the voice of Sam Crowther.

Then Sam Crowther lifted the screaming Ann Tinney, held her horizontal with the floor, across his two mighty arms, and suspended her above the casket. The awful arms reached up to grasp her in their deathly caress—as a woman might have held up her arms to receive her newborn child.

But at that moment Leon Plante—because his love for the girl, Ann Tinney, was greater than the strength even of the tentacles of the water, or because, as though to make the jest more joyous, the water had decided to release him—hurled himself forward, free of the gripping, unearthly bonds!

He hurled himself at the casket. He struck against the standing Sam Crowther—*and his arms went through the figure.* His only sense of having touched him at all, was that the area in which he saw the figure was icy cold.

Then, just as the casket lid was being lifted, to shut down upon Ann Tinney, imprisoning her inside it with whatever horror it hid, his hands struck the casket.

He was driving forward with all the desperate strength of his body.

The casket swayed. He heaved against it. He struck it with his shoulders, even with his head. One of the pedestals protested, as though its ebon wood were cracking.

The casket swayed. One side fell lower than the other. The casket, as he heaved at last, mightily, rolled from the pedestal, crashed resoundingly to the floor—the lid still open. And out upon the floor rolled two figures, horribly intertwined.

One was the figure of Ann Tinney. The other was the figure of a Chinese, with the dead face Plante had followed into the crypt!

Leon Plante, even as he gathered the girl in his arms—tugging, pulling, almost screaming in terror as the dead arms clung—even as he backed with her against the wall, stared at the apparition of Sam Crowther.

It was fading out. It was swirling like fine dust in a whirlwind. And the red ball over the casket, too, was whirling. And Leon Plante sensed that the whole crypt was filled with the miasma of a bitter, cruel disappointment. It was nothing he could lay a hand to; but he tried to figure it out in his mind, as the ghost of Sam Crowther vanished, and the red wind grew again into being.

Sam Crowther had been brought here and slain, and the red spirit of the dead Kwan had hidden his body, and enslaved his spirit as an instrument by which to bring Ann Tinney to the crypt.

"Hurry, Leon!" Ann whispered. "Hurry! Hurry! If we wait they will grow strong again and hold us!"

Terror gripped him, made him strong, gave him the power to move faster than ever before. He set the girl on her feet, caught her right hand, and literally jerked her feet from the crypt's floor as he dashed for the circular staircase leading upward.

CHAPTER FIVE

Rooms of Dread

BELOW them as they raced up the stairs the music of the musicians rose to a shrill, mad crescendo. They could hear the gathering together of the wind, the gurgling of the waters.

The gurgling of the water . . .

The rising roar of the wind . . .

Both came out of the tomb, where the spirits of the restless dead gathered their ghastly forces for a new assault on the heights from which they had fallen when they had died. The hands of the departed were fast in the ankles of the living, who fought against them.

Up and up, following the winding stairs. Both held their breaths, expecting at any moment that dreadful things would come in pursuit. That Sam Crowther, slave of the dead Kwan, would come after them to bear them back to a necrophilic mating by those in whom he had sworn he did not believe—who had died in his disbelief, and become the slave of the dead as punishment for his blasphemy.

They expected the water to catch them and drag them back, led to the attack by the body of Kwan, as a general leads an army to the attack, as the dead Kwan had attacked to lead Leon Plante into the depths.

They expected the wind to come, as it had come for Sam Crowther.

But Sam did not come, nor his spirit.

Nor did the wind.

Nor the gurgling water.

And the fact that they did not come was fast becoming more terrible than if they had! For they had experienced mad Sam Crowther, and the red wind, and the water; but what did they face now? What new terror was being born at this moment in the womb of the crypt of the restless ones? What ghastly new manifestation was being prepared to steal away their courage, their bodies, their very souls?

In his heart Leon Plante cursed Kwan Chiao for what he had done, for his challenge to Sam Crowther, for the invitation they had all accepted to their everlasting sorrow. Not this side the grave would they ever forget one iota of it. But Kwan, surely, never had expected such terror as their presence here had loosed. Or had he? Had there been some deeper reason why he had asked them? He loved Ann Tinney. Had he hoped in some way, here, with the help of his ancestors, to win her for himself? Leon shook his head. It couldn't be. They knew him too well; they were loved by him, he by them.

They ran like two mad people.

They looked often over their shoulders, back down the twisting parabola of the stairs. Not even sound came up now. The moaning of the wind had stopped, the awful gurgling of the water. They both believed that it was only a breathing space, that the wind and the water were merely strengthening themselves to renew the assault.

There was little they could do, save flee, and shut all doors behind them, knowing even this of little use because in the past all doors had been opened so easily by the red wind.

Now they were at the trapdoor, were through.

Leon slammed it down, fastened the catch which, somehow, had not been broken by the rushing wind. He looked about for something heavy to drag over the trapdoor, and was cognizant for the first time that the room was lighted.

In dread they passed through all the rooms to the supper room.

There, draped across the table, her clothing torn from her shoulders, so that her breasts gleamed in the light, was Gloria Gannet—her lips set in a soundless giggle, her legs dangling stiffly below the table level.

Dead on the floor under the table, was DeCarre.

Of Kwan Chiao there was no sign.

AND now the wind was rising out of the depths. This time it would be more dreadful than ever before. Both knew that. Leon Plante tried the outer door again, without success. Then he took the mad Gloria Gannet, placed her in a corner near the door, put two chairs in front of her, one for himself and one for Ann Tinney, and sat down to await whatever might befall. He knew that his eyes were wide with terror, mirroring the terror he saw in the eyes of Ann, but he could not hide it.

The water raged, by the sound of it. The wind shrieked. The house shook and trembled as though stirred at its foundations by an earthquake.

But with the sound of the wind and the water there now came another sound. It was the sound of many voices, out of the crypt. The voices of yelling men, the banging—Leon could think of no other sound to which to compare it—of flat swords against shields. *A marching host was coming up out of that crypt!*

They could hear harsh commands in sing-song Chinese. They could hear the scuffling of many feet. The marchers, invisible, terrifying, were being played to the attack by the flutes, the red instruments, the drums of a mighty orchestra.

On to the attack!

So said the marching feet; so said the commands in sing-song Chinese; so said the flutes and the horns.

So said the wind and the water which gurgled accompaniment to the onward march of the host out of the depths. His ancestors had been law-givers and great

men, Kwan Chiao had said. They, some of them, had also been generals.

Were they, behind the impenetrable curtain of death, marshaling all their dead servants, all their soldiers whom the dusts of time had claimed, into an army to attack the living? Leon thought so. He looked at Ann Tinney. She smiled at him wanly. She gave him her right hand. Courage began to pour back into him at her touch.

The next thing to happen seemed trivial. It was the entrance of Kwan Chiao. He came through the last door they had locked. His face was a mask of sadness, of fear and horror. But his lips parted in a tremulous smile when he saw them. He closed the door behind him, turned and put his face against it for a moment. Moaned words came from his laboring chest.

"God forgive me! They're dead—all dead!"

It seemed a strange thing, this Chinese calling upon an alien God for forgiveness.

And he kept repeating, "Dead! Dead! All dead—and we must follow them."

He turned to face Leon Plante and Ann Tinney, behind whom was still Gloria Gannet, unconscious, semi-nude as they had found her because there had not been time to cover her nakedness with clothing.

KWAN CHIAO came to them. His voice was sad with an abysmal sadness.

"All my fault," he half-whispered, bowing to Ann Tinney. "But I never thought it would be like this. I have the blood of many on my soul—and we must go, too. But there is time for me to tell you something: I love you, Ann. That is why I am going to do everything within the power of Kwan to save you. I know there could never be anything between us. Leon loves you. I have known it always, I think. And I love Leon Plante as one man might love another. I wish you to love him, too. Is it possible? Do you love him, Ann?"

She hesitated.

"I . . . I . . . don't know. I never thought of it. But it seems to me that of all of you he has been the most fearless. He has thought of me instead of himself. I believe I could learn. . . ."

The face of Kwan Chiao was transfigured by a kind of radiance. His lips parted in a little smile. He spoke softly.

"That is all I wish to hear, all I have wanted to hear since I knew you—that there was a possibility that your love would be given to Leon before marriage to someone else made it too late. Now, knowing that the two whom I love best love each other, I am not afraid. I will do that which will make all the Kwans turn in their graves. I shall defy even the spirits of *feng shui* to save you!

"Listen, my friends, soon they will come again. They will bring the ancient hosts of the past, the dead who were their servants, to serve them again. They allowed you two to escape once, perhaps because I prayed for you, to the God you serve. This time you cannot escape, else will *feng shui* be thrice disturbed, and my ancestors not find peace this side of eternity.

"Understand what that may mean? That the evil influences in this house may extend to all Chinatown, and from there thrust its avenging tentacles into the heart of New York. But even that I will dare for your sakes. Promise me this, and will to do it with all the strength of your souls, and with all the love you bear each other: that no matter what happens you will not leave the chairs in which you are sitting?"

They promised. No need to seek a promise from Gloria Gannet, for she could not pass them in their chairs. She was a prisoner who giggled hysterically in her unconsciousness—so that her breasts shook with her mad merriment.

Kwan Chiao whirled. He put his chest against the table at which they had eaten supper. He pushed the table against a far wall, clearing space there for battle. He dragged the bodies of Reynolds and DeCarre against the wall. And even as he worked, with the frantic speed of a man in the throes of despair, the lights in the room were dimming.

Now Leon noticed something, that Kwan had opened the first door. And beyond it, even to the room of the crypt's trapdoor, the doors were open, and all the lights in all the rooms were dimming. Leon and Ann could see the trapdoor opening, as though lifted by invisible hands.

Leon gripped her hand with a grip of steel. She leaned against him, and he put his arm around her shoulders. She gripped that hand with her free one, and whispered.

"If the world ends in the next few minutes, I shall go into eternity holding your hand," she said, "and repenting through all endless time that I was so blind I did not see the depth of your love."

He held her more tightly.

AND now, terror piled upon terror was pouring out of the open trapdoor. First water boiled out, as from an artesian well. It thrust its ghostly tentacles in all directions along the floor, as though it reached for something. And Leon spoke swiftly to Ann Tinney.

"Don't look, darling!"

She hadn't seen for, expecting some new terror, she had hidden her face against his shoulder.

The water came on, forming a sheet two feet deep on the floor—and atop the water, as though on some dreadful treadmill, appeared phantom shapes—the shapes of Chinese soldiers dead and gone, with ghostly banners waving as they marched again at command of their leaders—the ancestors of the Kwans!

"God Almighty!" whispered Leon Plante.

But he only held Ann Tinney the closer. Her warm flesh trembled against him. Her dry sobs shook both their chairs. Then she stiffened. A woman did not hearten her man with tears.

The water flowed on. Now Leon could see, in advance of the marching hosts and the water under their feet, the red pillar of wind, redder now than it had ever been before—red, he knew, with the added blood of Crowther.

Now Kwan Chiao raced to the first door. His hands were raised as Reynolds, hours earlier, had raised his hands, in a strange, awesome kind of exorcism. His words were in English, sing-song English, as he said:

"Back, O spirits of my honorable ancestors! Back to your graves, else I make thee a vow which will never be broken: that if ye touch so much as the hair of the head of these whom I love, I shall give no sons to worship at thy graves, and shall make it binding upon my progeny, to the end of time, that they bring forth no sons to worship at thy graves. How then, O Honorable Ancestors, can ye find peace beyond Purgatory?"

Kwan looked so little, so frail and insignificant in the face of that oncoming terror. Yet his face was alight with a firm resolve which overrode the fear both Leon and Ann could see so plainly there.

But the spirit-wave came on, manifested in the shapes, in the red wind, and the water which must have dripped from the hoary mists of time.

Kwan seemed to be beaten backward by the wave of opposition which rolled out to meet him as the hosts whirled nearer and nearer to the last door. Why had he opened the other doors? Leon thought

he knew why—to keep his ancestors from being angry at opposition, so that he might the more easily reason with them. A pitiful, puny overture of the living to the dead.

Leon and Ann were frozen in their places. Now Gloria Gannet was standing, behind them, giggling frightfully. But they did not turn to look at her.

Kwan was being forced back and back.

Now he whirled and plunged toward Ann and Leon.

"They are too strong!" he cried. "But this at least I can do: I can spare you the terror of what must come. It seems the most I can do. Look at me steadily, forgetting everything else you have seen and heard. Think only of me, and of my eyes. Cling fast to each other. I am hypnotizing you. Concentrate! Sleep! When you waken, if ever, let it be only at sunrise, when the spirits of my ancestors must go back to their crypt. In your sleep you will know nothing, feel nothing. Swallow your terror, lest you be visited with greater terror still."

Leon met Ann's eyes. Hers were big. She nodded at him. If there were no hope, at least they would not see each other's terror and soul-blasted suffering.

They faced Kwan again. In times past he had hypnotized them—could do it again, even in this hell. But even as he droned on, and made the cabalistic passes with his hands, the water came into the room, the red wind began to creep toward them as it had crept toward Reynolds, and the phantom hosts began to form for combat in the room. Leon, looking over the heads of the hosts, thought he saw yet other hosts, reaching back and back to infinity. . . .

"Sleep! Sleep!"

The world was withdrawing. Yet Leon fought against Kwan Chiao until he felt Ann's head fall against him, knew that she slept as Kwan Chiao had bidden her.

Then the whole terror vanished on a wave of a strong man's will, and Leon Plante slept, too, his arms tight around the figure of Ann Tinney. . . .

WHEN he awakened Ann Tinney was stirring. Both turned their eyes on Kwan Chiao, who sat, looking tired and drawn, in a chair before the table which had been pulled back into the center of the room. Dawn came through the windows whose blinds last night could not be lifted, but now had been—and through the street door which had been opened by someone with the dawn. Kwan Chiao smiled at them wanly.

There was that in his face which, to Plante, seemed the very sorrows which Lucifer must have known, when he looked up out of Hell to see how far he had fallen.

"I defied them, with success, my dearly beloved friends," said Kwan Chiao softly. "It is a sort of truce. I swore to give no future generations of sons to worship at their graves; they denied me peace beyond Purgatory; but it is worth the price that you are safe at sunrise. Leave me now, Ann and Leon—for I must make peace with my soul, as much as I may, that so many have died, so many of my friends, all my servants, to prove to you that *feng shui* is the All-Powerful of my people. Even your great police could not find so much as a shred of their bodies!

"Go now, for it is written that we may never meet again—and that, too, perhaps, is part of my punishment. Take heed of my words: Marry, and beget children, many children, but never tell them of this, and never speak of *feng shui*—or, if speak of it you must, treat it with reverence, as you would protect your yet-unborn loved ones from its vengeance! For its mark is on your souls!"

Stunned, they went forth from the Kwan-house, into the bright sun of morning, hand in hand—to see glowing dawn against the gaudily painted signs of Chinatown, as though to prove that all they had experienced had been real, as real as a nightmare come to dreadful life.

THE END

PRINCE OF PAIN

By Mindret Lord

Had Robert Brundage truly gone mad, that he saw those horrors that transpired in the laboratory of Prince Ahmed? So thought the world—yet there was still before his eyes the tortured white body of Rosalinde—and the mindless Thing that was to take her place. . . .

PRINCE Ahmed Sulieman Arvaht, Egyptian nobleman, sat in the richly furnished study of his house on the Avenue Malakoff in Paris and gazed at his visitor with cruel, thoughtful eyes. Peculiar eyes—somehow dreadful eyes that held depths of super-human intelligence but reflected no emotion, no feeling.

In a dark, suave way, the man was almost handsome. His short, neatly parted black beard would make it rather difficult to guess his age, but the lithe strength that one sensed beneath his beautifully tailored London clothing must certainly indicate comparative youth and a powerful muscular development.

Prince Ahmed's visitor was an older man. He was fat and had a greasy complexion. His face wore a constant smile. He concluded the account of his adventures in London, saying, ". . . so I think you may depend upon it that the American Ambassador, Mr. Vane will *not* return from England tonight."

Prince Ahmed nodded. "You have done well, my dear Zogeb. You are returning to Egypt this afternoon. When you arrive in Alexandria, you may tell our friends that my plans will be consummated within the next two days. The whole world should be under our thumbs by this time next year."

Zogeb laughed and shook his rolls of fat. "Yes, yes—under our thumbs!" he repeated. "By the way, do you mind telling me something of your plans to get the formula?"

"Not at all. . . ."

Zogeb's smile grew broader. "Then you will be using Ambassador Vane's own daughter as our aide! It is an amusing idea. But then, my dear Prince, you always had a delightful sense of humor. I remember the time you built a little fire on the stomach of that pretty spy—what was her name?—your comments were marvelous. I was in stitches." Giggles seemed to choke him for a moment, then he continued a little more seriously, "But what do you propose to do if the dear young lady is unable to lay her hands on the formula?"

Prince Ahmed answered, "I shall use another young lady who will certainly not fail."

"How do you mean?" Zogeb asked.

"I'll show you," he said. "Come along!"

PRINCE AHMED went to the door and threw it open. Standing just outside was a servant in native Egyptian dress to whom he addressed the terse phrase: "To the cells!"

Following the servant the two men traversed a long corridor and finally came to a halt at the blank wall at the end. The servant applied his finger to some part of the floor molding and the whole wall swung inward, revealing the top of a narrow, circular staircase, leading downward.

The row of cells was three stories below the level of the street. Prince Ahmed led the way past four of the barred cubicles which were occupied by three men and one woman. All were Europeans. At the fifth, he stopped and turned to Zogeb and said: "There she is. We will go in and sit down while I tell you my plan." He signed to the servant to open the iron barred door. As they entered the cell, Zogeb's pig eyes lit with appreciation and he licked his repulsive, fat lips.

The servant waited at the open door as Prince Ahmed and Zogeb sat on a wooden bench against the wall. They faced a young woman of twenty or so who was chained to the opposite wall by her slender wrists and ankles. She wore only one garment—a pair of rough, grey trousers. From the waist, up, she was nude. Across her ribs and swelling breasts was a crisscross of fading red weals—evidence of a recent whipping. In her eyes was mortal terror.

"I found her in Marseilles," Prince Ahmed said. "By European standards, I suppose she would be considered extremely good looking. I kept her because I thought a plasm of her might sometime be useful—much more useful than she, herself, will ever be. After the first hour or two, she is an unreliable hypnotic subject."

Zogeb giggled. "I see someone has been tickling her with a strap."

"Yes. The last time I came down here, she tried to bore me with her pleas and complaints. However, she seems to have learned her lesson, now, for she is quiet, enough." Prince Ahmed turned to his companion. "But to get back to my plan: as I was telling you, if Miss Vane fails to get the formula for me, then I think I can safely assume it will be in the possession of Mr. Robert Brundage, the young man at the Embassy who is her suitor. Well, after he retires for the night, I will hypnotize this young lady and have her introduced into his room by means of the window. At my direction, she will search for and find the document we want, pass it out the window to us and then she will suddenly drop dead—due to a certain pill she will have taken just before entering the room."

The girl in chains suddenly gasped with fright.

"Very clever," Zogeb chuckled. "Deceased young ladies tell no tales. And if there is any hue and cry it will center around the corpse instead of around the stolen formula."

Prince Ahmed nodded. "It will have the added advantage of involving young Mr. Brundage in trying to explain to his sweetheart and the police just how the body of a strange woman happens to be in his room. . . . But I must go, as I have many things to do." He stood up.

Zogeb lingered and Prince Ahmed, who had started out of the door, turned back inquiringly. Zogeb said, "I have nothing to do in the next two hours before my train leaves. If you don't mind I think I'll stay here and amuse myself." He looked at the girl and laughed.

Her eyes were on Prince Ahmed. "Oh, God! No!" she cried. "No!"

Prince Ahmed smiled. "Still the same old Zogeb! All right, amuse yourself—but mind you do nothing that will interfere with her performance tonight."

As Ahmed and his servant started up the circular staircase, they heard a sudden, agonized scream followed by the sound of hearty laughter.

A T TEN o'clock that night a party was in progress at the palatial Versailles home of the American Ambassador. Rosalinde Grantland and Julie Vane were in the latter's bedroom to which they had gone for a few minutes' rest from the crowd.

The two girls were perfect examples of opposite types. Julie was blonde and small—one might almost say fragile. She was like a beautiful china doll, come miraculously to life.

Rosalinde, on the contrary, looked as if she might have stepped out of a painting by Titian. Rosalinde would have delighted the Venetian master as a model, not only for her fiery hair, but also for the grace of her fully developed figure.

Julie was sitting at her dressing table, powdering her nose, when she looked up and asked, "How did you happen to come with Bob Brundage, Rosalinde? I didn't know you knew him."

Rosalinde smiled at Julie's reflection in the mirror. "Are you jealous?" she asked. "He is awfully nice, isn't he? I shouldn't say he was handsome—he's more the strong, athletic type. But he must have brains or he wouldn't be in the Embassy."

"You still haven't answered my question."

Rosalinde laughed and said. "Don't worry, dear—he's mad about you, I'm sure. I didn't know him. But father sent me up from Lyons with an envelope to give to someone who was to meet me at the station and say some silly code word. It turned out to be your Bob. He was going right back to the Embassy to deliver the envelope to someone else and he was kind enough to take me along and drop me at the Meurice. I mentioned that I was coming out here for the week-end and he said he was, too, and asked if he could take me. And that is the whole story—except for the fact that coming out here, he was very proper and I was just as seductive as I could be."

After a moment, Julie said, "I suppose we ought to go down, but I hate to."

"Why?"

"Because that awful man, Prince Ahmed something-or-other is coming. Why father invited him, I can't imagine —except that he's supposed to be terribly important in Egypt and rich as Croesus. I met him at a party once and he hypnotized me."

DOWNSTAIRS, Robert Brundage and his chief, A. J. McDonald, faced each other across a table in a small room off the drawing room. McDonald had a sharp, aquiline face and iron gray hair. Brundage was considerably younger— probably well within hailing distance of twenty-five.

McDonald spoke in an undertone as he withdrew from his pocket a plain, brown envelope which he passed across the table. He said, "This is the Blue Death formula which you got from Rosalinde Grantland. The office has put it into code. Incidentally, it is a new code and I don't believe it would be possible for anyone to decipher it. I've got to go, now, so I am giving the formula to you to hand to Vane the moment he arrives. Guard it with your life in spite of the fact that it would probably be useless to whoever might steal it. You never can tell."

Brundage tucked the envelope in his inside coat pocket. "I understand," he said, "but what is the Blue Death, anyway? Do you mind telling me?"

"All I can tell you is that it is an entirely new type of explosive which has just been invented by Harvey Grantland— the American scientist who has his laboratory at Lyons. I believe its principle is that its action is progressive—up to a certain point, at least. In other words, you drop a bomb of this stuff and it explodes like any ordinary bomb, but then the gas liberated by the explosion unites with the nitrogen in the air to form a new explosive which detonates instantly—and so on. One well placed bomb or shell of this Blue Death might easily destroy an entire city. You can imagine what such an invention would mean to any country that was in sole possession of it!"

McDonald stood up and said, "Well, I must be going. You won't be able to reach me tonight, but call me tomorrow. And for God's sake, don't let anything happen. Our department has been leaking like a sieve, lately, and I don't know how or why. All I do know is that we've lost three good men."

"Really?" Bob asked. "What became of them?"

"One after the other they lost their minds. One day they were clever, competent men and the next, they were abject idiots—fit for nothing but the asylum. It's got me frightened. I don't know what to think." He nodded a farewell and went out. It was a moment before Bob could shake off the feeling of apprehension with which his chief had left him.

AT NINE o'clock the next morning, Robert Brundage had locked himself into the library of the Vane home. He was at the desk, speaking into the telephone. Dark circles under his eyes told of a sleepless night and his brows were drawn together in a frown of serious concentration.

"McDonald?" he asked. "Thank God you got down to the office early! Something terrible has happened! Yes, I know the telephone is dangerous—I'll be as brief as possible. I woke up in the middle of the night and found a strange woman in my room. Lord knows how she got in. The door was locked and I was on the third floor. Anyhow, she had stolen the envelope you gave me. When I tried to grab it from her, she dropped it out of the window. Then, when I started after it, she threw her arms around my neck and died—yes, died. What did I do? What *could* I do? I realized it was no time for me to get into a mess so when I made sure she was dead, I took her down and put her in one of the cars in the garage. . . Yes, they've discovered it—the police are here and raising hell. No, I'm not under suspicion.

"The formula? No, it was gone. . . . I haven't any idea. I've searched everywhere. . . .

"Don't hang up! There's something else I want to tell you. When I went to my room, last night, I discovered someone had rifled my luggage and I found a woman's handkerchief on the floor. It was Julie Vane's—yes, Julie's. I don't know what it's all about. She's been acting strangely ever since that Egyptian Prince arrived last night. And she tried to get me to let her keep the Blue Death formula. She said she thought it would be safer with her. How did she find out? *I* don't know.

"Well, listen—Julie is trying to persuade me to go back to Paris with her and Miss Grantland and this Prince. She seems to think he can solve all this mystery in some occult way—I don't quite know how. But I suspect he's mixed up in it in some way. I'm for going to his house to see what happens. What do you think? . . . You do? Okay, then, I'll go. We're leaving right away, so if you don't

hear from me by, say, one o'clock, you'll know where I am and that I couldn't call you."

Bob repeated the address of Prince Ahmed's house on the Avenue Malakoff. Then he hung up the receiver and went out to join Julie and Rosalinde in Prince Ahmed's Renault limousine.

AS THEY entered his big, grey, stone house, Prince Ahmed said: "I will spare you the dubious pleasure of inspecting my poor dwelling, but will lead you, instead, directly to the room in which I find myself best able to concentrate. Permit me, ladies. . . ."

They followed him through several richly, if somewhat ornately furnished rooms and then down a stairway which led to a big, oaken door. Bob realized that they were below the level of the street. Prince Ahmed opened the door and stood aside for his guests to enter.

They found themselves in a comparatively small, windowless room which was furnished solely with four extremely heavy wooden chairs in a semi-circle facing one side of the room which was hidden by black velvet drapes that fell from the ceiling to the bare, stone floor.

Prince Ahmed said: "Will you please be seated? I am afraid you will not find these chairs very comfortable—but then for clear thinking it does not do to be too comfortable."

Sarcastically, Bob asked: "Just what sort of a performance is this going to be?"

"Patience! I will not keep you waiting long." The Egyptian clapped his hands together twice. Instantly there entered six tall, bronze-skinned servants, briefly clad in loin-cloths and sandals. Rosalinde seemed somewhat frightened at their sudden, silent appearance. Julie was still calm and apathetic.

Prince Ahmed spoke a few words in some oriental tongue. On the instant the servants sprang forward—two to each American—and pinioned their arms behind their backs! In a moment all three were tied securely and immovably in their chairs.

As the six servants finished their task and stepped away, Prince Ahmed, who had not moved from his chair, leaned back and smiled. "It will do you no good, Mr. Brundage, to curse and strain against your bonds. And you, Miss Grantland—please spare us your tears. They are quite ineffectual." With a slightly higher intonation, he turned to Julie and said: "Miss Vane! I release you from my control!"

Bob glanced at the girl and saw her give a sudden start of surprise. She tried to move her arm and seemed astonished to discover that she was tied in her chair. "Bob!" she cried, "What does this mean?"

"It means that this man Ahmed is making a damn fool of himself!"

Prince Ahmed raised his hand in a mild gesture. "Allow me to explain—"

Bob interrupted, "You'll have plenty of explaining to do later, believe me! Even if this *is* a practical joke."

The Egyptian looked at him sharply. "One more word from you, sir, and I shall be put to the necessity of having you gagged. Is that understood?"

Raging internally, but realizing his impotence, Bob subsided.

"Good. Now I will continue. The reason why you are here is quite simple. I want the cypher of the Blue Death Formula—the explosive which is the invention of your father, Miss Grantland. The formula which was put into such a careful and complex code by your office, Mr. Brundage. I intend to get the information I want from one of you. . . ."

He looked up and spoke some unintelligible words to the servants. Immediately they filed out of the room by way of a part in the middle of the black drapes.

Prince Ahmed continued, "While preparations are being made for you in there, it may amuse you to hear something of last night's little drama. In the first place, I had been reliably informed of the fact that you had the Blue Death Formula in your possession, Mr. Brundage. If you had been a good hypnotic subject—like Miss Vane, for instance—my task of acquiring the formula would have been rather more simple. But one look at you convinced me that you were not. However, I was prepared for such an emergency. A very strong and agile Nubian in my service managed to hook a rope inside your window with the aid of a greatly extended bamboo pole. Then, with a young woman hanging around his neck, he climbed the rope and dropped her inside your room. She, in her turn, waited for him to descend, then loosened the hook and allowed the rope to fall to the ground. The rest of the plan was very simple—though not quite so simple as it would have been if you had confided to Miss Vane where you kept the formula. Your reticence made it necessary for your visitor to search your room. Where, by the way, did you keep the envelope?"

"Under my pillow."

"Ah! No wonder you awakened—but to what a dilemma! You awoke to find your bedroom occupied by a very beautiful and sketchily clothed young lady. You cannot very well arouse the household. Neither will your chivalry allow you to attack her immediately. You have no choice but to try to persuade her to return your property. This gives her time to obey her instructions to drop the envelope from the open window where one of my men is waiting to catch it. Then, when you would like to rush off in pursuit, she further hinders you by succumbing to the poison which had been given her before she entered your room. Thus, a double object is accomplished. One: I have the formula. And two: you are in a very awkward predicament. But you quite surprised me by disposing of the body with admirable intelligence. I didn't mind sacrificing the girl because I had already made a plasm of her and—"

"What do you mean—plasm?" Bob interrupted.

PRINCE AHMED ignored the question, for the black velvet curtains were being pulled back. Now, for the first time, Brundage began to see the situation in its true and fearful light. The room beyond was a tremendous laboratory, but although he had some scientific knowledge, Bob could not guess the purpose of most of the elaborate apparati the room contained. One object he was able to identify as an electric furnace.

Prince Ahmed arose and said: "I see that all has been made ready for the pursuit of my inquiry. This is the little workroom in which I am able to perform certain experiments which would seem quite wonderful to the so-called scientists of the Aryan race. They are mere babies and are only beginning to learn what men of the East knew ten thousand years ago. Actually, their only contributions to science are in the nature of labor-saving equipment. To their mechanical ingenuity, I have added the knowledge and theories of the Orient—with results which I shall demonstrate. But perhaps you will save me the trouble by telling me what I want to know. Tell me either the formula of the Blue Death or tell me how to decipher the code in which it is written." He looked first at Rosalinde, who seemed to shrink into her chair.

Rosalinde said: "Honestly, I don't know. I don't even know what the Blue Death is supposed to be."

Julie said: "But Prince Ahmed—I know absolutely nothing about it."

He turned to Brundage who growled: "I certainly don't know what the formula

is—and that goes for the code, too. But if I did know, I'm damned if I'd tell you."

Prince Ahmed nodded without any appearance of concern. "Yes," he said, "it is just as I expected. Your patriotism will not allow you to divulge what you know. But there is something that is stronger than love of country, or honor—or anything. That is pain. And I will convince you that I understand pain."

He spoke to his dark-skinned servants who were standing at one side. Two of them leaped forward and an instant later Rosalinde had been released from her chair and was being held erect between them. The girl was gasping for breath and her eyes were wide with terror of she knew not what.

As Prince Ahmed approached her, he said: "I really must apologize for the seeming indelicacy of what I am about to do. The fact is that I must remove all your clothing, but I would have you understand that it is not for any lascivious reason. The motive is quite a different one, I assure you."

While he spoke, he carefully undid the buttons of Rosalinde's simple sports dress and let it slip to the floor around her feet. Just as calmly, he released her firm, finely-molded breasts from the confinement of a lacy brassiere. The girl struggled ineffectually. Bob pulled against the ropes that held his arms immovably behind his back until his muscles ached and his bones felt as if they were about to crack.

In a moment, Rosalinde was stark naked. In spite of his rage, Bob could not but admire the beauty of her graceful young body with its satin smooth skin and slender, flowing contours.

Now, at a word from the Egyptian, she was half dragged, half carried into the laboratory. Two chains which were suspended from pullies in the ceiling were attached to her wrists and two more chains anchored her feet to the floor, so that she was forced to stand motionless with her arms and legs stretched apart. This accomplished, Prince Ahmed faced Julie and Bob.

"Before I demonstrate to you the power of pain," he said, "I am going to allow you to see something which any scientist of your race would find it utterly impossible to explain. You asked, Mr. Brundage, what I meant by the word plasm. As you probably know, ectoplasm is a peculiar substance which is within the human body and which occasionally emerges from the psychic medium while in the trance-state. Ectoplasm has been seen, /felt, photographed, weighed. As it is consciously or subconsciously directed by the medium, it will carry out any given command— even to the extent of assuming the appearance and speaking voice of a dead person. But I think I may truly say that I am the only scientist living today who has ascertained the actual nature of ectoplasm. Ectoplasm is a fourth dimensional projection of a portion of the strength and material of the human body and I have found that it can be used in almost exactly the same way as the silver emulsion is used on a photographic film. In other words, I can duplicate life in ectoplasm—"

A moan from Rosalinde interrupted him and he turned back to her. He continued his exposition as he went to a table and gathered up a large bottle and a sponge.

"My comparison of ectoplasm with a photographic emulsion is a very apt one but you will understand it better when you see the process in actual performance. I shall explain it as I proceed." He poured a large quantity of liquid from the bottle he held, onto the sponge. "This is simply pure alcohol and I use it to make certain that the subject is absolutely clean before attempting to create her plasm. It is a curious fact that when the reproduction is made, dirt or extraneous matter appears on the plasm as imperfections in the skin."

Beginning at Rosalinde's head, he gave her a thorough bath in alcohol. When he had finished at her feet, he said: "There! I think that will do!"

HE STOOD aside and motioned to his men. Two of them brought to him an obviously heavy, metal object which looked rather like the helmet of a knight of the Crusades. At its top was a ring by which the men attached it to a chain that was let down from the ceiling just over Rosalinde's head.

Prince Ahmed said: "This helmet is made of lead that is over two inches thick. It will cover the young lady's head for the first part of the exposure and will protect her from the harm which the rays would do to her. It serves another purpose, too."

Rosalinde was staring wildly about her like a trapped animal. The frightful terror of the unknown had her firmly in its grip, as, slowly and carefully, the helmet was lowered over her head until the bottom edge rested on her shoulders. Since her face could no longer be seen, one could judge of her hysterical fear only by the spasmodic heaving of her breast.

The whole thing was becoming so fantastic, so cold-bloodedly horrible, that Bob had almost convinced himself that it was not real.

Prince Ahmed unlocked the fetters on Rosalinde's arms and legs. Then he stepped back and looked at her critically. "That helmet," he said, "will hold her tightly to prevent her getting out of focus. Now we are ready!"

He spoke at some length to his assistants. While several of them dragged a tall black box to within a few feet of the hanging girl, others arranged a great bank of various types of lamps to focus on her. Some of the lamps Bob recognized

—X ray—ultra violet—infra red—neon—carbon arc—but there were others foreign to him. Meanwhile, Prince Ahmed was busy at a large switchboard.

Suddenly the room was filled with the rising hum of generators and transformers. The Egyptian looked up and pointed to the black box. "That," he said, "is a glass case. It contains a supply of ectoplasm which was collected by the simple expedient of destroying a number of mediums before the material had had time to return to their bodies. In a moment I shall put out all the lights; the black cover will be removed from the glass tank and then various light rays will be concentrated on Miss Grantland's body. You will see the result."

He flicked a key on the switchboard and the lights winked out. The darkness was complete. There was a sharp buzzing followed by a dim, blue illumination as the X ray and ultra violet ray lamps sprang into life.

"Watch the glass tank!" Prince Ahmed called.

Bob strained his eyes in the darkness. At first he could see nothing. Then, as the light of the other lamps came slowly up, one by one, he saw some straight, red streaks appear in what seemed to be the empty air of the tank's interior. Gradually, these streaks became paler, then white. And suddenly terror grabbed at Bob's stomach as he realized he was staring at a headless skeleton.

Prince Ahmed said: "You see, by means of X rays among others, the young lady is being photographed from the inside out. First the marrow in the bones—then the bones, themselves. Now you will observe the formation of the circulatory and digestive systems. . . ."

It was true. As the laboratory was more and more flooded with the light reflected from Rosalinde's body, the thing in the tank became a woman without skin. It was a pulsing mass of crimson veins. The expansion and contraction of the heart and lungs were plainly visible. Bob heard an exclamation of horror at his side. Julie, too, found it almost impossible to believe her own eyes.

The transformation continued. In another few seconds the veins, lungs, stomach and intestines were covered with muscles and a thin layer of white fat. The skin appeared—skin as fine and delicately tinted as that of Rosalinde. Bob glanced quickly from the headless figure in the tank to the hanging, helmeted girl. There was not the difference of a single pore between the two.

By this time, the whole bank of strange lamps was in use. Prince Ahmed adjusted an instrument on the switchboard and the high note of the buzzing which had accompanied the weird demonstration died down to a lower tone. At a signal, one of the men operated a pulley which raised the lead helmet free from Rosalinde's head. For a moment she stood still—with frozen nerves and brain—staring at the headless duplicate of herself that confronted her. But even as she swayed and fell fainting to the floor, exact replicas of her head and neck sprang into being on the shoulders of the ectoplasmic woman.

The lamps dimmed out as the ordinary lights came on. Prince Ahmed left the switchboard and walked to the tank. He looked through the glass, then, smiling, he turned to Julie and Bob. "And so," he said, "we have the plasm, Rosalinde Grantland! An absolutely perfect reproduction—at least as far as appearance goes." He glanced at his silent, efficient helpers and made a gesture towards the real Rosalinde, lying senseless on the floor. They raised her up and locked her arms and legs in the same fetters that had held her, before. The helmet they unhooked and took away.

PRINCE AHMED continued in his lecture room manner: "Yes, the appearance is exact, but there are a few minor differences which are not visible. One is that for some peculiar reason which I, myself, am frank to admit I do not understand, the plasm is totally unable to reproduce its kind—or rather, humankind. Another difference is that the thing has no soul—no emotion—sympathy—call it what you will. It would almost convince one of the divine origin of the original.

"But most important is the fact that the brain of the plasm is of little use. It is incapable of sustained thought or of memory because, by using the leaden helmet during most of the exposure, I did not allow the full development of the interior grey matter." He faced around and gazed at the girl in the tank—the girl whom Grantland, himself, would have claimed as his daughter. "Look at her!" he exclaimed. "See how stupid she looks! Standing there with her hands at her sides—doing nothing—thinking nothing."

The Egyptian went back to the laboratory and gave a few terse directions. A hinged side of the glass case was swung out. The Prince took the girl by the hand and led her to where Rosalinde's clothing still lay in a heap on the floor. "Put these on," he said. "Then sit quietly in that chair."

As the plasm calmly carried out his command, he returned to stand in front of Rosalinde. She had not yet recovered consciousness. Her whole weight hung from her slender arms. Her head drooped forward and her eyes were closed.

One of the men wheeled over a white enameled metal table. On its top were a number of objects, among them an electric stove on which a pan of water boiled. The sight of it tore a terrible cry of protest from Bob's throat. "Damn you!" he shouted, "What are you going to do?"

Prince Ahmed looked up and addressed a word to the man at his side. The servant immediately picked up a roll of adhesive tape with which he proceeded to fasten Bob's jaws together so that he could not make an intelligible sound. The Egyptian said: "I will tell you what I am about to do now that your bellowing can no longer annoy me. I am going to persuade Miss Grantland to tell me all she knows about the Blue Death. Then I am going to kill her. It would not do for two Rosalinde Grantlands to be alive—and this one will be somewhat disfigured during my questioning. By the way—if at any time you decide to tell me what I want to know, just nod your head and all this will stop." He paused and waited for some motion of surrender but Bob could not tell what he did not know. He glared his hate.

Prince Ahmed shrugged. "Oh, well—you'll change your mind in time. You will beg me to listen." From the table he picked up a large hypodermic needle that was filled with some brownish liquid. "A little while ago," he continued, "I said that I understood pain. It is more than that—I am a genius in the infliction of pain. I can produce such devastating agonies as no one could believe human nerves capable of sustaining. What I am going to do now is rather a good example of my inventiveness. As you may know, in woman, the breast is particularly sensitive, yet it can be considerably damaged or even removed without seriously endangering life. Therefore, I choose that gland as a beginning for my experiment."

Bob dug his nails into the palms of his hands until they bled. He felt he wanted to be sick. Nausea made him weak. He did not actually faint but he was no longer fully conscious of all he saw and heard. The Prince, the hanging girl and the laboratory all seemed a vague, blurred picture—a wavering vision in a hideous nightmare.

What was he saying? ". . . liquid in

this hypodermic—highly irritating—acid—unnatural heat inside the breast—sensation of internal fire. . ." He was standing next to her—this couldn't be—it wasn't possible—such things didn't happen. He was holding her full, round breast in his left hand while he deliberately buried to the hilt the two inch needle point of the hypodermic in the center of the nipple. His thumb was slowly pressing down the plunger, emptying the liquid to the last drop. He was pulling the needle out. There's one drop of blood on the point of her breast. He's put the hypodermic back on the table. Now he's just looking at her—waiting for something. She's still unconscious—maybe she's dead. . . No, she's not! Her head has suddenly jerked up—her mouth is open wide. She's screaming!

THAT agonized scream swept away the cobweb edges of Bob's senses. For a brief interval, picture and sounds were clear again.

Prince Ahmed said: "Are you ready to tell me now, Miss Grantland, what you know about the Blue Death?"

Racking sobs caught in her throat and the girl could hardly speak. "I don't know, I tell you! I don't know anything about it!"

"Perhaps in a little while you will remember."

Without paying any attention to Rosalinde's hysterical moaning, nor to her cries of: "My breast! My breast! It's burning!" Prince Ahmed spoke to Bob.

"We will wait a minute," he said, "while the acid takes effect. The breast will swell considerably as the irritated glands enlarge. By the time I am ready to remove the skin, it will be very tight, indeed. Have you noticed how well-behaved the plasm is? She is looking on without interest or emotion. In some ways that is an improvement on humankind." He laughed and turned back to Rosalinde.

He had been right. One of her breasts was half again as large as the other. It looked red and hard. Spasmodic shudders ran over the girl's body. Her muscles were contracted with the frightful pain. A little stream of blood ran down her chin from where she had bitten through her lip.

Bob glanced at Julie, at his side, and saw that she was still staring with unseeing eyes. He wondered if she were mad. Next to Julie was Rosalinde—a Rosalinde with a vapid face and a faint, silly smile. Again he felt reason slipping. He turned back and, through an aching haze, he saw Prince Ahmed take the boiling water from the electric stove and pour it into a wide-mouthed bowl.

Bob felt that his brains had disintegrated. His skull held mud and thoughts moved sluggishly there, like worms. "There is a man, there, with a short, black beard. He is holding a bowl—a steaming bowl. A white-skinned girl is hanging by her wrists. He is taking the bowl to her. Julie is mad. I am mad—so all this doesn't matter because it isn't true. The man is raising the bowl and carefully inverting it over the girl's swollen breast. He's holding it there. I'm sick. God, I'm sick! I wish I could wake up or dream of something else. At last he's taken the bowl away. Her breast is white now—dead white. Now what is he doing? I've got to snap out of this—I've got an important appointment—*He's pulling the skin off her breast in one piece like a glove!*"

THE American Hospital in Paris—eight days later. A man is lying on a cot. His eyes are fixed on the white ceiling. At the foot of the bed there is a chart which reads: "Robert Brundage—Brain Fever—Temperature 100—Pulse 125 (Irregular)." All of which indicates, of course, that the patient is well on the road to recovery.

At last Bob's thoughts were beginning to take on some semblance of order. Not that his memory was clear—probably it would never be—and that was just as well. He tried to remember things as they happened—in their exact sequence.

Yes, Rosalinde was almost certainly dead when they shoved her into the electric furnace. . . Julie's clothes had already been stripped off when the servant came to say McDonald was there with the police. . . So they dressed her again while Prince Ahmed talked. . . He said something about dope and sprinkling them with whiskey. McDonald would think all three were drunk. He'd be disgusted. Dope would make explanations impossible even if he believed them. How *could* they believe Rosalinde was dead when she was there—alive? I wonder if I *am* really crazy or if I'm just coming out of a lunatic fit? . . .

Bob heard a noise at his side and looked up to see Julie gazing down at him with sad, serious eyes. She said: "This is the first time they've let me see you, Bob—and now they'll only let me be with you for five minutes."

He took her hand. "Julie—is it true?"

She knew what he meant. "Yes. I was half hypnotized, but I remember—too much."

"Rosalinde is dead?"

Tears filled her eyes. "Yes—but nobody will believe it. I've told the whole story, but they think I'm insane—they think I'm insane no matter what I say. And they think worse of you. You've been discharged. And that Rosalinde Thing has gone home—Oh, it's too horrible!"

"And Ahmed?"

"I found out he's gone to America—after that miserable formula, I suppose."

Bob sat up in bed and stared Julie straight in the eyes. "Julie," he said, "until we can catch that fiend and *prove* our story is true, our lives will be hell! Will you come with me to America—to fight?"

"Of course I will. We must—for our own sake and for the sake of the world. What would the Blue Death be in the hands of a devil like him!"

Bob drew her close and whispered, "Even if we don't win, Julie dear, I'll try to make you happy. . . ."

The nurse entered and interrupted a kiss that was both a promise and a pact.

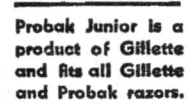

Novelette of Tingling Fear

One by one the men and women of that little storm-bound town died hideous deaths—by the gory knife of a fiend from the grave. Was Dan Draper's turn next? Was the golden-haired Mary Wilson going to be scalped alive, too—after the monster first defiled her lovely body . . . ?

SCALPS Of The LIVING

By George Edson

(Author of "The Cross of Blood," etc.)

FOR a while they had known only horror. But now something else clutched them—eerie, heart-squeezing fear. Dan Draper could feel it. And he knew that the two men standing here in this old country store with him felt it, too.

Neither of them had spoken since Ben Judson had gone for the sheriff. They kept casting furtive glances toward the door which led into Eli Hammond's living quarters at the rear of the building, then toward the front door and the windows. He knew what they were half-expecting to see. Over and over he told himself it was impossible, utterly absurd. Yet the creeping fear within him wouldn't be stifled.

He didn't *know* that it was impossible. There were people who told strange tales of the restless dead. . . .

Outside, the wind howled with increased fury. It battered at the walls of the building as if it strove to tear them from their foundations. Snow drove against the windows. That morning, threatening clouds had settled over the mountains; late in the afternoon they had swirled down on the little village in the valley. Certainly the storm was the worst in many years, and the dying chief had sworn he would come out of a storm. . . .

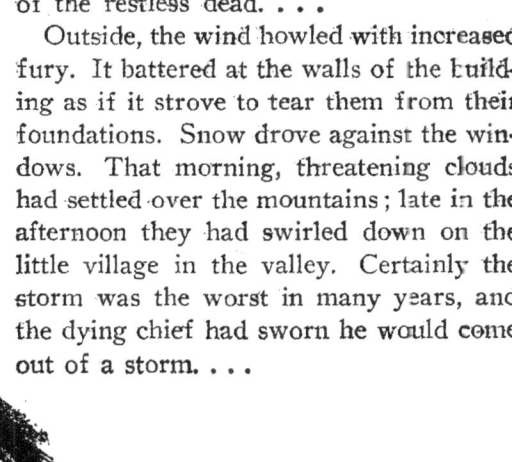

Suddenly the front door flew open. An icy blast of wind swept through the store and almost extinguished the kerosene lamp in the antiquated fixture hanging from the ceiling. For an instant Draper stood rigid, staring—then he relaxed. The white figure that lurched in out of the darkness was only Judson. And behind Judson stamped the burly sheriff, Eb Tait.

Draper realized that he brought out an audible exclamation of relief. And he heard similar exclamations from the two other men near him.

Sheriff Tait pushed the door closed, shook the snow from his coat and cap. Evidently Judson had told him where to find Hammond. Grimly, without any questions or greetings, he strode to the rear of the store and through the doorway into the storekeeper's living quarters.

None of the others followed. They had seen that gruesome sight once and did not want to see it again. They waited in silence.

Only a few seconds passed before Tait stumbled back through the doorway. His face was grey, sick; his eyes were filled with horror. Staring wildly from one to another, he babbled: "His head . . . his head . . . God! It—it looks as if . . ." The next words clogged in his throat.

Old Zeke Hodge, the hermit, mumbled something under his breath. Then he said hoarsely: "You don't need to tell us. We all saw his head. The top of it was hacked off with a knife or hatchet. Eli Hammond —was scalped!"

DRAPER shivered. Outside, as if to emphasize those last words, the wind rose to a shrill shriek. It sounded like the wail of some lost soul suffering excruciating agony. Or—and the chill pierced to the very marrow of Dan Draper's spine—was it more like the weird yell of triumph that the Indians used to utter after the kill?

"Holy Mother!" someone whispered.

"Maybe that's him out there!" A crazy tone had stolen into old Zeke's voice. "Yes, you know . . . all of you! You know he has come back just as he swore he would! Back from the grave . . . swingin' his bloody tomahawk! Storm of Death."

"Don't be a fool," Tait snapped. "That's damned nonsense. Only a silly legend."

But the sheriff's statements lacked the ring of conviction. And in his eyes Dan Draper could see the same fear that was in the eyes of the others. The same fear he knew was in his own eyes.

"Only a silly legend?" Old Zeke gurgled out a mocking laugh. "Yes, for nearly a hundred years. Now it's more than that. He swore he'd come back in the midst of a storm. This is the worst storm in anyone's memory. And"—Zeke pointed toward the rear of the store—"there's Eli Hammond whose father helped run the last of the Indians around here up into the mountains. He's lyin' in there dead —scalped. And I wager he ain't goin' to be the only one."

"Who found him?" Tait demanded.

"I did," the hermit said. "I'd hiked down to get some provisions. Eli wasn't out front so I went lookin' for him. Then Judson, Bedell and young Dan Draper showed up."

Draper had been facing the rear of the store. Abruptly he stiffened, whirled. His keen ears had caught a new sound which couldn't possibly have been the wind—a short, feeble cry. That cry had torn from a human throat.

He gained the door in three bounds, ripped it open. Snow drove into his face and blinded him. He swung one arm up to shield his eyes as he pushed through the drift on the porch. He heard the cry again, plainer. And then, when he made out the slight form struggling toward him, wild fear clutched his heart.

Mary—the girl he loved! What was she

doing down here? What had happened?

He fought his way to her, caught her just as she would have fallen. Lifting her in his arms, he turned and ploughed back to the store. The others who had grouped around the door, stepped aside and followed him across to the stove in the corner. John Bedell, who was Mary's uncle, grabbed a blanket from a pile on a table. He and Draper wrapped it around her before Draper lowered her to a chair.

She was unconscious, now. Her lips were blue, her pretty face so white that it looked frozen. Draper knelt beside her and chafed her white hands.

Presently she opened her eyes. For an instant they were blank; then mingled terror and anguish leaped into them. She moaned.

"What is it, Mary?" Draper was on his knees beside the girl. "What's happened?"

"Daddy!" Her voice was weak, husky. "He's gone! But blood . . . all over the floor! The barn . . ." She broke into sobs.

HORROR, an even more numbing horror than had come with the sight of Eli Hammond, gripped Dan Draper's brain. Mary's father gone! Blood on the floor! Had the thing struck again?

"He—he was at the barn so long that I began to worry. I went to see what was wrong. And—and I found the blood. I called . . . looked everywhere. Then I ran to the house to telephone. The phone wouldn't work. I started down here." Her tone became frantic. "Oh—you've got to find him! Maybe he's freezing out in the snow! He must have been terribly hurt!"

"Steady, dear. We'll find him." Draper spoke loudly enough to give the others a cue. He knew that Mary was in no condition to hear what had happened to Hammond, to bear the horrible dread that the same thing might have happened to her father. "Don't you worry. We'll find him."

But old Zeke ignored the cue. Laughing crazily, he gibbered: "What did I say? I told you Eli Hammond wouldn't be the last one. No. Nor will—"

"Shut up!" Draper twisted his head, glared savagely at the hermit. "One more crack out of you and . . ." He left the consequences to Zeke's imagination.

"What—what does he mean, Dan?" Mary quavered.

"Nothing." He tried to make the answer sound convincing. "Listen, dear. You're going over to your uncle's house with him and have your Aunt Martha do something to keep you from catching pneumonia. The rest of us'll go for your father."

"And we're starting now," the sheriff muttered grimly. "Come on, men."

Draper gave John Bedell a significant look and said: "Take care of her, John."

Bedell nodded. He was a tall, muscular man; he picked Mary up in his arms as easily as if she were a mere child.

"No—no!" She tried to squirm free. "I've got to go up and help! Please, Uncle John!"

But he held her and said gently: "They can do everything, Mary. You couldn't help. And you're already half frozen. I'm going to carry you right over to the house and have your Aunt Martha make sure you don't get sick. Your father wouldn't forgive me if I didn't."

It was only a short distance to Ira Wilson's little farm. Yet to the four men who struggled toward it in the storm that distance seemed interminable. Every step through the deep snow was an exhausting labor. Several times they even had to smash through drifts nearly up to their waists. The merciless wind battered at them, numbed their faces and blinded their eyes.

Draper forced his mind to think of the ordinary things which might have happened to Mary's father. He might have fallen, cut himself somehow. One of the horses might have kicked him, gashed him with a spiked shoe. There could be countless explanations for the blood. For his disappearance—he might have started for the house, dropped in the snow because loss of the blood had weakened him, been immediately covered.

Might and could . . . and it wasn't possible for any man to return from death. *It wasn't possible.* Yet Dan Draper couldn't stifle the gnawing dread within him. Who else would have killed Eli Hammond so horribly . . . ?

Eventually they reached their destination. First they went to the barn and through to the stable. A lighted lantern hung from a nail in one wall; its flickering rays showed them the bloodstains on the floor. The sheriff sent Ben Judson to see if Wilson had by any chance returned to the house, told Draper and old Zeke to cover the section between house and barn, remained himself to search that.

For several moments Draper tramped back and forth between the two buildings. Suddenly his foot struck something. Stooping, he dug away the snow. Then he called to Zeke, sent him for the others.

They came and helped him carry Ira Wilson's stiff body into the house.

There, in the lighted room, they stretched the body on the couch and stared down at it. Horror made them all catch their breath. The man's face had been frozen into a ghastly mask of agony. He had died just as Eli Hammond had died —suffering a hell of pain. He had been scalped alive.

CHAPTER TWO

Storm of Death

AGAIN on this awful night the wind rose to a wild, triumphant scream. The sound shuddered through the walls and windows and rocked the room. It lasted for nearly a minute—time during which the four living people there stood taut, motionless. Finally it faded to a whistling moan.

"That—that ain't the wind," Zeke whispered. "I've heard them redskinned devils yell when they were on the warpath. It's him—Storm of Death!"

"By God!" Sheriff Tait shuddered. "It —it does sound like an Indian's screech. Hell, it can't be! It's only the wind."

"Don't you wish you believed that?" Old Zeke chortled as he glanced around at each of the other three. "But you don't. You know it's the last of the chiefs— Storm of Death. He's carryin' out his threat. Before this storm dies all of us in this village'll be dead. Men, women and children. Like Hammond and Wilson. Scalped alive." The hermit leered at Draper. "Yes, Draper, even that pretty girl of yours. Her bloody hair'll be hangin' on the red devil's belt before he's finished."

A hot wave of rage surged over Draper. He clenched one fist, lifted it, took a quick step toward Zeke. Then, abruptly, he restrained himself. Why go for this harmless old critter? Maybe he was right. Two men had already died. Why wouldn't more die? Why wouldn't women and children die, too?

"We're doomed," Zeke intoned. "The last chief cursed this village and those who would ever live on the land from which his people had been driven. Storm of Death . . . people thought he was mad to've called himself that. He was comin' back in a storm, he told 'em. Comin' back as Death. Well . . . he has."

Draper felt the eerie chill probe to every part of his body. All his life he had heard repeated the famous legend of that last Indian chief who had died vowing to return for his venegeance. Once there had been something terrifying about it. He had often visualized the mad old warrior glaring down at the tiny village in the valley from the peak of the great mountain where he was supposed to have died. Then, growing out of boyhood, it had begun to sound silly—just the tale of a vain threat hurled down by a crazy old man. . . .

BUT now. . . . No! It was still silly! He was getting the creeps because two men had been so brutally murdered. Murdered . . . that was it. Some fiendish killer was trying to cover himself by playing on that ancient legend.

"Listen, Sheriff." He set his square jaw, pivoted. "And you, Ben. We can't dawdle around while someone else is being murdered. Don't you see the hoax? Some damned killer figures he can get away with his murders by terrorizing us. By murdering so that we can't help but be reminded of that legend."

Neither Tait nor Judson responded at once. On their faces could easily be seen the conflict that was raging beneath—the conflict between sane reason and primordial fear.

"Don't you understand that's what it must be?" Draper hammered at them. "Only one man ever rose out of his grave. This legend's just as foolish as it ever was. There's a killer in the village—a homicidal maniac of flesh and blood. We've got to get him. God! He may be after others this very minute!"

Judson, a man of methodical brain, said slowly: "Yes, that's got to be the explanation. Some maniac like Joe Labrecque. He was half Indian, too—and vicious. But he's still up there in the penitentiary."

"Labrecque." A speculative gleam snapped into Dan Draper's eyes as he echoed the name. "And he hates plenty of people in this village for sending him to the pen. Eli Hammond and Ira Wilson included. He said after the trial that he'd fix all those who had testified against him."

These weren't the only thoughts working through Dan Draper's mind. Another which he didn't put into words made the inside of him feel hollow: Labrecque had recently been attracted to Mary. Two or three times just before he had been arrested he had tried to force unwelcome advances on her. Finally Draper had given him a thrashing. He had caught the half-breed following Mary and had gone berserk at the obscene lust in Labrecque's eyes. If Labrecque *were* loose and roaming the village tonight . . .

"No," Judson mused, "Labrecque wouldn't go around scalping his victims even if he weren't in the pen. He's too smart. He'd know that suspicion would settle right on him because of his Indian blood."

"Labrecque's smart?" Sheriff Tait shook his head. "Not a bit of it. Call him smart to damned near kill old Silas Robbins in order to steal less than five dollars? And he'd be so conceited that he'd want us to realize he was getting his revenge. Joe Labrecque may be our man. He might've escaped."

"Phone the warden at the pen," Draper told the sheriff. "For God's sake, let's—"

"No use, Dan. Mary said the phone wouldn't work. Probably all the lines are down in this wind. We can't—"

"Labrecque!" The hoarse shout burst from old Zeke. "There . . . in the window! I saw him!"

The three other men whirled, stared at the window the hermit's shaking hand designated. They could see nothing.

"He's gone now!" Zeke babbled. "But I saw him! I swear it! For just a second . . . his face!"

DRAPER jerked into action. He rushed across the room and through the kitchen to the door. He yanked it open, plunged out into the storm, fought his way around to the side of the house. But the blizzard was like a curtain in front of his eyes when he tried to see any distance. He wallowed along to the window through which Zeke claimed Labrecque had been peering. He found no tracks; snow driven by this gale would probably have filled them by now if there had been any.

In a moment the sheriff, Judson and Zeke joined him. The sheriff said: "Zeke swears to God he did see the halfbreed. He can't've gone far. We've got a chance of catching him if we split. Ben, you and Zeke head for town. Dan, if you're game to attempt it alone, cover the trail over the ridge to the north end of the village. He might think he was fooling us by circling around that way. I'm going to trek up to the cabin where he used to live."

"All right, Eb," Ben Judson agreed. And he started off with old Zeke.

"It's not much of a chance," the sheriff muttered. "But, damn it, what else can we do? I'm sure Zeke was telling the truth. Labrecque was looking in that window. He escaped from the pen and committed these hellish murders. You know well enough that he'd had his eye on Mary. It's logical he'd be after her."

"He's not going to get her!" Draper's voice was grim, hard. "By God, he's not!"

The sheriff and Draper parted in silence at the foot of the ridge trail. Draper soon discovered that the task set for him was practically impossible. The wind screaming down from the mountains tore at him, made every few yards of progress through the heavy drifts of snow seem an endless distance. He could hardly see ten steps ahead.

HE stopped before he got to the top of the ridge. This was damned foolish. He'd never find Labrecque up here in this storm. And it would take at least an hour more to reach the village by this route. In that hour . . .

Abruptly he turned. Hell! He had been dumb! Sheriff Tait had been dumb! Labrecque, who knew every inch of this country, would have gone down the gully and across by the old mill. That way was sheltered, would be quick. He had learned that Mary wasn't at home. Wouldn't he go to her uncle's looking for her?

Cursing himself for a fool, Draper cut into the woods and wallowed down toward the gully. For some reason Labrecque must have left Wilson's after killing Mary's father—probably to settle another debt. Then he had returned for her.

God! Would it take him forever to reach that gully? If only he had some snowshoes. . . .

But eventually he did reach it. Sobbing for breath, he swung toward the village and pushed on faster. His mind conjured up a succession of horrible picture as he moved: The halfbreed leering at the helpless girl . . . gliding toward her . . . seizing her. . . . Draper ground out an oath.

He came to the sheltered part of the trail and forced his aching legs to run. He crossed by the old mill, smashed through a wide drift, saw the lighted windows of Bedell's house.

Terror clutched him when he heard a quavering wail. No! It was only the wind . . . only the wail of the wind!

Yet he drove himself more frantically toward the building. He didn't bother with stealth or caution. Lunging through the drift on the narrow porch, he grabbed the knob and heaved his shoulder against the door. It wasn't locked, burst open and let him stumble headlong into the hall. He spun toward the living room.

And then he halted. His eyes bulged from their sockets at the gruesome sight they saw. Horror pierced to the very depths of his soul, petrified him.

In a great pool of blood on the floor lay John Bedell and his wife. Death had set their faces in ghastly grimace of agony. Their heads—Draper swayed weakly—the tops of their heads were hairless, bloody. They had been scalped . . . scalped alive!

CHAPTER THREE

The Fiend From Hell

FINALLY Dan Draper jerked out of his horrified stupor, took two lurching steps into the slaughterhouse which had once been a cozy and cheerful room. Mary! Where was she? He had heard no sound of a voice. Had the fiend . . .? Was she, to . . .?

There were only those two silent corpses. The halfbreed wouldn't have killed her so soon.

"Mary!" Frenziedly he shouted her name. "Mary! Mary!"

But there was not even a feeble response.

He knew that Labrecque, if he had still been here, would have heard the front door crash open. He might have fled, might be waiting for the chance to add one more scalp to his collection. Draper drew his lips into a savage snarl and went grimly toward the kitchen.

He searched the entire house but found neither the girl he loved nor the monster who had her.

Then he remembered the wail he had thought was the wind. It must have come from Mary. Labrecque had taken her to a place where he could satisfy his desires at leisure! Oh God . . . where? The cabin where he had lived?

Madness burned in Draper's brain as he stumbled out of the house and started for the halfbreed's old cabin north of the village. Sheriff Tait had already gone there. But Tait would be no match for a maniac who could kill John Bedell. Labrecque would get him. And then Mary would be left to the halfbreed's mercy.

Mercy! Draper choked a curse into the wind blasting at him as he struggled through the storm. Labrecque had no mercy. In the end he would kill her. He had sense enough to know that no amount of mere suspicion could prove him guilty of these monstrous murders. He wouldn't let Mary live to be the damning witness to his guilt.

Some of the snowdrifts were so deep now that Draper could hardly batter through them. Time and again the force of the gale hurled him backward—as if it were toying with him. In his fevered mind the blizzard became a living demon who wanted to keep him from the girl he loved.

Labrecque probably had snowshoes. Draper made frenzied calculations. His own house was off the direct route to Labrecque's cabin but less than half the distance. He would gain by going for his own snowshoes. He veered to the left.

He had almost reached his house when he heard the feeble cry. It came to him in a moment during which the wind had died, came from the direction of his house —a cry of mingled terror and despair.

Mary! His heart pounded wildly against his breast. It had sounded like her voice!

HE SHOUTED a hoarse response. Gulping for breath, he bent his head and forced his legs to move faster. He ploughed through the mountain of snow at the foot of his driveway, stopped, peered up toward the house. He heard a second cry. Then he saw the form near the corner of the porch.

"Mary!" He plunged on again. "I'm coming!" To himself he sobbed: "Oh . . . thank God! Thank God!"

She turned toward him. She staggered two or three steps, fell.

"Mary!" He reached her, stooped, gathered her quaking body into his arms. "My dear! My poor dear!"

He took her up on the porch, let her feet slip down while he unlocked the door and then carried her inside. He stretched her on a couch in the warm living room. His throat constricted when he saw the stark whiteness of her face. She must be nearly frozen. She wore a thin coat, but it was open at the neck and showed only a nightgown underneath.

Rage flamed to an inferno within Draper. The fiend hadn't even let her dress. Draper glanced down at her legs and saw that he had at least let her put on shoes and stockings.

Draper hurried into the kitchen and returned with some brandy. He forced a few drops between her blue lips. She stirred a little, moaned.

"Mary," he murmured softly. "Mary, you're all right now. You're here . . . in my house."

She moaned again, shivered. Draper rose and threw more logs in the stove. He got blankets from his bedroom, spread them over her, tucked the edges under her. And presently her eyes opened. For an instant they remained blank; then terror, wild terror, jumped into them.

"Mary, you're safe." He slid one hand beneath her slender shoulder. "You're safe."

She stiffened, whispered: "Storm of Death . . . I got away . . . but he'll come for me. . . ."

The anxious lines furrowing Draper's face deepened. She was delirious. He prayed that the telephone connection between his house and the village hadn't been broken. He had to get the doctor; yet he couldn't leave her alone while Labrecque was still at large.

"Storm of Death!" Her whisper rose to a shrill cry. "He's coming . . . I hear him!" She tore one arm from under the blankets and clutched at Draper's sleeve. "I hear him!"

An eerie chill crawled up Dan Draper's spine as the wind outside uttered a demoniacal shriek. A wave of coldness seemed to be sweeping into the very room.

"Dan. . . ."

"No, no." His own voice was hoarse, unsteady. "It's only the—"

"Dan!"

She was staring at something behind him—staring fearfully. He heard a faint noise. He twisted. Lunging at him, a knife gripped in one upraised hand, was Joe Labrecque.

DRAPER didn't have time to climb to his feet. Ducking his head, he flung out both arms and dove for Labrecque's legs. The knife swept down at him and grazed his cheek just as his hands hit the halfbreed's ankles.

Labrecque's feet skidded out from under him. He pitched forward and landed on Draper's back. He slashed at Draper again.

Draper felt the blade of the knife dig into his side. The room whirled and went dark. Desperately he fought off complete oblivion. As if from a great distance he heard Mary scream. And through the cloud of darkness he saw that she had struggled up from the couch, that she was flinging herself at Labrecque. The halfbreed had risen; he caught her and smashed a fist into her white face.

"You damned . . ." Draper's voice clogged as fury at Labrecque's brutality and his own helplessness surged up like fire within him. He shook his head in a frenzied attempt to clear it. He managed to pull himself to his knees.

Mary had crumpled and lay moaning on the floor. Labrecque laughed. Then he turned, glimpsed Draper; the laugh trailed off into a hiss. He raised his knife.

Draper wobbled from his knees to his feet and straightened as the halfbreed sprang. He lashed out a wild blow. Luck was with him; the blow landed on the wrist of Labrecque's knife arm. The knife scaled into the air, clattered to the floor. But the halfbreed instantly changed tactics and clamped his hands around Draper's throat.

Draper tried to yank free, tried to tear the hands loose. Hot pain streaked over his body with every movement. He had lost so much blood that he was weak, faint.

He choked for breath. His lungs ached, burned. His head spun and eyes grew dim. He couldn't . . .

A pitiful whimper from Mary struck his ears, throbbed into his brain—and something happened. It was like a shell bursting inside him. He stiffened his legs. He jammed his chin down between the throttling hands and heaved both his fists at Labrecque's chest. He jolted back as they landed.

Labrecque's hold broke.

Dan Draper mustered all his remaining strength and swung his right to the halfbreed's swarthy face. Labrecque gurgled out a groan. His black eyes rolled, glazed; his jaw drooped. For a moment he stood absolutely motionless. Then he quivered and sagged to the floor.

Draper dragged air into his aching lungs. Thank God! Oh, thank God! The horror of this awful night was finished! Labrecque had committed his last atrocity!

MARY uttered a little cry. Turning, Draper stumbled across the room and dropped down beside her. He murmured: "Darling . . . darling, it's all over now."

But she had fainted. He pushed to his feet once more, lifted her, carried her to the couch. Then he glanced at his side and saw that the knife wound was pretty bad. It needed attention. First, however, he went back to Labrecque. The halfbreed lay still, looked as if he'd be out for a long while. But it would be best to tie him at once and take no chances. Rope—there was some in the shed.

He picked up Labrecque's knife, tossed it on the table in the kitchen. He knew exactly where to find the rope and didn't bother to get his flashlight.

Wind tore at him when he unbolted the door and stepped through to the open shed. He shivered. The storm was growing worse. He remembered how old Zeke had prophesied that before it died all the people in the village would be dead. Draper tightened his lips. The prophecy might have come true if he hadn't managed to conquer the killer. God only knew what further horrors had been in Labrecque's perverted mind.

He wondered if the halfbreed had been thinking of the old chief's curse. There was something weird in the idea that the last descendant of the tribe had almost succeeded in fulfilling the vow of the last chief. It was as if the command had issued from the grave. The yells of triumph the wind had . . .

Suddenly Draper froze. From the house had come a short, shrill scream. Mary! What a fool he'd been to leave her alone for even a moment with Labrecque! The breed had recovered, had . . .

Quivering, Draper twisted and lunged back across the shed. The lamp in the living room had been extinguished. But enough light filtered through the doorway from the kitchen to show him the gruesome sight. He choked.

Labrecque still lay upon the floor. But the top of his head was a horrible, gory mess. He had been scalped!

And Mary was gone!

For one awful instant hideous thoughts whirled in Draper's brain. Labrecque hadn't committed the fiendish murders. He had been murdered like the others. Mary had been alone in this room with him. Was it possible that she . . . No! Good God, no! But who?

Terror, the full force of the creeping terror he had felt before on this night of hell, stabbed to the depths of Dan Draper's soul. He knew now that the legend wasn't silly. It was true! The mad old chief *had* returned from the grave! That was the only answer. He had killed Labrecque. He had taken Mary!

Draper stumbled toward the front door. Then he heard a low moan. He swung around toward the bedroom—and halted.

Out of the darkness into the faint light filtering through the doorway from the kitchen sprang a monstrous figure with a horrible, painted face. An Indian! *Storm of Death!*

SOMEHOW Draper managed to recover enough control over his muscles to fling out a protective fist. He tried to duck away from the long knife that was clutched in the monster's hand. But his blow was too feeble, his body too slow, and the sweeping knife gashed the side of his head and raked down across the point of his shoulder.

For a split second he looked into the monster's eyes—looked deep and shuddered. They held a terrible consuming madness.

Abject fear filled Dan Draper's heart even as he ducked a second slash and struck again at the horrible face. He had no chance. He couldn't fight with this . . . this thing from the grave. Nor could he hope to escape that knife in the end. He was going to die—die as the others had.

And Mary . . . He visualized the knife hacking at the top of her pretty head. An insane frenzy seized him and swallowed the fear for himself.

Merciful Father! No! Not Mary—his beloved Mary!

He didn't try to duck any longer. Recklessly, crazily he rushed at the monster. And for a moment the monster retreated before the attack, used both arms in defense against it.

But even frenzy couldn't give Draper endless strength. Finally he weakened. The monster saw his opportunity and whipped up the bloodstained knife. In helpless fascination Draper watched. Excruciating anticipative pain pounded in his head. The knife started down. . . .

"Dan! Dan!"

Mary's quavering cry made the monster stay his hand a second. Draper dragged himself back two or three steps. He felt his knees give, his body sag. He groaned.

"Dan! Where are you?"

The monster's face distorted into a snarl. He glanced down at Draper, then turned and disappeared into the darkness. Desperately Draper tried to rise. He had to save her! He had to save her! He managed to get to his knees—but only to crumple again.

A scream came from the bedroom. One single scream which trailed off into a moan—then silence. . . .

And Dan Draper's heart became a cold lump of despair.

He didn't quite lose consciousness. In some dim limbo of existence where his mind could suffer a hell of anguish he lingered; half mad and half sane. The fiendish specter had murdered her. She was dead now—dead. . . .

But there had been only the one scream; she hadn't lived to go through agony. Soon he, too, would die. And somewhere he would join her. They would be together forever as they had planned.

He saw the massive form of the monster glide out of the darkness again and move toward him. It was Death approaching—the death he wanted. Yet he couldn't help cringing. Once more anticipative pain throbbed in his head. He wondered how long it would take him to die.

The monster came closer, lifted his knife. He made a gibbering sound deep in his throat. His painted features twisted into an expression of fanatical glee.

Draper shuddered. Nausea churned in the pit of his stomach. His mouth went dry.

"Dan!" This shout came from outside during a moment when the wind had abated. It was a man's voice. "Hey, Draper! You in there?"

The monster halted, straightened. He hesitated for an instant, suddenly pivoted and ran back into the bedroom. Almost immediately he reappeared. He was going out the front door. And on his shoulder he carried a burden—a limp human form. Mary!

Draper choked out a hoarse cry as the significance burst on him. Mary wasn't dead! Frantically he clawed up to his feet, stumbled toward the hall.

"Help!" he managed that feeble shout to the person outside. "Around front—quick!"

He plunged out into the storm after the fleeing monster. But he didn't even get through the drift on the porch. A wave of agony from his wounds crashed over him, made him reel. And he sank into oblivion. . . .

CHAPTER FOUR

Cavern of Lust

HIS next sensation was of crawling through a shadowy region of horror peopled by ghastly creatures whose heads were hairless, bloody blobs. He recognized all of them. But he was seeking one he couldn't find, had been seeking her during long ages of torment. Suddenly he saw her. . . .

The nightmare passed. Draper realized that he was still alive—remembered what had happened. He forced his aching eyes open. He was lying on the bed in the bedroom of his own house. Near him stood Ben Judson.

Judson leaned over and said: "You're going to be all right, Dan. That damned devil, Labrecque, nearly got you. But I've bandaged all the wounds. Stopped the flow of blood from that gash on your head. It's lucky I reached here when I did, though. Zeke strayed away from me in the storm and I got lost. Landed up here at your place." He scowled. "By God, we've got to get that murdering halfbreed!"

Draper ignored the pain streaking over his body and hammering in his head. He jerked up to a sitting position, choked: "Mary! Oh God . . . he took her! The Indian . . ."

"Labrecque took Mary?" Judson stiffened. "What do you—"

"Not Labrecque! Storm of Death . . . the old chief! He *has* come back from the grave! He's got Mary!"

"Steady, Dan." Judson spoke in a soothing voice as he forced Draper down again. "Don't try to move. You need to keep quiet. I'm going for the doctor. The phone doesn't work. Will you—"

"Let me go!" Draper fought free and struggled up to the edge of the couch. "You think I'm crazy—delirious. I'm not. Go and see for yourself. Labrecque's in the living room. I knocked him cold. Then the monster came and scalped him. Took Mary. God! Don't you understand? We've got to find her!"

SHE wasn't dead. That one thought revolved in his brain. The monster wouldn't have carried off a lifeless body. She wasn't dead. Other thoughts, horrible thoughts, grew out of that one. He had read stories about the dead mating with the living—gruesome stories which had once seemed absurd. Now he remembered that even then icy little fingers had crawled over him while he had read of those black things his reason wouldn't accept. Some primordial instinct within him had tried to speak to him, tried to tell him that the black things could happen.

This creature, cold with the clammy cold of death, had taken Mary for a mate. He would want her warmth, her life. He would suck it into his cold body. . . .

"It—it's true!" Judson had gone through the hall and looked into the living room. Now, white and trembling, he stared at Draper. And suddenly a gleam of suspicion came into his eyes. "He's dead! He was murdered like—like the others. You—"

"You fool!" Draper's voice was harsh. "I didn't kill him! Do something! Go down and round up all the men in the village. We've got to save Mary!"

Slowly, as Judson became convinced that Draper was telling him the truth, the suspicion in his eyes changed to fear. He shivered, cast a furtive glance toward the windows.

Dan Draper realized that no man in the village, since John Bedell had been killed, would help him hunt the fiendish specter from the grave. He would have to do it alone. Setting his jaw, he pushed to his feet and wobbled toward the shed. Snowshoes—he had to have them to go anywhere tonight. To go . . . where? Where would the monster have taken Mary?

Despair swept over him. He didn't have a chance of ever finding her. He didn't . . . He tightened his lips into a grim line. At least he would meet death trying. That was better than staying here with his terrible thoughts, better than living on without her.

He had almost reached the doorway when his legs buckled. He fell. His head hit the floor.

And once more oblivion swirled down over him. . . .

HE REGAINED consciousness to find himself back on the bed. But Judson was gone. Outside the storm still raged;

shrieking wind shook the little house and snow drove against the windows.

"Mary!" Draper sobbed her name aloud. Then, in a hoarse voice, he prayed: "Dear Lord . . . help me save her! Help me save her from . . ."

As if in answer to his prayer a memory of something that had happened long ago returned to him. Another boy and he had been wandering through the woods behind Zeke Hodge's cabin. They had discovered a cave. Coming out after exploring it, they had met the hermit and learned that the corpse of the Indian chief who had cursed the village was supposed to have been buried there. They had been so frightened that they had run all the way home.

That the last chief actually had been buried there was a common belief in the village. Several people had dug for his bones, found nothing. Yet the belief had persisted.

That cave . . . it might be the grave from which the monster had risen to stalk the village for his vengeance on this night of storm. That would be where he would take Mary. He would make her lie with him in the hole where his mouldering corpse had lain through all these years.

The hideous thought sent madness to Dan Draper's brain. He pushed to the edge of the bed and up to his feet. He stumbled into the kitchen, yanked on a mackinaw and heavy cap, got his rifle from the closet. He went to the bedroom for his flashlight, slipped it into one of the mackinaw pockets. Then he rushed out to the shed and found his snowshoes. With trembling fingers he fixed the thongs around his ankles.

Wind blasted at him as he clumped out into the blizzard. Snow lashed at his face, stung his eyes. His left arm, throbbing with pain from the wound on the point of the shoulder, hung limp and useless at his side. He held the rifle between his knees while he twitched up the collar of the mackinaw.

It wasn't more than a mile to the tiny cabin where old Zeke had lived ever since Dan Draper could remember. The cave was just a short distance from there.

"Dear God," he begged, "help me. Help me to reach her . . . to save her."

FROM somewhere Draper received new strength. It lasted while he fought more than half the mile to old Zeke's cabin through the terrific gale which battered ceaselessly at him. Finally, however, it ebbed. Twice his legs gave way and he crumpled into the snow. Both times he managed to drag himself up, struggle on again. But he had to slacken his speed.

The rifle he had taken seemed to weigh more with each step. In the end he dropped it. What could a rifle do to this monster who had risen from death? What could anything . . . No! He must not let himself think of that!

Above all he had to keep his courage. Keep his courage and trust God before whom this creature of the Devil in hell must be an abomination.

A third time his legs buckled. He sagged into the snow and lay there a moment. Stabbing pain from the wounds in his side and shoulder surged through his body. His head—Judson had said it was only a gash—hurt like hell. The cap was too tight over the bandage Judson had made. He ripped it off, flung it away.

What had happened to Mary by now? Over and over that question blasted at him. What obscene horrors had she already known? And back of that question another eternal one: Was she still alive?

Yes! Oh God, she must be! She must be!

Frenziedly Draper pulled himself up and plunged on faster. He had covered three-quarters of the mile. The rest of the way would be uphill, harder. He set his jaw.

That final quarter of a mile seemed interminable. He fell, dragged himself up, fell again, dragged himself up again. Pain slashed at every muscle, ground like an infernal torture machine in his head. His throat went dry and his lungs burned. But he pushed on. And at last he reached old Zeke's cabin.

The windows were dark. Zeke hadn't returned home after straying away from Judson on the way down from Ira Wilson's house.

Draper swung around to the rear of the cabin and into the woods. They gave him some protection from the storm. He drew out his flash, lighted it. With the aid of its beam he spotted occasional landmarks which the snow hadn't entirely covered.

He found the hill under which the cave tunneled, climbed until he reached a wall of rock. The trees had kept the snow from drifting against it. He moved along to the mouth of the passage into the cave. Stooping, he loosened the thongs and stepped off his snowshoes.

The blackness in that passage was so thick it seemed almost tangible. Yet Draper didn't use his flash. To give away his presence would be to destroy any feeble hope he had. He groped his way.

The passage wound upward for a short distance, then turned a sharp corner and plunged down into the bowels of the hill. The air grew damp, clammy; it took on the stench of decay. To Draper it was the stench of a grave—a rotting, unholy grave. He shuddered.

But pray God she was here! Here—and alive! If he didn't find her . . .

SUDDENLY he tripped in a hole, fell. He broke the fall with his right hand. And yet the palm of that hand didn't press against earth or rock. It pressed against something else, something . . . He uttered a stifled cry of horror. He had picked the thing up and knew what it was. It was a human scalp!

And the hair was long—a woman's! Whose? Cold sweat welled out of Dan Draper's pores as he ripped his flash from his pocket, snapped the switch. Relief burst over him. It wasn't Mary's golden hair. The strands, crusted with gore, were gray. The scalp must have belonged to Mrs. Bedell.

He dropped it, flicked off the flash, clawed to his feet. For a moment he stood there trembling. His flesh crawled. Nausea whirled in his stomach and made him feel like vomiting. He swallowed; then he gulped in a deep breath and continued on toward the main chamber of the cave.

That gruesome object proved he was on the right track. It proved that the monster had come here. He must have brought Mary.

Abruptly Draper slowed. He had rounded a corner and saw faint light ahead of him. Then he heard a low voice—a horrible, gloating voice. Crouching, Draper crept forward until he could look into the cavern.

He stiffened. In the flickering light from a small fire he could see Mary. She lay on her back, her coat pulled open and her nightgown torn to expose the white mounds of her breasts. She lay motionless except for those breasts which moved with her slow breathing and told Dan Draper that she was alive.

He peered around the cavern for the monster, saw him glide out of a shadowy recess beyond Mary. This first good view of him in light made Draper's throat constrict.

Leather garments blotched with blood clothed his massive form. Long black hair hung down over his shoulders. And his face—it was even more hideous when seen clearly. The streaks of paint daubed across it made it look unutterably evil, vicious; the mouth was set in a bestial snarl and the eyes glittered with lust.

He slouched over to Mary, stooped and lowered one hand toward her. He murmured: "Now, my pretty, our work's done. They're dead—the three of 'em. And your sweetheart, Draper. But I'll take his place."

Draper stared. Those words—they weren't stilted English or even antiquated English. They were modern. Who was this creature in Indian garb . . .?

CHAPTER FIVE

The Monster's Triumph

HE DIDN'T have time to wonder. The creature's foul hand touched Mary, slid down and ripped more of her nightgown from her. Rage crashed over Draper. It killed his pain, gave him new strength. He hurled himself into the cavern.

The monster straightened, whirled. He yanked his long knife from his belt.

Draper slipped under the thrust and took the shock of the monster's forearm on his shoulder. He smashed his right to the snarling mouth. Jumping back, he grabbed at the monster's knife arm and clutched the wrist. He wrenched it until the weapon dropped. But he went down when a bludgeoning blow caught the side of his head.

In a second the monster was on him. He rolled, pulled free. Only for long enough to drag in one quick breath. Cursing, the fiend followed him. Clawed at him, battered at him.

Draper's eyes dimmed. His throat clogged. But the vision of this devil's defiling hand touching Mary fired him with a maniacal force. He squirmed over to one side, threw himself to the other. For a fleeting instant the monster lost his balance. Draper took advantage of that instant and heaved his fist at the massive chest. The monster rocked backward, toppled. Draper stumbled to his feet.

The monster rose and charged. Draper jumped out of the way, lashed a hard blow to the painted face as it twisted toward him. He slipped under the monster's outstretched hands and drove a blow to the stomach—another. Then one more to the face. Bone crunched. The hulking body quivered, sagged.

Draper swayed. Through a mist swimming before his eyes he saw that the fiendish creature lay motionless. He gave a silent prayer of thanks; he knew that he couldn't have carried the fight any farther. Hot fire was coursing through his side and his shoulder. His head was splitting.

"Oh. . . ." That was Mary's voice. It rose to a glad cry: "Oh, Dan!"

Draper pulled himself around to go to her.

"Dan!" She brought that out in sudden terror. "Behind you—quick!"

He spun. The monster had fooled him, had crawled to his knife, was lunging up with it clutched in one hand. Draper steeled himself for the charge. He tried to raise his right arm; it seemed to be a thing of lead.

Despair surged over him. His muscles refused to work. He knew that he couldn't . . .

The fiend rattled out a laugh of triumph, swung up his knife, rushed. But one foot caught on a jagged edge of rock. He stumbled, fell. And his laugh of triumph turned into a horrible groan of agony. He writhed, flopped over on his back and suddenly went limp.

From his breast protruded the hilt of his knife. Somehow, in his fall, he had twisted his hand and pointed the long blade at his own chest.

Draper drew in a quick breath. The long black hair was only a wig; it had

pulled from the monster's head after he had fallen. And the real hair underneath that wig exposed his true identity. The hideous face was just a clever mask of make-up.

The monster was Sheriff Eb Tait!

DRAPER staggered over to him, bent and saw that he was dead. Dead by his own hand and knife which had fiendishly murdered five people on this night. Straightening, Draper turned and went to the girl he loved.

A sob tore from his throat when he dropped into her arms. He mumbled brokenly: "Darling—darling, you're safe now. Safe. Oh . . . thank God!"

She clung a moment, then pulled away from him. In a tone of anxiety she said: "You're hurt, Dan. You're—"

"I'll be all right," he told her. "I'm just weak from the loss of a little blood. I need rest . . . and a good nurse."

She gave him a tender smile. But almost immediately it vanished, and she whispered: "Oh, Dan. He killed them all. My father, my aunt and uncle. It—it was horrible. He was so strong that even my uncle didn't have a chance. He—he scalped them and let them die in unbearable agony. He got pleasure out of killing that way. He told me."

"I wonder why he did it," Draper mused. "Why should he want to kill them or your father or Hammond. I can't understand."

"He told me that, too. He was town treasurer besides being sheriff. He had stolen the town funds to speculate and couldn't repay them. The annual meeting of the selectmen would have come in a few days. He wouldn't have been able to account for that money. But he thought he could before new selectmen would have been elected."

"I see." Comprehension flashed into Draper's eyes. "The three selectmen were your father, your uncle and Eli Hammond."

"He had been planning this for weeks. Waiting for a storm to complete the hoax of that old legend. He killed Hammond first, then my father. And—"

"And that's why he had us separate and chase Labrecque," Draper interrupted. "He didn't overlook that valley trail to the village. He sent us in other directions and took that himself. Down to murder your uncle."

"He killed Aunt Martha just because she was there with Uncle John," Mary said bitterly. "He thought I'd recognized him through his make-up so he took me with him. I got away that once but he knocked me out at your house. I didn't come to until I was in this cave. He told me he carried me all the way here. He was strong—terribly strong. He intended to kill me after—afterwards."

Draper tried to conceal a grimace of pain with a frown. He muttered: "Labrecque's appearance was just a coincidence. He was out after you and to settle with me for the thrashing I once gave him."

Mary wouldn't be fooled, saw the grimace. She said: "Dan, we've got to have the doctor take care of you. But you can't go down to the village in this storm. You're too weak. I'm going to get him and make him come up here. And I'm going to bring some men to carry you down to your house. On a toboggan."

She pulled her coat more tightly about her, rose.

"No." He wobbled up after her. "We'll both get out of this hole in the ground and go down to old Zeke's cabin. We can get in somehow. And he'll be back there

pretty soon if he isn't already. We can send him for the doc." He smiled feebly. "I'm not going to let my nurse run away from me for a minute."

"But, Dan, do you think you're strong enough to make it to Zeke's cabin?"

He nodded. But he was too confident. Suddenly a wave of pain swept over him and he crumpled into blackness.

AT FIRST he was only aware of soft, cool hands stroking his forehead. Presently he opened his eyes, saw Mary bending over him. He smiled up at her. Then he noticed that he was in a bed and not lying on the ground in the cave.

Mary divined his question, answered: "You're at Zeke's cabin. I found him and he helped me carry you down here. He's gone for the doctor. I've dressed your wounds as best I could."

Draper sighed. His head ached like hell. But somehow, with Mary's hands on it, he didn't seem to mind the pain.

For a long while they both remained silent. Finally, as if she could hold it back no longer, Mary asked: "Oh, Dan, is the pain terrible?" Then desperately: "You've got to get well."

"I will," Draper promised. "For any day you schedule our wedding."

"A day very soon," she whispered.

He sighed again. Her hands were so gentle, so soothing. Gradually he became aware that there was no shrieking of wind outside. It was odd, he thought, that a storm which had been raging such a little while ago had died so soon. It was as if it had died with the man who had played *Storm of Death* . . . with the end of the horror that had been brought on the village.

THE END

COMING!

More gripping, eerie stories by master writers!

IN THE APRIL TERROR TALES   Out February 22nd!

THE BLACK CHAPEL

WHY has TERROR TALES become such a phenomonal, over-night success? The answer is simple. This magazine is presenting tales which satisfy a primitive, age-old urge in the heart of every red-blooded human—the keen desire to know fear. In this pampered era of ours, this strong old emotion, gripping and poignant, has well-nigh been lost. And modern man, like his forebears, needs its stark stimulation.

It is for that reason that these stories are grim and terrifying; they fulfill a real, present-day need. They provide vital fare for persons who want to fortify the steel of their souls.

The authors whose works appear in TERROR TALES are the foremost in the field—peerless masters of eerie, ravening fiction. There is a limitless variety in their work, backed by exhaustive research into the human fears and dread which were old when the world was new. Month after month, this is the place where you will find bold, outstanding terror stories —thrilling tales of eerie, spine-tingling mystery and chilling horror.

We are convinced that TERROR TALES is going to be your favorite magazine. In it, you will find stories of the supernatural, the bizarre, and the eerie— tales of dark deeds in the dead of night; and grim plans fomented by men of deadly purpose. You will never find a dull tale in it, nor can time lag while you are reading it.

This issue, for instance, is well-balanced fare for those who have a healthy appetite for stories of terror and mystery. Weird happenings from the far corners of the earth have been brought together here for the enjoyment of discriminating readers. They have been selected with the same fine finesse which a famous chef would use in preparing a sumptuous feast.

That, then, is the basic reason for the success of TERROR TALES. There are enough of you folks who recognize the need for strong emotional diet—people with true understanding of the essentials of sane well-rounded living—to create a demand for stories of terror, horror, and blood-chilling, spine-tingling mystery. It is for you hardy souls that TERROR TALES was conceived—it is for you that this magazine is published!

HOW NEW HAIR GROWS
and
WHY Men Go BALD!

Learn FREE!

Baldness may come from several causes. A germ called "Flask Bacilli of Unna" gets deep into the scalp, causing one of the most dangerous types of dandruff, yet is seldom suspected. The refuse it produces clogs the pores and hair follicles, causing the itchy scalp, falling hair and prevents the dormant hair roots from growing new hair. No wonder so many stay bald. All the hair tonics, ointments and soaps in the world will not grow new hair, as they treat only the surface conditions. But now a new discovery enables those with thin, falling hair and bald spots to harmlessly remove this clogged up thin outer skin of the scalp, thus permitting pores to breathe in air, absorb sunshine and receive the penetrating, nourishing, stimulating influence of a scalp food, thereby activating the dormant hair roots to function and grow new hair. It is believed in certain scientific circles this new discovery will revolutionize methods of growing hair. Full instructions on how to proceed are published in a treatise called "GROW HAIR," now being mailed absolutely free to readers of this magazine. Send no money. Just name and address to Dermolav Lab, Desk 400-E, 1700 Broadway, New York, N. Y., U. S. A., and treatise will come by return mail postpaid, free. If pleased tell friends.

KIDNEYS MUST CLEAN OUT ACIDS

The only way your body can clean out Acids and Poisonous wastes from your blood is through the function of millions of tiny Kidney tubes or filters, but be careful, don't use drastic, irritating drugs. If poorly functioning Kidneys and Bladder make you suffer from Getting Up Nights, Leg Pains, Nervousness, Stiffness, Burning, Smarting, Acidity, Neuralgia or Rheumatic Pains, Lumbago, or Loss of Energy, don't waste a minute. Try the Doctor's prescription called Cystex (pronounced Sisstex). Formula in every package. Starts work in 15 minutes. Soothes and tones raw, irritated tissues. It is helping millions and is guaranteed to fix you up or money back on return of empty package. Cystex is only 75c at druggists.